I0717975

DEADLY DECEPTION

WINDSTORM
PRESS

Praise for Deadly Deception

The world McLean portrays feels more real than real. I'll never see a dark spot in the night sky or a deviation in a roofline the same way again. Is it really a mere shadow, or is it a flier of some kind? A mysterious threat, career politics, conflicting matters of the heart, and the clash of family secrets coalesce into a fast-paced, compelling read. Emelynn Taylor is a wonderful heroine—complex, yet easily relatable to, as she continues to come to terms with (and survive!) the mixed blessing of her amazing gift.

—Ev Bishop, award-winning author of the River's Sigh B & B series

A stellar paranormal—with the heart of a romance and the suspense of a spy novel. J.P. McLean's series soars.

—Roxy Boroughs, award-winning author of The Psychic Heat series

Constant danger doesn't scare Emelynn Taylor as much as the lies she's told. This compelling fifth installment of the Gift Legacy series hinges on a high-stakes battle of wills to hide Emelynn's gifts and unique life. Exposed secrets, hidden enemies, and a new, gut-wrenching reality for Emelynn create a gripping read you won't want to put down.

—Debra Purdy Kong, award-winning author of
The Casey Holland Mystery series

Praise for The Gift Legacy

“ A profoundly intelligent story of a captivating young woman whose victories and struggles with a unique gift will grab your every emotion.
—Jennifer Manuel, award-winning author of
The Heaviness of Things That Float

“ JP McLean possesses her own unique gift: the ability to bewitch her readers with her boundless imagination.
—Elinor Florence, Globe and Mail bestselling author of
Bird’s Eye View

“ A deftly crafted, impressively original and inherently compelling read from first page to last.
—Midwest Book Review

“ Danger, suspense, and mystery all bundled into one perfect read.
—Urban Lit Magazine

“ Exciting action and conflict of loyalties make this a fantastic page-turner.   —Kristina Stanley, author of
the Stone Mountain Mystery Series

“ JP McLean’s adventure fantasy series, while full of tense and dangerous moments, is also playful and expansive.
—Bill Engleson, author of *Like a Child to Home*

“ Unique and compelling—a must read for fans of supernatural thrillers!
—Lisa Voisin, author of The Watcher Saga

“ An intelligent novel, generously sprinkled with beautiful, subtle humor, and written by a natural storyteller. What a treat!
—J.F. Kaufmann, author of The Langaer Chronicles

Titles by JP McLean

The Thorne Witch Novels

The Never Witch

Hexborn

The Dark Dreams Novels

Blood Mark

Ghost Mark

Scorch Mark

The Gift Legacy

Secret Sky

Hidden Enemy

Burning Lies

Lethal Waters

Deadly Deception

Wings of Prey

The Gift Legacy Companion

Lover Betrayed (Secret Sky Redux)

Novellas

Crimson Frost (A Supernatural Noel)

DEADLY DECEPTION

The Gift Legacy
Book 5

JP McLean

Deadly Deception
The Gift Legacy ~ Book 5
First Canadian Edition

Copyright © 2019 by JP McLean
All rights reserved.

ISBN
978-1-988125-19-0 (Paperback)
978-1-988125-20-6 (MOBI)
978-1-988125-21-3 (EPUB)
978-1-988125-22-0 (PDF)

Edited by Nina Munteanu
Copy edit by Rachel Small
Book cover designed by JD&J with stock imagery
provided by Konstantin Kamenetskiy © 123RF.com
Author photograph by Crystal Clear Photography

This is a work of fiction. All of the names, characters, places, organizations, events and incidents, other than those clearly in the public domain, are either products of the author's imagination or are used fictitiously. Any resemblance to actual persons, living or dead, is entirely coincidental and not intended by the author.

No part of this publication may be reproduced, recorded, stored in a retrieval or information browsing system, or transmitted, in any form, or by any means, without prior written permission from the publisher or, in the case of photocopying or other reprographic copying, a licence from Access Copyright, www.accesscopyright.ca, 1-800-893-5777, info@accesscopyright.ca.

Excerpt from *Wings of Prey* copyright © 2019 by JP McLean

Cataloguing in Publication information available
from Library and Archives Canada

WINDStorm PRESS
BRITISH COLUMBIA, CANADA
WWW.WINDSTORMPRESS.COM

For the beta team: Jean, Eleanor, Kathy, John, Gee, Sue, Cathy, Sally, George, Denis, Colleen, Anna and Lorna. Thank you for your keen perception, careful input, grace and humour.

Adapt or perish, now as ever, is nature's inexorable imperative.

—H.G. Wells

CHAPTER ONE

The stately Tudor-style home looked much like the others we'd visited, though *visit* might be a stretch. For Sebastian Kirk, *B&Es* and *visits* were synonymous—a quiet evening's entertainment. Come to think of it, *Sebastian Kirk* and *distasteful* were also synonymous. That I was here with him in First Shaughnessy, one of Vancouver's wealthiest neighbourhoods, was temporarily unavoidable.

Homes here started in the three-million-dollar range. Security-company stickers mounted on lawn stakes and ground-floor windows advertised the best targets, and they were abundant.

The entry point I'd chosen was a second-storey dormer. The window's curtains had been left open, and from my vantage point in the maple tree fifteen feet away, the small room beyond appeared unoccupied. That it was nighttime and dark as pitch didn't matter to the likes of us; our night vision was better than a cat's.

Sebastian focused his close-set eyes and adjusted his watch. "I'll give you five minutes."

"This is the last one," I said. The chill in my voice matched that of the April night, which had already painted a coat of dew on the slate roof. A maple catkin tickled my face as I checked my footing on the tree's branch.

Sebastian had chosen a sturdy limb on the other side of the big maple's trunk. Higher up, of course. He pulled his cuff down over his watch. "If you can locate it in five minutes, we'll move on. Otherwise . . ." He shook his head and turned the corners of his mouth down in a frown worthy of a schoolmaster addressing an errant student. My two-week commitment to his mentorship had dragged on for more than a month. Sebastian had proven harder to get rid of than a cold sore on prom night, and his B&E lessons left me wanting a bath in a vat of antibiotic ointment.

Each home we broke into was a classroom. Over the past few weeks, I'd followed him and his laser pen in silence as he pointed out motion detectors, tripwire laser beams, trigger plates and infrared sensors, most of which were nearly impossible to spot—but Sebastian had the knack. Years of practice, no doubt. I pulled out my phone and set the stopwatch.

"After you," he said. He'd decided that tonight I would demonstrate how clever a teacher he was, and to spice up the challenge, he'd made sure the owners were home, a detail he knew made me uncomfortable.

Once again, I dissolved my corporeal body into a fine mist and then pushed through the tiny cracks surrounding the dormer window. I sensed Sebastian's ghosted presence close behind me as I passed through the small room and into the hall beyond. The scent of grilled lamb lingered. I made a mental note of the motion sensor mounted in the corner of the ceiling and drifted toward the only room with double doors. I paused to steady my nerves. Violating the private spaces of strangers didn't get easier with repetition. I sucked in a breath and wafted through the doors. The king-sized bed's occupants lay back to back. Soft snores reverberated in my chest like jackhammers. I looked away from their peaceful faces and made a careful circuit of the room and adjacent ensuite. The closets and artwork concealed nothing.

A home office was the next most likely room for a safe. I slipped back into the hall, relieved to leave the slumbering homeowners behind, and dove headlong down the staircase. Sebastian followed me into the office. A sweep of the room ruled out all likely locations except the desk. Drifting close to the floor, I circled the pedestals. Decorative brass locks protected the drawers on the business side of the desk, but it was the magnetic contact sensor on the opposite side that gave away the safe. It had been cleverly hidden behind a false panel.

"Found it," I whispered. I solidified the molecules of my ghosted arm to check my time: four minutes and thirty-seven seconds. At four minutes and thirty-eight seconds, my near celebration ended with the jarring blare of an alarm. "Damn it!"

"Shh," Sebastian hissed. He plucked a pen from the desk and dropped it to the floor.

How could I be so careless? Sebastian would use this to glom on to me for another week. I flung my ghosted form at the office window and hauled my wispy butt to the backyard. A neighbour's dog had taken up an incessant bark to match the alarm's shriek. Behind me, one by one, the home's windows lit up. I drifted across the neighbour's backyard and over their rooftop to the next street, where we'd parked, and re-formed inside Sebastian's SUV.

He'd beaten me there. "That was an amateur mistake. I would have expected more of you by now." The wind had tousled his dark hair. He smoothed it forward with his palm.

I'd been so anxious to beat his time that I'd re-formed my hand and most of my arm to get at my phone. Ghosts could do many things, but in ghosted form, we existed as molecules, vapour, and neither molecules nor vapour could pick up a phone to check the time. Re-forming had triggered the motion sensor. Sebastian would dangle my error in front of my face for weeks.

"Yes, well, what can I say? B&Es don't come naturally to me."

"Your snide remarks are uncalled for. You were sloppy."

I tugged at the fingertips of my gloves, hating that he was right. He'd demonstrated half a dozen times how little it took to get caught. Not that we'd actually *get* caught; we were Ghosts, after all. But still, the alarm's abrupt blare had left my heart racing. "I'm sorry. I'll do better."

"I hope so. ICO may not know the extent of your *gift*, but they expect an operative who can get them what no one else can. That's the deal they made. We're all counting on it." International Covert Operations was a clandestine government-sanctioned organization that held the secret of our gift hostage. The government, I'd come to learn, took a conveniently tolerant view of blackmail when they were the ones benefiting from it.

"You don't need to remind me." I'd been the one who'd exposed the gift. The fact that I'd done it to save a man's life hadn't garnered me any leniency. Working for ICO was my penance. I stared through the darkened side window. Early April promised warmer nights. This wasn't one of them. "Can we go now?"

"You in a hurry?"

"It's two in the morning. I'm tired, I'm cold and I just ruined the night for a lovely couple who did absolutely nothing to deserve it. So yes, please, I'd like to go home."

Sebastian exhaled a heavy sigh. "Your performance tonight proves you're not ready to move on, but I'm willing to negotiate." Leather creaked as he turned in his seat.

I narrowed my eyes. "Negotiate what?"

"You've just set up the perfect scenario for your next lesson, but it has to be tonight."

"What do you mean?"

"In about an hour, that *lovely couple* back there will be done with the security company and the police. With no sign of an intruder, they'll assume the pen they find on the office floor inexplicably rolled off the desk and triggered the alarm. After they go back to bed, I'll show you how to get a combination for a safe without even asking."

"You want to wake them again?"

He forced a placating smile. "It's for a good cause."

I looked away. The man had no conscience. I hoped I'd never turn out like him.

He continued. "Some of these home safes are fireproof, which means they're airtight. You can't just ghost an arm, reach in and take what you want."

I hated when he talked down to me. As if I didn't know that airtightness was the only thing that stopped us. I stuffed my tongue in my cheek.

"But with a little manipulation, owners generally oblige and open them. I'm prepared to demonstrate tonight." He checked his watch. "Unless you'd rather repeat this exercise some other time?"

When it came to manipulation, Sebastian was a master.

Two hours passed before the lights in the couple's bedroom suite went out again, and we waited another hour to be sure they'd settled. Daylight threatened in the eastern sky as we broke in again, this time through the office window.

I drifted to the ceiling to observe, as Sebastian had asked. The moment he re-formed, the alarm wailed in protest. Knowing it was coming didn't stop me from cringing. Sebastian knelt down and casually cracked open the false panel on the desk. He then ghosted and joined me at the ceiling.

Within moments, a red-faced man with a hairy baby bump burst into the room and flipped on the light. Thank god he'd put some pants on. He rushed past the desk to the windows. After a careful examination of the window sensors, he punched a code into his phone. The alarm cut out. Seconds later, the phone rang. "I'm in the office now. The windows are fine. Must be something wrong with one of the motion sensors." He dragged his hand through dishevelled hair. "No, we've had enough for one night. I'll leave it off. Send someone over to have a look in the morning."

The man hung up and swept a scrutinizing gaze around the room. His wife appeared in the doorway clutching at the lapels of her robe. "What happened?"

The man walked around the desk, toward her. "It's got to be a malfunction. They'll send someone around to fix it."

The woman settled a hand on her husband's chest. Soft pillows cradled her eyes. "I'll never get back to sleep, now," she said. "Would you like me to make a pot of coffee?"

The man's shoulders sagged. "Sure. Might as well."

She turned to leave. He reached for the light switch and, before turning it off, took another look around the room. As his gaze passed over the desk, he hesitated. "Honey," he said, stopping her. "Did you notice the desk panel open on the safe earlier? After the first alarm?"

She stepped back into the room and looked at the offending panel. "No. I thought you checked it."

"So did I." The man returned to the desk. He crouched before the panel and opened it to expose the safe. I sensed Sebastian leave my side. Then the man punched in the code and opened the safe. He flipped through the papers on each shelf and ended with a satisfied *harrumph*. Finished his inspection, he closed the safe's door then straightened, hiking his pants. "It's in order. I mustn't have latched it properly." He draped an arm around his wife's shoulder and flipped off the light before closing the door. Their footsteps echoed down the hall.

Sebastian and his self-congratulatory smile accompanied me on the drive back to my car, which I'd left at our rendezvous point hours ago. We'd pulled another all-nighter. The sun was up and my bed called.

"Good night," I said, opening the door.

"I'll phone you tonight with a new address."

"I can't tonight. I have a dinner date."

"Oh? Is James in town?"

Sebastian could be so bloody nosy. "No," I said. He raised a questioning eyebrow I didn't dare walk away from. "If you must know,

Avery's invited me over." Avery Coulter headed up the local covey. I hated bringing up his name. I owed Avery my life and didn't want Sebastian's focus on him. I jumped out of the SUV.

Sebastian leaned over. "Covey business?"

"No. Just dinner." Sebastian was now a bona fide member of the Vancouver covey. Avery had had little choice but to admit him when Sebastian moved into the jurisdiction, but I didn't like it. The small group of Fliers was my family. We protected the secret of the gift, and one another, and I didn't trust Sebastian. It irritated me that he'd bought his way into my circle of friends.

"Fine. Take the night off. I'll be in touch."

"Thank you," I said, barely keeping the snark out of my voice. He waited until I'd started my old Volvo then pulled out and passed me.

Relief washed over me, as it always did, when I was sure he'd gone. I pulled out my phone and checked for messages. There were none. James didn't usually leave me hanging for this long, but when he was working a case, he cut off communication. I didn't think his being a private investigator, no matter how dedicated he was, justified his no-contact rule, but he disagreed. He insisted it was for the safety of us both and wouldn't budge despite my pleas.

Our relationship didn't spend a lot of time in neutral—we either raced with the needle in the red zone or we idled. We'd been idling for too long. I missed him. Maybe that was his goal. He'd left me with a decision to make: he'd proposed. But his proposal glossed over a shitload of potholes. Living and working in different countries would cause a few flat tires, but the family he wanted to start threatened to break the undercarriage. And his habit of disappearing for weeks on end was a washout big enough to stop a transport.

Working with Sebastian, as disagreeable as the man could be, helped me keep my mind off James and his proposal. There was no denying Sebastian's skills. He'd been born into one of the nine founding coveys, which had ruled our kind through their Tribunal for hundreds of years. He'd been an enforcer for them during his younger years, and a political player ever since. He could deliver a painful *spark* or a deadly *jolt* with no more effort than it took to flick a speck of lint from his sleeve. As off-putting as his lessons were, he'd taught me things I'd never pick up in grad school.

But I needed a night off, and I was looking forward to seeing Avery. I'd only visited with him a few times since Carson Manse and his

Redeemers torched my cottage and attacked the Tribunal at Cairabrae. The surviving Redeemers had scattered after the attack. We didn't know their identities, but they knew mine. Association with me had proven dangerous, so when Avery insisted I join him for dinner tonight, I knew it was important to him. After I'd rested, I'd put Sebastian's lessons in motion and make absolutely certain no one tailed me to Avery's place.

Traffic at dawn was light, and I soon pulled into my building's underground parking garage and took the elevator to the top floor. My condo occupied the southwest corner. I closed the door behind me and set the perimeter alarm. In the bedroom, I pulled on an eye mask to block out the sun and crawled into bed.

When I woke, the eye mask was lost in the sheets and late-afternoon sunlight streamed across the room. With a feline stretch, I turned my face into the warm rays. I couldn't go to Avery's until dark but hated to waste the end of such a beautiful day. I decided to go for a run. But first, a cup of tea. I hopped out of bed and padded to the kitchen.

Molly's baby shower invitation lay on the kitchen counter. She'd taken Cheney's last name, Meyer. It still looked strange to me. She was due the month after next. I'd met Molly in kindergarten. We were best buds until seventh grade, when my father died and my mother moved us to Toronto.

Last year, I'd returned to Summerset, and Molly and I had reconnected. The reunion had been a blast but all too brief. She knew nothing about the gift, or about the Redeemers who targeted Fliers, especially those like me, who were Ghosts; she just knew that one of the men responsible for terrorizing me was still at large. Until that threat was gone, the best thing I could do for her as a friend was to not expose her connection to me. It was the story of my life these days, and it was wearing thin.

I smoothed my hand over the invitation, picked up my tea and wandered to the bank of windows in the living room. Outside, in the planters on the balcony, a tall dandelion bloomed brilliant yellow, hiding among the daffodils. A weed camouflaged—just like the Redeemers. The Tribunal was focused on removing the Redeemer threat, but it seemed to be taking forever. I'd already had to bow out of Molly's wedding, and when she and Cheney bought a sweet little storybook bungalow in Summerset, I'd had to decline their housewarming party invitation. Molly was my little corner of normal, and I wanted her back.

Sadly, that wouldn't happen today. I finished the tea and a cup of yogourt and got ready for my run.

After a warm-up in the fading light on the West Mall, I wound my way east. My goal was eight kilometres. Every laneway and dumpster was familiar to me. I'd used them to practice what James and then Sebastian had taught me. The Redeemers might know my name, but they'd never again get my address. And they'd be snowboarding in hell before I'd ever let myself be taken by them again.

When I reached Sixteenth Avenue, my reversible jacket was pink instead of navy, my leggings were hiked up to my knees, I'd donned a Toronto Blue Jays baseball cap and my white sneakers were camouflaged with black nylon. There were days I actually wished someone would tail me just so I could evade them.

I continued east toward Point Grey and decided to swing past Sebastian's place before turning for home. I'd never been invited inside, but I knew where he and his wife, Kimberley, lived. They'd chosen an expansive glass-and-concrete home that looked like something Arthur Erickson had designed, which was entirely possible considering the neighbourhood.

Mature plantings obscured the home from the road. As I approached their driveway, I spotted a man getting into a sports car at the top of Sebastian's circular drive. My curiosity got the best of me. I passed the driveway and stooped to tie my shoelaces. From under my cap, I watched the nose of the man's black BMW approach the sidewalk. He stroked his goatee as he looked both ways, and then drove off. I didn't know him.

I continued on my run as twilight settled in and all the way home wondered what business the man had with the Kirks.

CHAPTER TWO

Colin buzzed me in from the security desk. "How you doin'?" he asked, flashing a flirty smile. I might have been flattered if I hadn't known he flirted with all the female tenants, even Myrtle Beckerman, and she was in her nineties.

"Never better," I replied, and pushed the elevator's call button.

"You take care. Have a good night," he said, as I stepped into the elevator. Once inside the condo, I set the perimeter alarm again and proceeded to the shower. I dried off and donned the Flier uniform: dark-coloured everything, from head to toe. Fashion wasn't a consideration when you had to blend into the night sky. Colour options included funeral black, charcoal grey, midnight blue, mud brown and the deepest forest green. Exciting.

I activated the condo's security system and then ghosted up to the rooftop. The winds could be brutal on the roof, but it was calm tonight. I gathered the wisps of my ghost together and re-formed. I would fly to Avery's, but not in ghosted form. That took too much energy. Thirty minutes in ghosted form and I'd drop from exhaustion, if the winds didn't scatter me over the Pacific first.

I secured my racing goggles, tightened my ponytail and rechecked my coordinates on the wrist-mounted GPS I never went anywhere without. All set, I thought. Euphoria brought a smile to my lips. Flying never lost its charm. It was the single most exhilarating thing I'd ever done. I called to my crystal talisman and a surge of power pulsed under my skin. Alcohol and opiates weren't even in the running as far as highs went. Not all Fliers had talismans, but every Ghost did. Each carried clear crystals, heirlooms passed down through generations. But unlike all the other Ghosts', my crystal wasn't physical. It was as much a part of me as my heart but as untouchable as my soul.

I held it in my mind's eye. It felt warm to the touch with six smooth sides and a prism cap on each end. It thrummed with a pulsating energy I could siphon off with a gentle squeeze. I drew a little more energy from it, severed my bond with gravity and flew straight up from the centre of the rooftop.

At three hundred feet, and silent as a prayer, I was almost invisible. I'd come to learn that people rarely looked up. And if they did, I'd look like a shadow. If they thought to look closer, their minds would create a scenario that made sense to them: an optical illusion, a smudge on their glasses, one too many glasses of wine. I turned west, crossed over Marine Drive and then headed out over the Pacific.

Avery lived and worked from his home in St. George, a respectable neighbourhood south of Vancouver. He was a medical doctor with a small home practice of clients who were mostly Fliers. But he was more than a doctor to me. He'd found me. He'd taught me what it meant to be a Flier and how to use my incredible gift. He'd played guinea pig to my clumsy early efforts to jolt and spark and had spent countless hours helping me hone those deadly skills. He'd picked me up, patched me up and dusted me off so many times I'd lost track. I loved him like a father.

I followed the rope of headlights along Highway 99 until I got close, and then swept in to find his house. A large white *X* on his rooftop startled me. What the hell? I dropped into his back garden and gazed through the kitchen's French doors. Avery looked up from behind the kitchen island. A slow smile crept across his face. He sauntered around the island and opened the door.

"You find it okay?" He struggled to keep a straight face.

When I got close enough, I smacked his arm. "Smart ass." I walked into the kitchen and he closed the door behind me. "So glad my terrible sense of direction amuses you." He'd cut his hair in an Anderson-Cooper style, and his blond looked as good as Anderson's grey.

"To no end," he said with a chuckle. He reached behind me and gave me a one-armed hug. "It's been a while."

"Mmm, what smells so good?" I'd yet to eat anything Avery had made that fell short of delicious.

"Prime rib. It's not ready yet." A glass of red wine sat on the island beside an assortment of vegetables.

"Nice. Will Victoria be joining us?" Avery had been dating Victoria Lang, another Flier in our covey, for months now.

"She'll be here shortly. Can I get you a glass of wine?"

"Thanks."

He pulled a glass out of the cupboard and poured from an open bottle.

"The new cabinets look good." His kitchen had been shot up during an assassination attempt. On me, naturally.

He looked around the room as if admiring it for the first time. "It needed an upgrade. Victoria chose them." He handed me the glass. "Have a seat while I put the salad together."

"Can I help?"

"Yes, you can entertain me. How's it going with Sebastian?" He took a sip of his wine, set it down and took up a knife.

I pulled out a chair, sad to see that the century-old oak tabletop had been replaced. The table looked better without the bullet damage, but that old-world charm was gone.

"We've moved on from surveillance techniques and avoidance tactics to locating safes. Inside people's homes. At night. While they're sleeping."

Avery wrinkled his nose.

"Yeah," I said. "That's how I feel about it too. Got to give him credit though. He's very good at it."

"Sounds like he's growing on you."

If I'd had wine in my mouth, it would have snorted out my nose. "Hardly."

"Yeah, me neither. Still insists I keep his Tribunal connection from the others. It's not right. The covey has a right to know." Avery took his frustration out on a carrot. "How's he dealing with the changeover of power in the Tribunal?"

"I'm the last person Sebastian would discuss that with, and Mason hasn't mentioned it in a while." Mason Reynolds was an uncle of sorts, which made Mason's father, Stuart, a quasi-grandfather. The family claimed me when they learned that Mason's only sister, Jolene, had given me her gift, and with it, her life. The Tribunal's leadership rotated through the nine founding coveys every five years. Mason was next in line.

"When's the big day?"

"End of the month. Unless the Redeemer business delays it again."

"Any news on that front?"

"None. Which doesn't mean nothing's happening, just that Mason hasn't told me. Keeping me in the dark is his way of punishing me for not taking the seat the Tribunal offered me." The offer had been a thank-you from the Tribunal for my part in ending the siege at Cairabrae—a siege at which the Redeemers had planned to strip the Tribunal members and their families of their gifts assembly-line style and put an end to their lives and their rule.

Avery chuckled. "I thought having to accept Sebastian's mentorship was your punishment."

"That too."

He picked up his wine and took a sip. "Maybe you should reconsider your decision about the seat."

I caught his eye to see if he was joking. He wasn't.

"It's just a thought," he said. "Being on the inside might be advantageous. Maybe you could influence how they operate."

"That's a big maybe with political players like Sebastian. I don't have the temperament for their brand of politics. I think I'd rather work with Sam, a man I trust and respect. At least with Sam, despite the ICO angle, we can do some good."

"How is Detective Jordan?"

"Unusually quiet." Sam Jordan was my handler at International Covert Operations. I'd exposed my gift saving his life. "We should be working another case by now, but there's been internal squabbling between power brokers at ICO. Sam's doing crossword puzzles until it settles down."

Sam was a good cop and had my back. He was one of a handful of people who knew I was a Ghost, and he hadn't told anyone, not even General Cain, the man he reported to. All ICO knew was that I could fly and there were more like me. ICO had agreed to keep our secret and not go after others of our kind, as long as James and I "volunteered" our services to aid their investigations.

"Has James started on another case?"

I nodded and twisted my wine glass. "He's doing his usual incommunicado routine, though he's never been out of touch this long. I wish he'd call."

"He's good at what he does. I'm sure he's fine."

Maybe I'd give Sam a call and see if he'd heard anything from Tim Beale, James's American handler.

A door opened beyond the kitchen, toward the front of the house. "Hello," Victoria called out. "Anybody home?" Interesting. Either Avery had left the door unlocked, or she had a key. Avery dried his hands and left to greet her.

Their laughter preceded them into the kitchen. Victoria wore a simple turtleneck and jeans, but nothing looked simple when she wore it. She had an elegance and grace that elevated ordinary to extraordinary. Avery couldn't keep his smiling eyes off her.

I stood and greeted her with a hug. "You'll have to forgive me, Emelynn," she said. "The roof decoration was entirely Avery's idea." Victoria would have been the one to carry out the actual decorating, as Avery had lost his ability to fly when he was a boy.

"Don't worry," I said. "I'll get him back."

"I do hope so. If you need ideas, I have plenty."

"So much for loyalty," Avery grumbled. He set a bag on the counter and reached for the cupboard.

Victoria was telling me about her struggle with the roll of paper towels that made up the *X* on the roof when the pop of a cork interrupted us. I glanced over and watched Avery pour three flutes of champagne.

"A celebration?" I asked, as Avery approached and handed me a glass. He offered the next flute to Victoria. She accepted it with her left hand. That's when I saw the sparkling ring of diamonds on her finger. I gasped and looked to Avery. It seemed a chore for him to take his eyes off Victoria.

"Yes. Victoria has lost her mind and agreed to marry me."

I stood speechless, fighting back unexpected tears. No one deserved happiness more than Avery, and that he'd found it with someone as special as Victoria felt perfect. *They* felt perfect.

I blinked back the tears. "That's wonderful news," I said, and tipped my glass to theirs.

"Thank you, Em." Avery reached an arm around Victoria's waist and kissed her temple. "Now, you two go talk wedding while I finish dinner."

Victoria and I sipped champagne at the table. Her cousin would be her maid of honour, and Avery's long-time friend and lawyer, Gabe Aucoin, had agreed to be his best man. It would be a small affair, and though they hadn't set a date, they were thinking of a fall wedding.

My mind drifted to another wedding—Molly's. Would I have to stay away from Avery's as well?

Dinner was spectacular: prime rib, tender with just a hint of garlic, and rosemary potatoes, divine. In the midst of pouring a puddle of gravy over my second Yorkshire pudding, my phone rang.

"I'm sorry," I said, embarrassed by the intrusion. I pulled the phone from my pocket. "It's Sam. I've got to take it." Avery nodded. I stood and walked down the hall to answer it.

"Hi, Sam."

"Something's come up. How soon can you meet me?"

Sam's manner hadn't improved during our downtime—he was brusque as ever. "I'm well, Sam. Thanks for asking."

"It's important, Emelynn. How soon can you get there?"

There was a twenty-four-hour Denny's on Broadway. Meeting at that location was our protocol. "I'm not at home, and I don't have my car. Forty minutes?"

"Put a rush on it," Sam said, and the line went dead. Sam Jordan was a sweetheart under that gruff exterior, but he fought it like a champion.

I returned to the kitchen but didn't sit. "I hate to eat and run, but it looks like the dry spell is over. Sam finally caught another case. I gotta go."

"Don't worry about it. Go," Avery said. He stood and gave me a hug. "Be careful and stay safe."

"I will. Congratulations again."

I turned to Victoria. "You've made this man very happy. Thank you."

Arm in arm, they walked me out the French doors to the garden.

CHAPTER THREE

Even in thermal clothing, the cold seeped through to chill me. A deserted lawn-bowling club on Fir Street provided cover for my descent. I drifted down, stuffed my hands in my pockets and turned north.

At the blip of my phone, I checked the message that had landed in my junk-email folder: *We ship same day free; Cialis, Viagra, Vicodin for $9.* Despite the randomly generated sender's name, I knew it was my mother telling me she'd Skype me at 9:00 p.m. That was five minutes away, and midnight for my mother in Toronto—late for her to call.

I spotted an alcove in the apartment building across the street and headed for it. James had set Mom up with an untraceable phone identical to mine. He'd devised the Viagra procedure so we could keep in touch without fear of exposing our connection. She'd only agreed because Sam had convinced her of the need for caution. He hadn't mentioned the Redeemers by name but had warned her that our connection could be exploited by the criminal at large who had me in his sights.

I paced, waiting for her call. At nine o'clock precisely, it came through. She wore a tan trench coat I recognized, and it made me laugh. "Where are you this time?" It was a running joke. She might be the smartest woman in any room, but James's technological wizardry stumped her. She didn't understand how he masked her location and didn't quite believe it worked. She talked with me from coffee shops, in cabs, and huddled in bus shelters but never from home.

"Ladies' room," she said, and a tired smile bloomed.

"That's a first," I said. Her expression quickly lost its humour. "What's wrong?"

"Sweetheart, I don't want to alarm you, but I'm at the police station. Someone broke into my apartment."

I stopped pacing. "Oh my god, Mom. Are you all right?"

"I'm fine. I was at work when it happened."

"How'd they get in?"

"The police think through the underground. Probably slipped in after a car."

"That underground's been a problem for years. Was anyone else's place broken into?" I checked my surroundings, hoping my presence wasn't drawing attention.

"No one else has reported anything, or at least not yet, but Emelynn, the police think I was targeted."

"Why?"

"Because nothing is missing, at least nothing I can think of."

"That makes no sense."

"It might be related to work. There have been a few break-ins at the labs. The university's security team assumes it's related to the drugs."

She was a behavioural research scientist at the University of Toronto. A big part of her research was testing drugs. "You never mentioned the break-ins before. What happened?"

"A few months ago, after Dr. Stein's lab got hit, my lab and a few others on the same floor were broken into. I swear these people think we leave the damn drugs in candy jars on the coffee tables."

The hit on Dr. Stein's lab was something I'd set in motion. I'd had no choice. It was due to an innocent mistake my mother had made. She'd passed on some of my father's research to her colleague, Dr. Stein. She didn't know Dad's research involved the anatomy of a Flier's eye and the second lens that identified us. My mother was an innocent—she knew nothing about the world of Fliers Jolene had made me a part of.

"What do the police think?"

"They're investigating. They lifted dozens of fingerprints. They brought me down here to look at some mug shots to see if I recognized anyone. I didn't."

"So, what now?"

"I'll go home I suppose. Clean up the mess. The apartment looks like a tornado's gone through it. There's fingerprint powder on every conceivable surface."

"I'm sorry, Mom. Do you want me to catch a flight out and help?"

"No, don't worry, sweetheart. Dr. Coulter needs you more than I do. I can handle a bit of cleaning."

Avery had been the one to suggest I use him as a decoy employer. Mom knew him, and she thought I was his medical assistant. It was the perfect cover for my work with ICO. "Have the locks changed as well, Mom. Just in case."

"I will. I'll call you when I learn more."

"Love you, Mom. Talk to you soon."

I slid the phone back into my pocket and, once again, headed north, toward Broadway. With the Denny's sign in sight, I removed my gloves and hat and shook out my hair. Sam would see me arrive, but wouldn't come in until he was certain I hadn't been followed. I took a seat by the emergency exit and ordered a coffee.

Avery's prime rib was no longer sitting so well. I'd thought Mom and Edgar Stein had a budding romance, though Mom denied it. I remembered him as a willowy man with long fingers, a scholarly gentleman. He didn't seem the burglar type, but Dad's research would have been life altering for the person who published it. Its disappearance must have been a blow. Maybe he'd hired someone to go looking for it. Then again, drugs were a solid draw for the criminal element. I was probably overthinking it.

Twenty minutes later Sam jogged across Broadway. A black watch cap covered his brush cut. His broad shoulders filled the doorway. He exchanged greetings with the waitress as his gaze swept over the restaurant's interior. He took the seat to my right having never once looked at me and dragged off his hat. The waitress followed with a cup and poured him a coffee.

"Refill?" she asked. I nodded, and she topped up my cup.

When she was out of earshot, he turned to me. "So . . . how are you?"

I jerked my head back and grinned. "Careful, Sam. That sounded an awful lot like a social grace."

"I hope you enjoyed it because you're not going to enjoy what comes next." He pulled out his cellphone, swiped across the screen and pushed it across the table. "Watch that."

It was closed-circuit TV footage. "Where is this?"

"St. Paul's Hospital."

I pushed play. A woman wearing scrubs came into view, her back to the camera. She approached a closed door and checked her surroundings in a way that told me she shouldn't have been there. And then poof! She disappeared. I glanced at Sam.

"Keep watching."

Moments later the same woman reappeared with a bundle in her arms. She walked toward the camera then passed underneath, out of sight. The video ended.

I pushed the phone back to him. "O . . . kay. What did I just see?"

"A kidnapping. Newborn." Sam's nostrils flared. Law enforcement types were pretty tough, and Sam was one of the toughest, but I'd learned that crimes involving children or one of their own cracked even the most hardened.

"The parents must be frantic."

"The mother's a fifteen-year-old street urchin. Dropped the kid and ran. Don't even have her name, and I doubt the father knows he has a kid. The baby's a ward of the court. No one's going to miss him."

The way Sam paused before that last comment caught my attention. It seemed as if something had hit a nerve deep inside him. It reminded me how little I knew about Sam Jordan.

"When did it happen?"

Sam checked his watch. "Almost three hours ago."

"What's wrong with the video footage? It looks like it's been spliced."

"Noticed that, did you? We're operating on the assumption the camera malfunctioned. But . . ."

I searched his face, hoping I was wrong. "You think she's one of us?"

Sam shrugged. "I know what you can do." He did—first-hand in fact. I'd ghosted out of a failing helicopter while gripping his hand, and he'd ghosted along with me. It had saved our lives.

He looked back to his phone and swiped through more photos. "I took these stills from the film of the kidnapper entering and exiting the building." He pushed the phone back to me. The cop in him studied me as I swiped through them. "Do you recognize her?"

I slid the phone back. "No."

Sam looked down at the table. "Would you tell me if you did?"

His question took me aback. Would I? I'd never imagined I'd be in this position.

When he looked up, I met his gaze. "If she were one of us, I'd get the child back."

He didn't respond, simply held my stare from under a furrowed brow. I looked away and stacked the empty creamer pots.

Sam exhaled. "If she's like you, I don't suppose we'd be able to incarcerate her anyway."

Would he feel any better if he knew how much worse the Tribunal's punishment would be? I resisted the urge to apologize. "Send me the files. I'll ask some people."

"The first few hours are critical. Do it as quickly as you can."

"I will. I'll call as soon as I learn anything." I stood to leave but hesitated. "Are we good? You and me?"

Sam managed a rare, though weak, smile and nodded. "Yeah. I can read you pretty well. I know you didn't recognize that woman. We're good. Let's get that child back and show him that someone cares."

For the second time tonight, his words revealed a crack in his armour. "Don't forget to send the pictures."

"Right," he said, and bent to his phone as I turned and walked out of the restaurant.

I pushed the doors open into the cool night and paused when I reached the sidewalk. A brief buzz from my phone told me Sam's attachments had arrived. I turned west and considered my options. The kidnapper wasn't a Ghost—of that I was certain. Despite what the film suggested, and what Sam feared, no Ghost worth her crystal would re-form within sight of a security camera as obvious as that one must have been. No way. There must have been some kind of blip with that security camera. Still, I would check it out for Sam as I'd promised.

The team that caught the case would be running the kidnapper's image through facial-recognition software and checking licence plates on every car caught on film in the vicinity. I couldn't help with that, but I could at least eliminate the Ghost angle and ease Sam's mind.

I crossed to the north side of Broadway and walked west. There were only two people who could confirm that this woman wasn't a Ghost: Mason or Sebastian. Neither option appealed to me. Normally, Mason would have been my first choice, but his time and temper were stretched between heading up the search for the remaining Redeemers and preparing to take on the Tribunal's leadership. I didn't relish earning his ire for a simple ID.

Sebastian would be as good a resource. I'd have to tell him about the case eventually anyway. Since he was the current head of the Tribunal, I was obliged to keep him apprised of any work I was doing for

ICO. When Mason took over that position, Sebastian would lose the inside track. I was convinced that's why Sebastian had offered to mentor me—with me glued to his side, he had a better chance of staying in the Tribunal loop after the spring caucus. I hoped he wasn't holding his breath.

I picked up my pace and turned north toward Granville Island, where I knew of a few secluded spots ideal for a takeoff. Parked vans and sharp corners provided opportunities to check for tails. No sign of one, yet something didn't feel right. It could have been paranoia from the weeks of intense training, but I trusted my gut and changed course.

Back on Broadway, I deked into a busy pizza shop and slipped into their bathroom. Immediately, I visualized my crystal and squeezed it until it melted like an ice chip, heralding my ghost. I blew out of there and hung around outside long enough to convince myself I'd had a case of the heebie-jeebies. But just to be safe, I drifted on a westerly breeze and didn't re-form until I was blocks away, at the side of a lonely garage. I pulled my hair into a ponytail, snugged my hat back on and ran to Vanier Park. Deep in the park's shadows, I took to the air and charted a course toward Sebastian's place.

The large spaces between the Point Grey properties provided solid cover to land in. Once on the ground, I pulled out my phone. Disrupting Sebastian's evening would be a satisfying bit of payback, but I wasn't foolish enough to show up completely unannounced. As I walked up his drive, I dialled.

He answered with his usual haughty-with-a-side-of-sickly-sweet. "Emelynn. This is an unexpected surprise."

"I'm sorry about the hour. Detective Jordan's put me on a case, and I need your help."

"Tonight?"

"I'm afraid so. It'll only take a minute."

He exhaled a loud and impatient breath. "All right. I'll be at your place in thirty minutes."

"No need. I'm on your front porch."

The silence echoed in my gut. He opened the door with the phone to his ear. One look at his stone-chiselled features told me I'd overstepped. He pocketed his phone and looked beyond me, then left and right.

"Come in." It wasn't a request. He closed the door. "Follow me." I bent to remove my shoes. "Leave them," he barked. I wiped my soles on the doormat and trotted after him. He pushed open the door to a small library and motioned me inside. "Wait here. I'll be back in a moment." He closed the door and his footsteps trailed away.

I took a moment to consider the double standard. How many times had Sebastian barged in on me unannounced? What the hell was he hiding? I blinked out of sight and hurled my ghosted form through the library door. Politeness wasn't even a consideration. James had taught me not to hesitate. Sebastian had taught me to use everything at my disposal. My skills were no match for the likes of Sebastian, but I had one advantage that Sebastian didn't: neither he nor anyone else could sense my ghosted form. Unfortunately, he knew it—we'd had to work around it during his mentorship—so I'd have to be quicker than he was and beat him back to the library.

Hushed whispers led me to a sleek kitchen at the back of the house. Sebastian's wife, Kimberley, stood with her hands on her hips. Her perfectly curled bottle-blonde hair and trim Lululemon-clad body seemed a poor match for Sebastian's dark presence, but she squared off with him, nose to nose, like an opponent in a boxing ring. Hardly the loving couple I'd seen in public.

"I don't care. What if Wade had seen her? It's bad enough you took her under your wing like some helpless"—she twisted her mouth, searching the room for words—"foundling, but now she thinks she can just show up here?"

Helpless? Foundling? Where the hell was that coming from? And who was Wade?

Kimberley tossed her arms in the air in a dramatic show of exasperation. "She's not Jolene!"

Jolene Reynolds? My Jolene? Mason's sister?

Sebastian narrowed his eyes and leaned in closer. "And she's not deaf. Kindly keep your voice down. I'll make sure she understands, and see her out."

I bolted out of there as Kimberley called after him, "Please do."

Shit shit shit! I raced down the hall a breath ahead of Sebastian's stomping heels and re-formed on the other side of the library door just as he opened it. The door banged me in the ass. I jumped out of the way with a start.

Sebastian scowled and looked me up and down before closing the door.

"Is something wrong?" I asked innocently.

"In future, I'd appreciate it if you didn't drop by without my approval. Kimberley hasn't been the same since Cairabrae. Unexpected visits aren't welcome."

Any unexpected visits? I wondered. Or just my unexpected visits? "I hope I didn't upset her."

Sebastian waved his hand, dismissing the notion. "You needed my help. What with?"

Oh yes. I'd almost forgotten. I pulled out my phone, opened Sam's video attachment and handed the phone to Sebastian. He pushed play.

"A few hours ago, a newborn was kidnapped from St. Paul's hospital. The woman in that footage is responsible." I studied his face for signs of recognition and saw none. "Swipe forward and you'll find a few more photos."

Sebastian looked through them and returned my phone. "And?" he said.

"Detective Jordan would like to know if we recognize her."

"Why would he think we'd recognize her?"

I wrapped my lips around my teeth and took a breath before answering. "The police are operating on the assumption that the glitch in the video footage was a camera malfunction. Detective Jordan isn't."

"Apparently the detective doesn't think very highly of us."

As usual, Sebastian had missed the human element. "A child is missing and the first few hours are critical. He's willing to risk insulting us if it means getting the child back."

"I see." Sebastian straightened and turned toward the door. "You can tell the detective she's not one of us."

I cocked an eyebrow. "Really? You're absolutely certain?"

Sebastian stilled and slowly turned back around. "Yes. *Really*," he said, the *how dare you question me* clear. "She is not one of us."

"You know every Ghost?" I hadn't meant for it to come out as an accusation.

Sebastian hollowed his cheeks and lifted his chin. "There is always the possibility of a rogue, but it's unlikely. Are you sure you weren't followed here?"

"Yes, I'm sure. Why?"

"That footage is weak. Jordan could have set you up. It would be quite a coup if General Cain got the identities of a few more of us. We don't need to give ICO any more leverage."

That was a stab at me—I'd given them their current leverage. I chose to ignore it. "Detective Jordan would never do that. He wouldn't break my trust."

"Maybe not knowingly. But Cain would without hesitation." Sebastian frowned and shook his head. "He'll be looking for a crack to exploit in our next contract negotiation." He grasped the doorknob. "Now, if there's nothing else?" When I didn't respond, he opened the library door. "Let me walk you out."

He closed the front door behind me and watched my retreat through the glass side panel. The intensity of his glare burned my back all the way to the street.

Chapter Four

Thoughts crashed around in my head like bumper cars. Was Sebastian right? Would ICO betray me? Or even Sam? And what was up with Kimberley? She resented the hell out of me—that was clear—but why? Surely she didn't think I had the hots for her husband. I shuddered. Targeting husbands was their daughter Tiffany's modus operandi, not mine. Besides, arrogant egomaniac wasn't my type.

The tone of Kimberley's voice when she'd mentioned Jolene was unmistakable. Kimberley was jealous of her, which made no sense. No one had heard from Jolene since the day she gifted me, more than ten years ago. Given the fifty-fifty chance Jolene had had of surviving the gifting, not even her family still believed she was alive. So why such a vehement reaction from Kimberley? And who the hell was Wade?

Once safe inside my condo, I dropped to the sofa and called Sam. "She's not one of us."

"Okay." I heard him draw a long breath. I wished I could have seen his face, to get an idea of his thoughts. "At least I know what we're *not* dealing with."

"Any breaks in the case?"

"The AMBER Alert produced a lead. A vehicle description—older-model Mercedes sedan, tan. We're combing through the city's traffic cams to find it."

"How can I help?"

"Keep your phone on. It's going to be a long night."

"I will." I would have hung up, but I needed to clear up a nagging doubt. "Sam, before you go, tell me, how did you learn about the kidnapping?"

"Every cop in the city was briefed. Child abductions are high priority."

"Did ICO ask you to take the case?"

"No. I got tired of waiting for them to sort out their shit. This one's on me. Why?"

"Is anyone testing the hospital's security camera or the footage to determine if either has been tampered with?"

"It's not a priority. Where are you going with this?"

I hated to add my voice to Sebastian's concerns, but it could be important. "If the film was spliced, someone's gone to a lot of trouble. Maybe they knew you'd see it and wanted you to think the kidnapper was one of us. Maybe they hoped you'd come to me and I'd lead them to more of our kind."

Sam's silence told me he was giving it serious thought. Eventually, he said, "ICO wasn't driving this case, so what you're suggesting implies someone besides ICO knows about your ghosting capability. And also knows that I know."

The weight of yet another potential leak settled on my shoulders. Had someone been witness to Sebastian's *mentoring*? "It's not impossible. Can you make testing that film a priority?"

"Not without drawing attention. Everyone assumes the camera malfunctioned—only the afflicted would think otherwise."

"Then I'll have it done, but I'll need the original digital file. Can you get that for me?"

"Yeah. You going to ask Moss to have a look?"

"James is working, and you know how he is. I haven't heard from him, have you?"

"No. Big case?"

"I wish I knew. If you're talking to his handler, find out, would you?"

"Sure. Let me know what you learn about the footage."

I disconnected and contemplated my next call. With James out of reach and Sebastian's welcome mat rolled up and put away, I'd have to turn to Mason. He'd have the right connections to examine the film, but I didn't like the idea of being in his debt. Asking for his help gave him leverage over me that he wasn't above using. But he was my only option tonight.

He answered on the second ring. "Emelynn. What's wrong?"

"Nothing like jumping to conclusions, Mason."

"You never call this late. What's going on?"

He had a point. I took a breath and dove in. "Sam called me in on a kidnapping case. I could use your help. I need the name of someone who can analyze some security camera footage."

"Why isn't Sam using his ICO resources?"

Crap. I'd been so distracted by asking Mason for his help that I'd missed the hole I'd stepped into. "There's a possibility—slim possibility—that Sam and I have been exposed." I spilled the story, leaving out Kimberley's contribution, and prayed he didn't explode.

"Sebastian's suspicions are well founded. ICO pushed hard for more recruits during negotiations after Cairabrae and didn't get them." Thankfully, his tone was level and calm. "If that film has been planted, and it's not ICO, then we're dealing with a new threat. Either way, you and Sebastian are going to have to get to the bottom of it. I can't lose my focus right now."

"All I need is a contact."

"I'll send an introduction. His name's Navin Patel. He's one of us. Send me the film, and keep Sebastian apprised."

"I'm not involving Sebastian."

"Sebastian isn't your enemy. You're going to want him on your side if it turns out that the film leads to a leak."

"I swear you get your jollies shoving that man under my nose. Do you know how irritating he is?"

Mason laughed. "Yes, and you can add arrogant and sanctimonious to the list, but you might need him, so try not to piss him off."

"I'm curious, Mason. Do you ever ask him not to piss me off?"

A long chuckle rang out. "Perhaps I should. His reaction would be priceless."

"I bet. Speaking of Sebastian, did he have a connection to Jolene years ago?"

"That's a blast from the past. How'd that come up?"

"It didn't. Just something I overheard. It's true then?"

"Yeah, they dated." I cringed. I thought Jolene had better taste than that. "It was before Jolene met your father. It never went anywhere. I haven't thought about that in years. Brings back memories though. Sebastian was full of himself even back then."

Jolene was eight years older than Mason. I tried to picture him as the little boy he would have been at the time, the girlfriend's baby brother. "They probably had to take you with them everywhere they went."

"Oh, I'm sure I had my moments, but oddly, I don't recall a single one."

"Sure you don't," I said, raising an eyebrow he wouldn't see.

"Sebastian was a big support after Jolene and your dad lost their son. When your dad moved back to Canada, Sebastian checked in on her from time to time. Of course, he was married to Kimberley by then, but he was a good friend to Jolene."

How good a friend, I wondered? Maybe Kimberley had reason to be jealous.

"Make sure Sebastian knows what's going on, Emelynn. I can't afford to be blindsided."

"All right. I'll let you know what Navin learns. And one more thing," I said, and then told him about the break-in at my mom's apartment.

"They were probably after narcotics," he said, "but just to be safe, I'll send Paul Rossi to take a look around, listen in on Dr. Stein. Rossi's the man who recovered your father's research from Stein's lab. He's familiar with the territory. He'll make sure there's not more going on."

"You'd do that?"

"Damn it, Emelynn. I shouldn't have to keep telling you that you're family. Laura's your mother. We won't hesitate to protect her."

"I'm sorry. Thank you. Maybe I'll invite Mom out here for a visit, get her away from Toronto for a while." She was married to her work, but given the break-in, I might be able to convince her to take a short vacation. Besides, she hadn't yet seen my new condo.

"That's a great idea," Mason said. "I'll let you know what Rossi reports."

"Okay. How's your dad?"

"You know Dad. He keeps busy with the cattle and the ranch. It helps. He misses Mom." Mason's mother had been one of the casualties when the Redeemers stormed Cairabrae. A vivid memory flashed in my mind—her overturned wheelchair, her frail body sprawled helpless on the floor beside it.

Five minutes after we hung up, an email dropped into my inbox. It was Mason's introduction to Navin. Within the hour, I had the original footage from Sam. I sent it on to Navin and copied Mason. The only thing left to do was wait. I pulled a blanket around my shoulders and curled up on the sofa.

Sam's call woke me. "The tan Mercedes has been located."

It was three in the morning. I sat up and yawned. "Where?"

"The parking lot of the McCleery Golf Course. Macdonald Street, off Southwest Marine Drive."

"You sure it's the right car?"

"Not yet. Forensics is going over it now. We've got every cop available knocking on doors, checking with the cab companies. The kidnapper might have met someone. Dumped the car. Do you want to go out there with me? Take a look around?"

"Sure. Give me ten minutes."

"I'll meet you in the parking lot of the botanical garden."

"Circle the lot," I said. "I'll come to you."

I splashed water on my face and brushed my teeth. From the condo's rooftop, UBC Botanical Garden was a short hop west. Shrubs, fragrant with spring blooms, lined the driveway into the garden's parking lot. I flew over and perched in a nearby fir tree until I spotted Sam's unmarked vehicle approach. When he drove past, I ghosted and dove into his car, re-forming in the passenger seat.

Sam swung his head around and the car swerved right. "Damn it, Emelynn! If you're going to do that, you need to warn me."

"I thought I had. I said 'I'll come to you.'"

"No one thinks that's what that means," he growled. I apologized, noting his beard stubble, and chalked up his outburst to lack of sleep.

Sam drove to Southwest Marine Drive and headed south. The police had closed Macdonald Street. He flashed his credentials at the policewoman manning the blockade.

"Abbott on site?" he asked. She nodded and waved him through. A large white tent had been erected over the Mercedes, and floodlights on poles lit the area as though it were a carnival's midway. Sam parked at the end of a long row of police cars.

"Here," he said, and handed me clip-on ID.

"Visitor. Really? You couldn't do better than that?"

"Classified operative would kinda defeat the purpose, don't you think? Let's go."

I followed him out of the car and trailed his long strides to the RV unit parked close to the tent. The door was open. He stepped inside and I followed.

"Abbott," Sam said, addressing a man hunched over a map with two other men. They wore side arms, and bulletproof vests with *POLICE* stamped on them.

Abbott looked up and straightened when he spotted me. "Jordan. Who's this?"

"Taylor."

Abbott extended his hand. I shook it. "I've heard your name. I'm John Abbott. Welcome. We can use all the help we can get."

"What do you know?" Sam asked.

"Car was stolen. No surprise there. A cabbie caught the vehicle on his dash cam in the vicinity at 19:45. She must have driven straight here from St. Paul's. The engine was cold when we found it. She could be anywhere with that kid by now."

"Has the door-to-door turned up anything yet?"

"Nothing. We're doing a grid search of the golf course. She could have fled on foot or met another vehicle. The Fraser River's close enough, so she could have slipped away in a boat. We've got a UAV in the air aiding the search."

Sam frowned at the mention of the UAV, whatever that was. "Any activity in the twenty-three hundred block?"

"None. We've got surveillance on it."

"Good. We'll have a look around. I'll be in touch." Sam shook Abbott's hand then ushered me ahead of him.

When we were out of earshot, I asked, "What's a UAV? And what's in the twenty-three hundred block?"

"A UAV is an unmanned aerial vehicle. A drone." The parking lights on Sam's unmarked blinked. We split up and headed to our respective sides of the car.

I looked across the roof at him. "You seemed worried back there when Abbott mentioned they were using one."

"No, we use them all the time. Had a thought is all." He ducked into the car, and I did the same.

"Care to share?"

"Drones make a distinctive sound. Like a pissed-off beehive. You ever heard one?"

"Sure, on YouTube. Why?"

"Just wondered."

When he didn't elaborate, I buckled up. "So what's the significance of the twenty-three hundred block?"

"One of the homes in that block has been identified as a stronghold for a suspected human trafficking ring. Finding the kidnapper's car this close to it is a major concern."

"Are you saying the baby might have been sold?"

"That's one possibility. The kid's a ward of the court so it won't be a ransom. Let's go for a drive."

Sam drove out the way we'd come. He lifted two fingers from the steering wheel to acknowledge the policewoman at the barricade and then turned south.

"Can you get a search warrant for the house?"

"Not a chance."

"How about just knocking on the door?"

"We wouldn't get past the guardhouse. Can't get near the place. The best we can do right now is stop anyone driving in or out of the place and collect IDs."

Sam pulled to the right and parked by the curb. He switched off the lights and handed me a pair of binoculars. "It's the house with the black gate."

Fortress was the word that came to mind when I scanned the area behind the gate. Tall hedges obscured the property from every angle. The gate provided the only visual through to the house. A security guard sat inside a small hut to one side of the gate. Above the hedge, security cameras jutted out from the corners of the house.

"How did you learn about this place?"

"The Combined Forces Special Enforcement Unit has it flagged."

I returned his binoculars. "Does ICO have someone embedded with that unit? Maybe we could get more details about the place?"

"If ICO has someone inside, they're not telling me." He stared out of the windshield, scanning the cars along the street.

I turned in my seat. "So this is why you brought me here."

He swivelled his head and met my gaze. "If that baby's inside, you're his only hope."

I looked back to the fortress. "Is Abbott using a drone for surveillance?"

"No. Drones would be overkill. There's only one way in and out, and it's through that gate."

"Where's the surveillance team Abbott mentioned?"

"In that van." He tipped his head toward a windowless black van parked across the street. "Can you get inside the house?"

"I think so, but not in sight of Abbott's team."

Sam signalled and pulled out. He turned west on Fifty-Fourth Avenue and parked.

I released my seat belt. "If he's in there, I'll bring him out."

"Be careful." I turned to go and Sam stopped me. "Emelynn, brace yourself. The place is flagged for a reason."

"Thanks. I'll be fine." I brushed off his warning with a flash of bravado I didn't quite feel. "While I'm in there nosing around, you start thinking about how we're going to explain it all if I find him."

"That's the least of our worries," he said, and picked up the binoculars. "Go do your thing."

I put on a brave smile then squeezed my crystal and blinked out of sight. After I breezed out of the car, I headed back across Southwest Marine, straight for the front door of the house. I blew through it. All was quiet inside. I did a circuit of the main level. Dark hardwood floors gleamed in the moonlight. Original paintings with thickly textured brush strokes adorned the walls, and an intricate Aubusson tapestry served as the focal point in a formal dining room. The scent of lemon furniture polish lingered in the air.

This home was as well-appointed as anything I'd seen in the First Shaughnessy neighbourhood. Nothing about it suggested human trafficking ring. I took my time in the kitchen, searching for baby bottles or formula, but found nothing. That didn't mean anything. I'd learned houses this size often had fully-equipped nurseries. I headed upstairs and counted five bedrooms but no nursery.

Whoever the owners were, they were away. The house was unoccupied. I didn't hold out much hope of finding the baby in the basement, but the dumbwaiter in an upstairs laundry room provided easy access. I dove down the shaft and burst out on the bottom floor. The heady fragrance of laundry detergent announced another laundry area, larger than the one upstairs. Adjacent, I found a fully-stocked wine room and behind another door, a pantry with enough food to feed a football team—for a month. Large storage rooms held jumbled Christmas decorations, outdoor furniture and the typical excesses and debris of the wealthy.

After I'd done a full circuit of the basement, I paused. Something wasn't right. I drifted up the staircase and came out into the kitchen, and from there pictured the basement layout superimposed on the floor. Either I'd missed something downstairs, or the basement was half the size of the rest of the house. Perhaps I'd overlooked a door to an underground garage?

I headed back down the stairs and retraced my path, poking into every room. How strange. Behind the back wall of the pantry and adjacent wine cellar, there should have been more basement. I examined the suspect walls in both rooms and found no evidence of a door. If it weren't for Sam's suspicions about this house, I'd have chalked up the missing basement to a construction problem. But I couldn't leave it at that, and I had one other option: I could blast my ghosted form at the wall. If there was a hidden door, the wisps of my ghost would seep through the cracks around it. I started in the pantry and threw myself against the wall. My ghosted form flattened out. Nothing there. I pulled myself together and repeated the exercise in the wine cellar. Jackpot.

I landed in a narrow hallway, closed in and sound dampened. Bare light bulbs hung unlit from a low concrete ceiling. Three doors lay to my right and three to my left. Behind me, the outline of the opening I'd come through was visible. One of the floor-to-ceiling wine racks had hidden it.

I spun around and stilled, listening for sounds of life, but heard only silence. Steeling myself, I ghosted into the first door on the left and sucked in a breath. A bed dressed in fresh linen lay centred against the far wall. Intricate ironwork in the headboard and footboard suggested turn of the century, but what gripped my attention was the steel cuff on a chain that had been draped over the top of the footboard. I traced the other end of the chain to an eyebolt embedded in concrete in the floor at the foot of the bed.

This was why Sam had warned me to brace myself.

Memories of another room with a chain and a cuff flooded me. A musty odour threw me back to the stained mattress and squalid trailer where I'd been held, tortured. Carson Manse's face flashed before my eyes. Panic threatened, squeezing my lungs. Breathe, I reminded myself, and tamped down the horrific memories. I took another deep breath and turned to leave. To one side of the door, a jailhouse stainless-steel sink and toilet had been installed. I held in a scream and burst out of there.

Only the thought of finding that baby kept me looking. I moved to the second door and pushed inside. This room had two beds. Same set-up. The remaining rooms were similar, but no baby boy, thank god. I raced back the way I'd come and flung myself at the hidden door.

A gust of wind pushed me into the cedar hedge. I couldn't remember getting outside. I pulled my ghosted form through the fragrant boughs and barrelled down the street toward the refuge of Sam's car.

Once inside, the shakes started. I couldn't re-form. I swallowed. "Sam," I said.

He shot his head in my direction.

"Drive, please," I said. "Get out of here."

He immediately reached for the keys in the ignition and started the car. "What the fuck happened in there?" he said, looking through me. He did a quick shoulder check and pulled out then hit the gas.

I inhaled a shaky breath. "Give me a minute. Just keep driving."

"Emelynn. Talk to me. Did you find him?"

"No. No one's in there." I struggled to calm myself. It was the only way I'd be able to re-form. He glanced in my general direction. I wanted to reassure him that a disembodied voice sounded just as strange to me.

The concern on his face was touching. "What did you find?"

"Six rooms. Hidden in the basement behind a false door in the wine cellar. They're cells. Each room has a bed or two, a toilet and a sink. All the rooms are fitted with shackles."

"So the intel on that place is right. There must be another access point. Did you find any other exits besides the one to the wine cellar?"

"Sorry, Sam. I didn't look. I got out of there as soon as I was sure the baby wasn't inside."

Sam took a right and slowed on the darkened street. We passed a forested area on our left. Fear finally loosened its grip. With my breathing under control, I concentrated and re-formed. It had been months since I'd had to work so hard to return to my corporeal form. The effort left me feeling vulnerable and a little frightened.

Sam looked over at me and smiled. "Hey," he said, as if he hadn't seen me in weeks. "You okay?"

"Thanks, yeah. I'll be fine. I wasn't expecting it, that's all. The chains, the cuffs. It brought back some ugly memories." I was grateful Sam knew my history. It meant I didn't have to retell the nightmare of my kidnapping, and the whipping I'd endured at the hands of a madman in a filthy trailer in the woods.

"You did good work in there. Now that we know the traffickers aren't active, there's hope the baby wasn't sold. We'll find him."

"The woman who took him might still have him. What do we know about her?"

Sam rubbed his eyes. "She's not a hospital employee, and last I checked, the facial-recognition software hadn't spit out a match. Let's head back to Abbott and get the latest."

Abbott had no further information on the kidnapper. Sam stood with his hands on his hips staring at Abbott's map and the circle drawn around the trafficking stronghold. He pressed his lips into a thin line. I felt his frustration, but there was no way to tell Abbott the house was a waste of his resources.

Sam shifted his feet and switched his focus. "She'd have to be pretty desperate to kidnap an infant," Sam said. "An addict, maybe, or connected with the criminal set. If she's working for someone else, they may have recruited her from the street. I'll send a team to the Downtown Eastside with her photo."

"Good plan," Abbott said. "Set it in motion and then get some rest. Come back in a few hours."

The sun was still firmly below the horizon when we got back to the car. "Where do you want me to drop you?"

"Drive by my condo," I said, "but don't stop. I'll *do my thing*."

"Thanks for the warning." He grinned and started the car. He gave the steering-wheel wave to the officer manning the blockade and turned north. "I'll catch a few hours' sleep and call you with an update."

When I got home, I crawled into bed. It wasn't sleep I craved—it was oblivion.

Chapter Five

The patter of rain on the bedroom window woke me. It was 7:00 a.m. Almost twelve hours since the kidnapping. Oblivion hadn't lasted nearly long enough. The memories dragged up from the stronghold had faded, but I knew from experience it would take days to suppress them completely. Distraction helped. It would be ten o'clock in Toronto. I sent my mom a message—a fifteen-minute Viagra warning—and stepped into the bathroom. While the coffee brewed, I video-called her.

She was in her lab. Shadows had moved in around her eyes. "How you doing, Mom?"

"Just fine, sweetheart," she said, lying like a trooper. "Got the apartment back in order last night. Still can't find a darn thing missing."

"That's good, right? Did you get the locks changed?"

"Yes. The police gave me the name of a twenty-four-hour locksmith."

"It can't be easy for you, staying in the apartment after what happened."

She tipped the phone away from her face. "Mom?"

She didn't answer, but I heard her sniffling. It hurt to hear her cry and know how vulnerable she must feel.

"The daffodils are already blooming here," I said. "The tulips aren't far behind. Why don't you take some of the holidays you've been saving for the last decade and come visit, see the new condo?"

I let the quiet linger between us, hoping she'd consider it. After last night, I could use a little Mom time. When she turned the phone back around, she'd wiped away the tears. "I'd like that, sweetheart. Very much. I'll make the arrangements and send you my itinerary."

"Let me do it, Mom. It'll be an oddball routing, but safer. Just a minute." My laptop was already on. I brought up Google Maps and found what I was looking for. "Go home and pack a bag then book yourself into the Hyatt on King Street. You'll fly out tomorrow from Billy Bishop Airport. I'll email you the details."

"I take it this is one of James's tricks?"

I laughed, making light of a reminder that left me longing for James's arms around me. "You don't think I come up with this stuff on my own, do you?" Neither my mom nor I would be safe if our relationship was uncovered. Redeemers operated without the burden of a conscience. They'd kill her to get to me without hesitation. "Can't wait to see you, Mom, and if anyone asks, tell them you're taking a week off and staying with friends in Montreal." I told her I loved her and then hung up.

James . . . why hadn't he called? I vacillated between angry and worried, with worried getting more and more of my time. Where was he?

Then I got busy and booked my mom's trip. First was a return flight to Montreal, but she wouldn't use the return portion. Instead, she'd take a limo from the airport to the train station, and from there, an express train to Ottawa. I booked her a hotel in Ottawa. The day after that, she'd fly from Ottawa to Vancouver. I sent the details on to her. It was a routing James would have approved of.

Before I made my next call, I scrambled two eggs and poured another cup of coffee. Once fortified, I dialled Mason and told him about Mom's visit.

"I'm glad to hear it. I'll update Rossi."

"Thanks. It'll be good for Mom to get away, and I could use the company, though it does present a challenge. She thinks I work for Avery, not Sam. I'll have to do some juggling."

"You'll manage. On another note, I looked at the film clip from the kidnapping. Who's the woman?"

"We don't know yet. She doesn't work for the hospital. They're still trying to identify her."

"What did Navin learn?"

"He hasn't contacted me yet."

"Call him. He should have something for you by now. And until we know for sure whether or not that film's been cut, keep a low profile. No demonstrations."

Heat rushed to my face. Had going into that traffickers' stronghold last night been a mistake?

"And one last thing. Why haven't you updated Sebastian?"

"Because it was four in the morning when I got home. No way am I waking Sebastian at that hour to tell him what? No news is good news?"

"Navin's involvement is news. And since when did anyone on the Tribunal, let alone the current head of it, punch a clock?"

"Wait a minute. How do you know I haven't been in touch with Sebastian?"

"How do you think? He called. He wasn't happy. What did I tell you about being blindsided?"

Sebastian and Mason were in the grips of a power transfer, and there were days I feared ending up as roadkill in the middle of it. "That man's impossible. I hope you—"

I jumped at the knock on my door. Security hadn't called to announce a visitor. "Someone's at the door. Want to guess who?" I gazed down at my nightshirt and bare feet, and with a shake of my head, plodded to the door and glanced through the peephole.

I switched off the alarm and opened the door. "I've got to go, Mason. Sebastian is here." I hung up on him, frustrated with both of them.

"Sebastian. This is an unexpected surprise," I said, parroting the words he'd spoken to me the night before.

"I doubt that." He looked down at my nightshirt with disapproval and brushed past, inviting himself in. I held my tongue and followed him down the hall.

"Just when were you going to report in?" he asked, without breaking stride.

I stopped short. "There are so many things wrong with this conversation I can hardly sort out where to start."

I braced myself as he turned around. He squared his jaw. "You brought me into this, remember?"

I raised my hands to my hips, and my good sense fled. "First, I can't believe you don't have a hernia from the enormous double standard you're carrying around. And second, you are not my boss. My asking for your help doesn't put you in charge of the case. And third, I don't generally wake people in the middle of the night to tell them I have nothing to report."

He tilted his head with a curious look that told me he thought I'd lost my mind. Maybe I had. He'd lashed out at me before, so I knew my *block* wouldn't protect me from his jolts, but his arrogance galled me.

"That's not what I hear."

What the hell had Mason told him? I dropped my arms in defeat. "Make yourself at home. I'll be back in a moment." I turned and trotted to the bedroom. I yanked on the clothes I'd worn the night before, pulled a wide-toothed comb through my hair and went out to pacify the arrogant ass.

He stood where I'd left him, staring out the windows to the Pacific.

I crossed my arms and spoke to his back, dribbling out the details of the previous evening. He didn't interrupt.

When I finished, he spoke. "Did you tell the detective you're having the film analyzed?"

"Kind of hard not to when he's the one who handed over the footage. I told you before, I know him. He can be trusted."

Sebastian didn't turn around. He shook his head. "Unless he's involved, in which case telling him was a mistake, you've just given him fair warning that we're on to him."

I held my tongue. Sebastian didn't know Sam like I did.

"What has he learned since you saw him?" he asked.

"I haven't heard from him, but I didn't expect to. He was up all night." Sebastian's head dipped and moved from side to side again. I imagined a scowl on his face.

"Who's the child?"

Each of his questions was a pin, and I was the voodoo doll. "The mother lives on the street. No name, no info on the father. She abandoned the baby, which makes him a ward of the court."

"What did Navin Patel have to say about the film?"

"I haven't called him yet."

Sebastian turned around. "Why not?"

I covered my face with my hands and moaned. This was why he was listed under *D* for Dick in my phone. Just then, my phone vibrated to life, dancing on the coffee table. I reached for it. "He must be clairvoyant. It's Navin."

Sebastian nodded to it. "Put him on speaker."

Was *pushy* included in the definition of *arrogant?* I wondered. "Hello, Navin. You're on speakerphone. Sebastian Kirk is with me." This time, I saw Sebastian's scowl. I didn't care. Anyone dealing with Sebastian deserved a warning.

Navin greeted Sebastian. "Hello, Mr. Kirk."

"What'd you learn?" I asked.

"My guess is it's been doctored."

"Your guess?" I said. I'd been expecting something more definitive than speculation.

"It's impossible to be one-hundred-percent certain. The clip passed every test, except one. I've identified an abrupt change in pixel luminosity values at the points where the camera cuts in and out. Could be a shadow from something out of the camera's range, like a door opening or closing, but the pattern doesn't look natural to me."

Again, I voiced my concern. "I wish you sounded more certain."

"With today's technology, it doesn't take a genius to manipulate pixels. My opinion is that this clip's been tampered with. That's as certain as you're going to get."

"Good enough," Sebastian said. "Goodbye, Navin." No doubt Sebastian would have hung up on him if he'd held the phone. Fortunately, he didn't.

"Thank you, Navin," I said, and then hung up politely.

Sebastian stared through me and crossed his arms, stroking his chin between his forefinger and thumb.

I dropped the phone back on the coffee table. "Even if Navin is right," I said, "we don't know who doctored the film or why, and at this point, a child is still missing. Sam and I are working a kidnapping case, not some conspiracy."

Sebastian stood a few inches taller than I was and used that height to glower down his nose. "That naïveté is why I spend my precious free time mentoring you. If you want to be one of us, you have to think like one of us."

"I am one of you. It may not have been by choice, but here I am. And you're the one who put my name forward when ICO threatened to expose us."

He pinched up his face and stepped forward. "Your carelessness is the reason ICO threatened us."

I raised my hand, palm out, shut my eyes and counted to three. "How many times did I warn you and everyone else that the party at Cairabrae was a mistake? A foolish, frivolous goddamn cocktail party that put us all at risk when the Redeemer threat was so great? Hell, even Sam knew it was a mistake, and he didn't even know what we were then."

Sebastian's face flushed. He clenched his jaw, turned on his heel and stalked back to the windows. It was Sebastian who'd insisted on the party. "Welcoming me to the fold," he'd said, but it was a thin excuse to satisfy petty Tribunal curiosity about the woman Jolene had gifted. Mason and his father, Stuart, had only gone along to keep everyone happy. Their collective arrogance nearly killed them. I knew Sebastian blamed me, he'd said it often enough, but I was sick of him dismissing his own role in it.

After a moment he looked to the floor. The storm had blown itself out. Sebastian and I would probably never see eye to eye, but surely we didn't have to butt heads all the time. I walked to the kitchen and poured us each a coffee.

"Peace offering," I said, when I returned. I handed him a cup.

He accepted it without a smile or a thank-you and took a seat on the sofa. He stretched one arm across the back, lifted his ankle to rest on his knee and savoured a sip. "When I say you need to think like one of us, I'm not talking about being a Flier, or even a Ghost. You've been offered a seat on the Tribunal. That seat comes with expectations."

I'd promised Mason and Stuart that I'd keep my options open, so I hadn't told Sebastian I had no intention of accepting the Tribunal's offer.

Sebastian continued. "Expectations that I'm afraid would tear you apart. You're too soft. But it's not your fault. You weren't raised as one of us."

Did that even qualify as a backhanded compliment? I wasn't sure, not that it mattered, but I did find it curious that Sebastian was steering me away from taking the seat.

"You're right." Neither my mother nor my father had been a Flier, so I hadn't been born this way. Jolene had gifted me, and not telling my mother about it was a mistake I regretted every day. "I wish I'd had the chance to know Jolene."

"Navin's findings are usually sound," Sebastian said. A jarring change of subject. Was it the mention of Jolene? "Let's assume the film has been edited. Who benefits from it?"

Though it irked me to admit it, Sebastian had asked exactly the right question. I sipped my coffee and considered it. "Someone may have helped the woman and then cut themselves out of the clip."

"In which case, they were framing the woman. Otherwise, they would have simply erased the entire film. The woman is of no interest to us. Who else?" Sebastian's lack of empathy bordered on sociopathic.

I tried again. "Someone trying to make the hospital's security look bad? A rival security company?"

"Then why haven't they taken advantage of the news cycle yet, and made a public case for themselves? Who else?"

"Sounds to me like you've already thought this through."

"As you should have. That's the difference experience makes."

I ignored his remark and restrained an eyeball roll. "What do you think?"

"I already told you what I think. Someone wanted your detective to see that film, assume it was one of us and use you to expose more of our kind. ICO is the most likely culprit."

"Sam doesn't think it's ICO. He picked up the case on his own after he saw that film."

"Then someone else knows about us. Either way, the detective and quite possibly you are being tracked. I do hope you haven't done anything foolish for the wrong people to see."

He wasn't the only one. A chill descended, and I wrapped my arms around my torso.

"Arrange a walkabout with the detective as soon as it's dark. Phone me with the details. I'll be there."

"Watching the watcher?"

"Exactly. We'll see how good the detective's instincts are. Now, I must go."

"Before you do, you should know my mother will be arriving day after tomorrow for a visit. She'll expect security downstairs to announce visitors."

"Yes, I recall. She doesn't know about your gift. How long will she be here?"

"I don't know yet. A week, maybe more."

"Noted. Call me when you've spoken with the detective."

Sebastian faded away, and within moments I could no longer sense his ghost. He'd left.

CHAPTER SIX

Waking Sam would have felt a little too much like obeying Sebastian's orders. Instead, I scoured the Internet for information on the kidnapping. It had made the news, but with no photos of the infant and no grief-stricken parents begging for his return, it didn't take up as much space as it should have. Sam's comment came back to me. *No one's going to miss him.* Sadly, that seemed to be the case.

Just before noon, I finally called Sam. He'd already been to the golf course where the car was found and had returned to the police station. "The car's in the lab. No match on fingerprints. No ID on the woman. No ransom demand. No sightings." His frustration punctuated the negatives. "And every minute that ticks by lessens our chances of finding him."

"I have some news, but I don't think you'll like it. The CCTV footage has been edited."

"You certain?"

"Apparently as certain as it's possible to be about pixels and digital film."

"You're right. I don't like it. However, it means someone else could have been involved. It's a new lead. I'll push Abbott in that direction and find out who had access to the camera's feed."

"Sam, what if that *someone else* is ICO?"

"That's the second time you've brought that up. Do you know something I don't?"

"No. The Tribunal doesn't trust them, but that's not news."

"I can guarantee you the feeling's mutual, but I hear you. I'll follow the evidence and won't rule out anyone. If any of the ICO players had a hand in it, they won't be the only ones with trust issues."

If ICO was manipulating Sam, trust would be the least of our worries. Exposure presented a much greater threat. "There may be a shortcut to finding out who's involved," I said.

"I'm listening."

I explained Sebastian's plan without mentioning his name. Continuing to pretend that Sam didn't know Sebastian was one of us felt like a game, but it was a game Sebastian insisted on, and I wasn't about to cross him.

"I'll go along with this plan as long as you and your contact understand that the child is our first priority. Whether the film's been doctored is irrelevant as long as that baby's missing. If we get a lead on the kidnapper, that's the direction we go. I won't give a rat's ass who's watching us."

"I agree. The child comes first." Sebastian and his sociopathic tendencies could bite me.

"And if we get a hot tip between now and dark, all bets are off and you're with me."

"Agreed."

"Good. Abbott's team didn't get anything from the Downtown Eastside overnight. How about we canvas the Granville corridor? I'll bring some photographs." We agreed to meet at sunset, just after eight o'clock.

When I got off the phone, I called Sebastian and gave him the game plan. The whole missing-child bit blew right on by. "Cover as much ground as you can," he said. "I want whoever is watching to have to hustle to keep up."

I touched base with Sam as darkness approached. We were still on, and after weeks of evasion training, I left the condo confident I hadn't been followed. I didn't show myself until I walked out of the shadows on Sixteenth Avenue. Whether Sebastian was already tagging along was unclear. He'd been vague on details, and I couldn't sense him.

I took public transit and caught up with Sam on the pedestrian mall on Granville Street, where he'd parked his unmarked. He exited the car as I approached. A navy windbreaker with *POLICE* stencilled on the back didn't hide the protective vest he wore underneath. Other than his brush cut, I'd never seen him wear anything that identified him as a cop.

"Nice jacket. You got one of those for me?"

"No, but you do get a vest." He nodded toward the passenger seat.

I strapped the Kevlar on under my jacket.

Sam pulled out a flashlight that could double as a baseball bat and secured it to his vest. "I'll ask the questions. You keep a step behind. And here." He handed me his spiral notepad. "Take notes."

"First a visitor and now a secretary. I'm not sure—is this a promotion or a demotion?"

Sam's sense of humour was locked up tight. "Even if it sounds like gibberish, write it down."

We headed north on foot. Sam stopped and talked with everyone on the street, including every homeless person who didn't scurry away ahead of us. His respectful tone earned him some eyes on the photograph of the kidnapper. Some deftly hid their vices in the folds of blankets or oversized coats. Others were off in drug-induced utopias and wouldn't open their eyes. Sam palmed five-dollar bills like they were Monopoly money, and received grateful nods in return. We turned around at Pender Street and canvassed the other side, all the way to Smithe. The number of homeless people, especially teenagers, astounded me. Sam's assurance that it used to be worse didn't make it any better.

We completed the four-block loop without a single hit on the kidnapper's photograph and returned to Sam's car. "Any word from your observer?" Sam asked.

I glanced at my phone. "Not yet."

"Let's go for a drive. If someone's following, we'll flush them out." Sam drove the length of the pedestrian mall and then wove his way out of the downtown and south over the Burrard Street Bridge. He turned west onto Fourth Avenue. Traffic slowed, narrowed by post-rush-hour street parking.

"Something you said before has been on my mind," I said. "The child's a ward of the court, so no teary-eyed parents pleading on TV for his safe return. No one from the hospital's putting themselves in the limelight, and same goes for whichever government body is responsible. Not a lot of outside pressure to get his kidnapping solved quickly." I put Sebastian's style of question to the test. "Who benefits from that?"

Sam braked for a left-turning vehicle. "Someone who thought a ward of the court was easy pickins."

"Which raises the question—how did they know he was a ward of the court? It has to be either a hospital insider or a technical whiz capable of breaking into hospital records. A tech geek would certainly explain the doctored film."

Impatient, Sam squeaked around the vehicle and detoured right, taking us on a tour of a residential block. "A tech geek with the right skills may also have been able to access the Special Enforcement Unit's database," he said. "Maybe the kidnappers intentionally left the suspect's car in the vicinity of that trafficking stronghold." Sam kept a keen eye on his mirrors as he rejoined traffic on Fourth Avenue. "Which means they wanted to observe us in action as long as they could."

Though neither of us had put voice to it, I had no doubt Sam was thinking the same thing as I was: the kidnapping was edging closer to resembling a deception, and someone well-connected was orchestrating it.

As we approached Blenheim Street, my phone buzzed. It was a text message from an unknown caller who could only be Sebastian. *Two men. They're using drones.*

"Pull over," I said, and scrolled down to the pictures Sebastian had sent. The drone looked like a four-armed spider on steroids, black with no identifiable markings. Below that was a photo of a man placing a drone into the back of a white van. The last picture was a close-up of the licence plate. I passed the phone to Sam.

Sam swiped through the photos with the thumb of his right hand. Without warning, he smacked his free hand against the steering wheel. I jumped. He pinched the bridge of his nose.

"What is it? Do you recognize him?" He returned the phone and then reached over and punched at the keys of his onboard computer as if they were punching back.

"No, but yesterday at the golf course, it wasn't Abbott's drone that worried me—it was because I remembered hearing one the night we met at Denny's. I never spotted it. Dismissed it as a toy. I shouldn't have."

A thought wormed into my mind. I stilled my hands, remembering my own paranoia that night. "I felt like I was being followed that night, too," I said. "Couldn't shake the feeling, but didn't think of a drone."

I turned to face him. "This is bad, Sam. If someone has me on film, ghosting . . ." I couldn't finish the sentence.

Sam sucked in a slow breath and exhaled. "We're not there yet. And you ghosted from inside the car. That would have been nearly impossible to catch on film. If they got a shot it was from a fair distance."

Nice try, but we both knew distance wasn't a problem with a good-enough lens. I texted Sebastian: *Where are they now?*

"Send me those photos," Sam said.

The phone was in my hand when it buzzed. I almost yelped. *Apartment roof, northeast corner.*

"What is it?" Sam asked.

"The drone is still following. It's up there," I said, nodding toward the grey, wood-clad apartment building.

My phone buzzed again. *They're tag-teaming two drones.* I passed on the information to Sam.

"The batteries in those things are only good for twenty minutes, give or take." Sam ran his finger down the computer screen. "The van's licence plate is registered to a numbered company at the south end of No. 2 Road in Richmond." He put the car in drive and pulled back into traffic. "How about you and I go take a look?"

"Now? They're watching. They'll know we're coming."

"Good. I hope they're sweating, and if they've seen you in action, they will be. Text your contact. Next time they switch out the drones, I want face shots."

Me? Give Sebastian an order? This night was going from worse to someplace considerably south of worst. I texted Sebastian our intentions and politely requested a better photo of the men. Then I forwarded Sebastian's photos to Sam's phone.

Sam turned north on Blenheim.

I flipped through the photos again. "Are these drones the same type as the ones Abbott uses?"

"I don't know, but I'll make a point of finding out."

At the buzz of my phone, I checked the screen. "They're down one drone," I said, passing on Sebastian's news. How had he managed that? I wondered.

Blenheim was a quiet residential street with roundabouts and four-way stops. Sam drove it like a cabbie with a twenty-dollar tip in the balance. Six minutes later, he flicked on his grill lights, blipped the siren and sped onto Southwest Marine heading for the Arthur Laing Bridge into Richmond.

My phone buzzed. *They're collecting the drone. You have a five-minute lead.*

"Won't help," Sam said, when I told him. "They'll have figured out where we're headed by now and warned whoever's on the other end."

"Then why are you driving like a madman to get there?"

"Sending them a message. I want them panicking, making mistakes." Sam raced down No. 2 Road, weaving around the traffic, blipping the siren and cursing under his breath when vehicles wouldn't get out of his way. As we approached the lights at Steveston Highway, he slowed and glanced at his GPS screen.

Half a block later, he swerved to the right and screeched to a halt on the apron outside the garage door of a warehouse. His grill lights lit up the front of the building with flashing colour. "How about we go say hello. See who they sent to greet us?"

"I think you're enjoying this."

He swung his door open. "I want to know who these bastards are." He leapt out and marched to the entry door on the left of the garage. Jiggling the handle, he glanced in the window beside it. He carried on without hesitation, walking the breadth of the building and then turning down the side. I followed as he made a circuit of the tall, one-storey structure. The exit door at the back had a lock but no handle. No windows other than the one on the front.

When we arrived back on the concrete apron, a second car was parked beside ours. The occupant was still behind the wheel. Sam walked behind the blue Honda and glanced down at the licence plate. I followed.

The driver door opened, and a woman emerged, a look of alarm on her face. "Officer. What's going on here?"

"You the owner?" Sam asked.

"My husband and I, yes."

"What kind of business?"

"Transportation, warehousing. Is there a problem?"

"May I see some identification?" Sam produced a notepad and flipped it open.

The woman scowled but bent to the car and rifled through her purse. She straightened with her wallet in hand, pulled out her driver's licence and handed it to him. Her feet were bare inside a pair of paint-splattered Crocs, and she wasn't wearing a jacket. She rubbed her arms.

"You got here pretty quick." He made a note of her licence and handed it back.

She pointed to a security camera. "I saw you pull up. I live around the corner."

"You should have called 911 instead of charging over here."

She started to talk, but Sam cut her off. I knew exactly how she felt, having been in her shoes opposite Sam back when he'd been Detective Jordan to me. He played the intimidating-cop card well.

"You have vehicles in there?"

"Yeah. We rent them out."

"You rent drones as well?"

Her brow creased. "Drones? No."

Sam pulled out his phone and swiped the screen. "Can you tell me who rented this vehicle?" He handed her the phone and I caught a glimpse of the photo of the white van's licence plate.

She glanced at the photo and then back at Sam. "Why do you want to know?"

Sam returned the phone to his pocket and shifted his jacket to expose the butt of his gun in its shoulder holster. "We would appreciate your cooperation."

Her gaze flashed from Sam to me as she weighed her options. "We don't want any trouble," she said. The woman turned back to her car, reached in and pulled her keys from the ignition. She closed the car door and walked toward the building.

Sam and I remained silent as she unlocked the door, turned on the light and headed to the only desk in the tidy showroom. Obviously well acquainted with the space, she turned on the computer and pulled a binder from the shelf behind. Laminated picture boards of cube and cargo vans decorated the walls. The computer beeped to life and she typed on the keyboard. Satisfied with what she'd found, she flipped through the binder and settled on a page. She turned the binder around to face us.

"Mr. Smithford rented that unit. He's been a regular for six months. Always returns the vehicles clean and on time. He's a good customer."

Sam pulled out his phone and took a picture of the page, which included the man's driver's licence. "When is Mr. Smithford expected to return this vehicle?" he asked. I pulled the book closer and took my own photo of it. A prominent jaw and bald head put me in mind of Mr. Clean. I doubted he was that.

"It's out for the month, but he can renew the rental with a phone call." Sam raised an eyebrow. "As I said, he's a good customer."

"Thank you for the information." Sam tucked away his notepad and nodded me toward the door. "Next time you see trouble around here, call the police. That's what we're here for."

CHAPTER SEVEN

Back in his unmarked, Sam ran Smithford's driver's licence. "Clean as a nun's habit. Did your contact get a better shot of the men?"

I checked my phone. "Nothing yet. Do you think the woman in there is involved?"

"No, but she wasn't monitoring that security camera either. Someone alerted her. She might suspect Mr. Smithford isn't totally legit, but as she reminded us twice, he's a good customer." Sam put the car in gear and pulled back onto No. 2 Road.

"Where are we going?"

"Smithford's address."

We parked at the curb outside Smithford's house on Cambie Road. "Let's go," he said, and we climbed out. He came around my side and we hastened up the front walk together.

"What if he's in there?"

"He won't be." Sam rang the doorbell.

A diminutive Chinese man answered. His equally diminutive wife hovered in the doorway behind him. "Yes," he said.

Sam flashed his badge. "I'm looking for Mr. Smithford."

The elderly man shook his head. "No. No Mr. Smithford here. You have the wrong address."

Sam pulled up Smithford's photo on his phone. "Do you know this man?"

The grey-haired man lifted the glasses that hung from a chain around his neck and propped them on the end of his nose. He tipped his head back to examine the photo. "No. Not familiar. Who is he?"

"Like you said, wrong address." Sam thanked the man and we returned to the car.

"Now what?"

"I go back to the station, get an ID on the elusive Mr. Smithford and touch base with Abbott about his drones. I'll call you when I have something. Where do you want me to drop you?"

"Main and Sixteenth. I'll get home on my own from there."

My phone buzzed. I pulled it out and looked at the caller ID. California was all it said. I didn't recognize the 619 area code. I answered, but there was no one on the other end.

"Who is it?" Sam asked.

"One of those annoying robocalls," I said.

We spent the drive working out suspects. I dismissed his suggestion that it might be the Redeemers. They would have no use for drones. He dismissed my suggestion it was organized crime. "Not their style," he said. I removed the protective vest and dropped it on the back seat.

"Has to be an insider," I said. "If it's not ICO, could it be someone in the local department?"

"I can't see it. Could be higher up the chain."

"I thought ICO was as high up as it got."

"Not high—hidden, as in black ops. Only a select few know that ICO exists, let alone what it does."

"Maybe it's someone connected to the infighting that's had us stalled."

"Could be. It's an old rivalry. ICO is military intelligence. CSIS is civilian intelligence. General Cain embedded me in the civilian side to mask the military's involvement. Could be the mask slipped."

"Territorial squabbles? As if our jobs weren't complicated enough. Whatever happened to *the greater good*?"

"Looks like it's under the bus keeping *common sense* company. You and I are on our own. We have to find out who's messing in our business and shut them down."

We didn't pinpoint that *who* before Sam and I parted ways.

If my instincts were correct, Sebastian wasn't far away. Meeting on Main Street was infinitely better than having him drop into my condo.

Sushi restaurants were more plentiful than coffee shops on this stretch of Main. I chose an unpopular one, took a table for two and ordered tea and a spicy tuna roll.

My instincts hadn't failed me. Sebastian strolled into the near-empty restaurant moments later looking as if he'd come off a *Matrix* movie set. He spotted me and waved off the hostess. My waitress approached from the other direction and delivered the pot of tea and the tuna roll.

Sebastian waited until she'd left before taking the seat opposite.

"Hungry?" he asked. His sarcastic tone prompted me to pop a piece in my mouth. The rice was still warm. "What did you learn?"

I finished my bite and reached for the teapot. "The man who rented the van calls himself Smithford, but the address on his driver's licence isn't his. Sam is working on an ID right now."

"You can save him the time. He won't be able to ID him. The two men in the van tonight were military."

"How do you know?" I pushed a cup of tea across the table to him.

"I've worked with enough of them to spot the training. Tell the detective. He'll understand. If he has any sense, it should shake him out of the notion that this is a child abduction."

It must be hard for Sebastian to have to deal with *idiots* like Sam and me, I thought. If I actually bit my tongue each time I held it, I'd have a callus on it. "Did you get a better shot of the men?"

He pulled out his phone, clicked through a few screens and put it back in his pocket. A moment later my phone vibrated against the table. If he'd intended to make me feel as if I had a communicable disease, he'd succeeded. I glanced through the photos. "That's Smithford," I said, pointing him out. The other man had short, dark hair and a swarthy, pocked complexion. "What's this?" I asked, indicating a picture he'd sent of a small rundown house with an attached garage.

"The van is parked in that garage. It's on Spires Road in Richmond."

"Did you go inside?"

He raised his eyebrows. "I'm glad you think so highly of my skills, but I don't perform miracles. I detoured to follow the van, doubled back to locate you and the detective at the warehouse, and followed you here. You imagine I also found the time to go inside that house and investigate? I think I've done quite enough."

Well, when he put it like that. Suitably chastened, I adopted a look of chagrin.

"Perhaps now the detective can do his job and find out who's behind this."

"I'll talk to him."

"I want to know what he learns immediately." Sebastian stood and left without another word.

I toyed with my phone while I ate another piece of spicy tuna. Despite Sebastian's arrogant manner, I couldn't fault him. He'd stepped up. Maybe Mason was right and I didn't know all there was to know about the man.

I texted Sam what I'd learned, sent him Sebastian's photos and then finished off the sushi roll while I awaited his response. The waitress cleared my plate and I poured another cup of tea.

Sam phoned. "The house on Spires is a rental. Owners live a few blocks away from it. How about I pick you up and we go take a look."

"Just you and me? Don't you think we should bring backup?"

"I've seen you in action, remember? You can take care of yourself and I've got a gun. Until we know who's behind this, there's no one here I can trust."

Twenty minutes later, he pulled up at the curb and I jumped in.

"What's the plan?" I asked, buckling up.

"Put on your vest. We'll hit the landlord first."

The clock on the dashboard read 11:27 p.m. Disturbing people's sleep was turning into a nasty habit.

"I know I shouldn't be happy about these guys being military," I said, "but it eliminates the possibility of someone new knowing about us."

"Wish I could agree, but all field intelligence operatives are highly trained, military or otherwise. We can't eliminate anyone."

The tiny bubble of hope I'd been floating on popped and I plunged back into shitload-of-trouble territory.

We found the landlord's address and parked on the street. The house was dark inside, but a car sat in the driveway.

"Let me do the talking," Sam said, and we got out. I followed him to the front door. Three angled windows lined the top edge. He rapped his knuckles so hard against the heavily painted wood I expected to see blood. Eventually, a light came on, and moments later we heard shuffling inside. "Police," Sam announced.

The middle-aged man who opened the door squinted against the light. "What is it? What's wrong?" he said, rubbing one eye and then the other. He wore flip-flops and tugged at the sleeve of a neon-green housecoat he'd pulled on over his pyjamas.

Sam had his notepad out. "Are you Huang Yeung?"

"Yes," he said, nodding and blinking fiercely.

"We're here as a courtesy. Earlier this evening, we detained two young men in the neighbourhood of the rental you own on Spires

Road." I looked sideways at Sam. "They broke a few windows, turned on some outdoor taps and shoved the hoses in basement windows. No one's answering the door at your rental. We suggest you go over and make sure it's secure."

"Jesus! . . . I mean, thank you, officer. Yes, I'll—" He stepped to his right then paused and swung back. "Yeah, I'll go right now." This time he stepped to his left and turned back into the house. He'd left the door ajar, distracted no doubt, with visions of water damage and rising insurance premiums.

Sam and I trotted back to the car and climbed in. "How long did it take you to come up with that whopper?" I asked.

Sam pulled his seat belt across his chest and clicked it into place. "You think this is the first time I've had to gain access without a warrant?"

"Isn't this risky? That man doesn't stand a chance against Smithford and his buddy."

"He'll be fine. Smithford knows him, and he has a legitimate reason for being there."

"Except for the fact that no one knocked on his tenant's door."

The corners of Sam's mouth curled up ever so slightly. "They probably just didn't hear it."

Yeung re-emerged still wearing the pyjama pants, but he'd pulled on a field jacket. It was an improvement on the housecoat. He got in his car, backed out of the driveway and made the turn toward Spires.

Sam took a different route, sped the entire way and approached from the other end of the street. He flipped off his headlights, coasted to the curb three houses away and cut the engine. Then he retrieved a pair of binoculars from a pocket on the driver door and scoped out our surroundings.

We watched Yeung pull into the driveway. He kept his head down and fumbled with keys as he climbed the stairs to the front porch.

"I sure hope he knocks first," I said.

Sam watched through the binoculars. "He's knocking." Yeung grabbed the rail and bent to the right to look into the window. He straightened and then stooped. "Looks like he dropped the keys. He's knocking again."

Yeung turned and jogged down the stairs. "Where's he going?" I said. Yeung stepped across the lawn and turned into the side yard.

"Checking for broken windows," Sam said. "Curious they didn't answer his knock."

"Do you think they can see us?"

Sam didn't answer. He kept his binoculars focused on the house. A few minutes later, Yeung came around the other side of the house and went straight to the garage. "He's unlocking the garage," Sam said. Seconds later we heard the rattle of the garage door opening. From this angle, I couldn't see a vehicle inside.

"Where's the van?" I said, startled by the sight of the empty bay.

This time when Yeung jogged up the front steps, he didn't knock. He immediately inserted the key, opened the door wide and charged inside.

"Shit!" Sam hurled open his door and ran across the road. He pulled his gun from its holster as he crossed the door's threshold. I hurried to catch up.

The living room lay to the right of the front door. It was bare. The dining room beyond was also bare. I looked left into a den and then a bedroom. There wasn't so much as a dust bunny. Sam followed Yeung down a staircase off the hall, calling out and identifying himself. I poked through the kitchen cupboards and opened the fridge. Empty. I checked under the sink. No garbage.

"He signed a lease," Yeung said, emerging from the basement. Sam's gun was back in its holster. "I don't rent for less than a year. I told him."

Sam pulled out his phone. "Is this the man you rented to?"

Yeung glanced at Sam's phone. "Yes. That's him." A quizzical glare crossed Yeung's face. "Why do you have a photograph of my tenant?"

"The vandalism?" Sam said, reminding Yeung. "We looked up the plates on their vehicle. A white Mercedes cargo van, right?"

"Yes. Brand new." He shook his head. "He had good references."

Sam swiped to the photo of the second man. "What about him?"

"That's his brother, Ed." Sam and I glanced at one another. Brother? Not in any gene pool I knew of. "He lived here too."

Sam opened the front hall closet. Empty.

"He had furniture, right?" I asked.

Yeung thought about it. "Less than most. He worked in sales. Said he spent a lot of time on the road."

"Any broken windows? Water in the basement?" I asked, aiming for a bright spot in Yeung's night.

He shook his head. "No. The trouble-makers didn't hit here, thank god. No damage."

Sam jammed his hand in his pocket and came out with a business card. He offered it to Yeung. "We're sorry for your trouble here tonight, Mr. Yeung. I hate to see you taken advantage of. Perhaps we can help. Unofficially, you understand." Yeung's face brightened. "As soon as you get home, email me the rental agreement and anything else you have on Smithford or his brother. References, credit checks. We'll see if we can find where Mr. Smithford has moved."

Yeung dipped his head with a little bow. "Thank you."

Sam rested his hand on Yeung's shoulder. "This is strictly between you and me, because officially,"—Sam shook his head—"I couldn't do it."

"Yes, yes. Just between you and me," Yeung said with a smile that nearly split his face.

We left Yeung in the house and returned to the car.

"They knew we were coming," Sam said. "How?"

"The woman at the warehouse. She told us Mr. Clean was a good customer. She probably phoned him."

"Mr. Clean?" Sam said, raising an eyebrow.

"Well, Smithford's not his name." I picked up the binoculars and absently checked on the neighbours.

"Smithford would have known the vehicle rental agreement wouldn't point to this address," I said. "So why clear out of here? There must be a connection between Smithford and this place that he knew we'd find."

Sam drummed his fingers on the steering wheel. "Unless they knew they were being followed. Could be someone saw your contact."

I lowered the binoculars. "Not a chance. Sebastian is scary good at this." His name was out of my mouth before I could stop it. Sam stilled his fingers. I closed my eyes. Damn it.

Sam resumed drumming and had the good grace not to mention my slip. "They vacated a perfectly safe hideout, in record time, and left not even a scrap of paper behind. These guys know what they're doing, which means Yeung's information will be a dead end."

"I think we have to concede the obvious. The simplest answer is probably the right one. ICO have the skills and resources. They knew about the gift or some of it. Maybe they speculated there was more to it. They definitely knew James and I weren't the only two."

Sam studied my face. Behind the stern facade, thoughts turned and twisted. I knew because I was thinking the same ones.

"They know I'm a Ghost," I said. "I fell for their trap back at that stronghold and showed them. That's why Smithford and his partner cleared out. They knew once we were on to them they'd have nowhere to hide. This is my fault."

He twisted in his seat. "If it was a trap, we both fell for it. Someone on the inside is responsible, but I'm not ready to concede ICO just yet. And we can't forget that a child is still missing."

My train of thought jumped the tracks and I swivelled my head to gaze out the windshield. With so many moving parts in this charade, how could whoever *they* were possibly look after a newborn? "Maybe the child isn't missing. Sure, they wanted to make it look like that, but why take on the complication of a newborn if they didn't have to."

"What are you thinking?"

"They didn't need to take the baby, just park him somewhere where he wouldn't be found for twenty-four to forty-eight hours. Just enough time to get the info they were going after. The bundle in that woman's arms as she left the hospital could have been a pillow for all we know."

"Shit!" Sam reached down and started the car.

"Where are we going?"

He did a quick shoulder check and screeched away from the curb. "The hospital." On the way, he called Abbott on the radio. We headed north on No. 3 Road and Sam tested the speed limit into Vancouver. By the time we'd arrived at St. Paul's, the hospital was awash in a kaleidoscope of flashing red and white. Sam parked in the fire zone. We got out and approached the main entrance. Sam badged us past the police constables who barred the doors. The hospital had been locked down.

Despite the early hour, the hospital buzzed with activity. Inside, a throng of uniformed police, scrub-clad nurses and aides were being dispatched with speed by a man in a white coat with a clipboard. Abbott stood at his side and motioned Sam and me over. "We've already searched and secured the basement levels. The teams are moving from top to bottom now. If that child is still here, we'll find him."

Sam and I stepped aside and let the man do his job. Abbott was in constant contact with his teams, talking alternately into his shoulder mic and a hand-held radio and jotting down notes on what looked like floor plans secured to a clipboard of his own.

Sam and I made like patients and planted ourselves in uncomfortable chairs in the waiting room. Fifty minutes later, Abbott's shoulders slumped and he raised his eyes to the ceiling. The white-clad man at his side took off at a gallop and disappeared into the stairwell. Sam and I stood and walked lockstep to the lip of the waiting room. Abbott closed his eyes and didn't move. When his radio finally squeaked, he lowered his chin and a slow smile spread across his face.

Sam wrapped his arm around my shoulder and squeezed. "They found him," he said, and exhaled a heavy breath. We stood in accord, two colleagues relieved of a heavy burden. I snaked my arm around his waist and squeezed back.

It took another thirty minutes to learn the details. A "nurse" had placed the kidnapped newborn with a new single mom who'd suffered a hemorrhage bad enough to keep her on bedrest and extend her hospital stay. She'd been told the baby's mother had died during delivery and they needed a wet nurse. The young mother had no reason to question the nurse, and her child's bassinette was big enough for two. The young mother had been more than happy to help the poor motherless babe.

Sam shook Abbott's hand and patted the backs of several of the uniformed officers before we made our way back to his unmarked. He got in and rested his arms on the steering wheel. "You were right," he said, as I clicked my seat belt into place. "Some bastard's been playing us and I want to know who the fuck it is."

He started the engine, fastened his own seat belt and pulled out.

"So what's the plan?" I asked.

"A video call to Ottawa. It's time I had a discussion with General Cain, and I want to see his face when I do." Sam reported our ICO activity to the general, much like I reported to Sebastian.

I pointed to the clock. "It's barely five in the morning there."

Sam signalled a turn. "He wanted timely reports."

"He won't be in his office at this hour."

"I'm not calling his office."

Traffic was non-existent as we left the downtown. Ten minutes later, Sam parked on the street near Olympic Village on First Avenue. He popped the trunk. "You coming?" he asked, and got out.

I didn't ask the obvious, simply followed. I removed my vest and dropped it in the trunk. He pulled out a computer bag, locked the car and led me to a townhouse with a red door. Sam's keys jingled in his hand. This was his place, or so it would seem, and it struck me as odd that I'd never imagined where he lived.

He unlocked the door, pushed it open and reached inside to flick on the lights. "After you," he said, gesturing. He stepped in behind me, locked the door and kicked off his shoes. A closet and a staircase going up lay on the left. A small, sparsely furnished bedroom lay on the right.

I slipped out of my shoes and followed Sam down the corridor. It spilled out into a sleek kitchen, which was open to the dining and living rooms. "You didn't tell me you lived with Martha Stewart," I said, stunned by the contemporary colour-coordinated décor.

"Don't be impressed. It came like this. It was a show suite."

"I like it." I raked my gaze over the space looking for clues to Sam's personal life. There wasn't much: a beat-up recliner that Martha hadn't picked out and a stack of newspapers.

"It's close to the station," he said, oblivious to the compliment. He stepped into a small den opposite the kitchen. I slowed and looked around. A drain rack on the counter above the dishwasher held a few pieces of cutlery, a cup, a plate and a mismatched bowl.

I crossed into the den, where Sam had shrugged out of his jacket and now stood with his shoulder holster in view. The computer bag lay on his desk. He turned on a lamp then walked around the desk and sat in the swivel chair behind it. "You're not here," he said, unzipping the bag. He pulled out the computer and opened it.

"Sit there and don't move." He pointed to a modern leather-and-chrome guest chair. One wall of the small office was glass and looked out into the living room. Another was lined with neatly framed photographs of children's sports teams.

The screen lit Sam's face. "Not a word from you," he warned, tapping on the computer's keys. He plugged in a headset and wriggled the buds in his ears. It seemed I would hear only one side of this conversation.

"General Cain," Sam said. "I hope I haven't disturbed you."

Sam narrowed his eyes. "I'm not sure 'congratulations' is the right sentiment."

"Someone went to extraordinary lengths to make it look like a kidnapping and yet the child never left the hospital," Sam said. "He was never in serious danger. This wasn't a kidnapping, it was a set-up."

"That's what I'd like to know," Sam said. "I've emailed you two photographs. The men in those photographs employed drones to keep tabs on me and my operative during the investigation. And there's no doubt in my mind that those men are military. If you sent them, I'd like to know why."

Sam dropped his gaze to the desk. "I don't mean any disrespect."

I furrowed my brow.

"Not you," Sam said. "But whoever set us up employs trained military, has the skills to infiltrate encrypted databases and was in place six months ago. If it isn't ICO, it's someone in your line of business."

"And you'll let me know?"

"All right. Next week then." Sam pulled out his earbuds and closed the laptop.

"He knew the child had been found. Congratulated us." Sam remained deathly still, his stare focused on the laptop as though he could see through it to the desk below. "Says he doesn't recognize the drone operators."

"Why do I get the impression you don't believe him?"

Sam slowly coiled the earbud wires. "It's always the little shit that trips you up."

"What are you talking about?"

"I'm Cain's contact. So who told him the child had been found?"

"Someone from the station?"

"No one at the station knows I report to Cain. Officially, I'm the communication liaison between the RCMP and CSIS. A civilian position. Cain is military."

"So Cain knows who's behind this."

Sam scrubbed his face with his hands. "Yup, and whoever it is set us up. And worse? Cain knows it and he's shutting me out. Told me to take a fucking week off. Bastard!" He slammed his fist on the desk. "What kind of lowlife uses a baby for this shit?" He shoved his chair back and leapt to his feet. "You and me? That newborn? We're all fucking pawns."

I'd never seen Sam so angry, and the violence of it shook me. He paced in front of the glass wall while I made a futile attempt to melt into my chair.

When he stopped pacing, he put his hands on his hips. "You know the problem with pawns? They're a means to an end. They're expendable." He looked at me with fire in his eyes. "I got news for them. We're not playing that game anymore."

A thought whispered across my mind and snapped me to attention. "Oh, no!" I straightened in my chair. "James! He's been off the grid. What if Cain or his buddies are pulling the same crap with him?" I wasn't the only one with secrets ICO didn't know about.

Sam locked down his eyebrows, pulled out his phone and then hesitated, his thumb hovering over the screen. "I don't know Beale. I've met him, but that's all. He could be a part of this."

Sam dialled. "Hey, Beale. Jordan here. Wrapped up another case. Interesting one. Call me for the deets." He hung up.

"He wasn't there?"

"No," Sam said, perching his butt on the edge of the desk.

And we were back to waiting—waiting for Beale to call, waiting for James to call, waiting for my house of secrets to implode. "How do we find out who Cain's been talking to?"

"If our suspect called him from the station, the digital call logs might ID him. It's a long shot. I can't imagine anyone dealing with Cain would be stupid enough to leave a trail, but it's my only move."

"You never know. They were stupid enough to get caught by us. What do you think they were after?"

"My guess? They want to know what you're capable of. What they might be up against."

I gathered my courage and stood. Sam looked at me. "I'd better get back. Report in."

"What are you going to tell Mason?"

Sam erroneously believed I reported to Mason. He had no reason to know that Sebastian was the current head of the Tribunal, and correcting Sam's misperception would expose Sebastian, not that I hadn't already hit my thumb with that hammer. "I'll start with the child. Give him the good news. But he needs to know we've been compromised. Cain and whoever he's been talking to are a threat to us. We have to protect ourselves, or at least prepare."

"Don't tell him about investigating the traffickers' stronghold. He doesn't need to know that."

"If there's evidence of me in action at that house, ICO will use it. He'll find out soon enough."

"Maybe they have proof, maybe they don't." Sam rammed the computer in its bag none too gently. "You think I don't know what goes on in your inner circles. I have a pretty good idea. Don't tell him."

I wondered if Sam's "pretty good idea" was even close. The Tribunal dished out retribution with an unforgiving hand and no chance of appeal. If they had proof that I'd further exposed us, who knew what price I'd pay? I wasn't anxious to find out. "If I can avoid it, I will. But I won't lie to him."

Sam nodded. "I'd better get to the station, go through those digital logs before they disappear. Can I give you a lift?"

I declined Sam's offer. A long trip home would give me time to clear my head. Telling Sebastian that General Cain knew we'd been compromised and wasn't sharing the details would not be a fun conversation. It also meant our deal with ICO was a farce. Once again, the secret I'd had a hand in exposing was in jeopardy.

I pulled up my hood, stuffed my hands in my pockets and walked to Broadway, where a night bus would still be running. The cool air put a spark in my step. Street traffic was sparse. I slowed at the first bus stop I came across and glanced back. With no bus on the horizon, I continued walking toward the next stop.

Sebastian, like most of the Tribunal members, didn't think the world would accept the free existence of our kind. At best, Fliers would be treated like privacy-trouncing drones. And when people learned the second lens in our eyes was as good as a weapon, who knew how they'd react? It wasn't as though there were a safety or a trigger guard.

It seemed like a lifetime ago that Avery had found me and opened the blinds to shine light on the wonder of this gift. I remembered the disconnect I felt after experiencing flight for the first time, knowing that Jolene had given this gift away. Mason believed his sister had gifted me in a suicide bid. Now I wondered if she'd simply gotten tired of having a target on her back.

Life seemed so much simpler when I was just a woman who had a problem with gravity. How I longed to go back to my cottage in Summerset, close the door and shut out the world.

With the next bus stop ahead, I turned. Instead of a bus, a cab approached. On impulse, I thrust out my hand and hailed it. The cab rolled to the curb and I jumped in.

"Where to?" the cabbie asked, looking at me in his rear-view mirror.

"Summerset," I said. "Cliffside Avenue."

Chapter Eight

Familiar landscape rolled past the windows as the cab turned onto Deacon Street. This was where Summerset locals strolled on warm summer evenings. It was where they bought their Starbucks, shopped for groceries and filled their prescriptions. It was where I'd bumped into Molly, working at Rumbles bookstore, after my ten-year absence.

I directed the cab to the cul-de-sac on the south end of Cliffside.

"Here, miss? Are you sure?" I couldn't blame the cabbie for his confusion. It was a dead-end street—a forlorn place to be dropped off in the early morning hours.

"We overshot the driveway. My fault. I'll walk back," I said, gesturing to my neighbour's house to the north. I paid the cabbie and got out. He turned around in the cul-de-sac and I waved to him as he disappeared down the street.

I rambled up my driveway, past the garage, and looked out at the gap in the treeline the house used to fill. Carson Manse and his Redeemers had taken so much from me: this home, my freedom, my peace of mind, the safety of my friends and family. And now ICO wanted a piece of me. Where would it end?

The ocean below the cliff rumbled in a quiet, steady rhythm. I couldn't see the water, but I could smell the brine on the night breeze. Grass now grew in the square of scorched earth that used to be my family's home. It was a different shade of green than the rest of the lawn. The property was now mine, though you'd never guess it from the deed. A complicated maze of holding companies paid the taxes.

Mother would arrive soon. Would she want to see the property? I wondered. She'd had mixed feelings about it since the day my father died, but she'd kept it. It was where she and my father had started their life together. The first home I'd ever known. We were once a family here. The memories were hard for her, even after all these years. They were hard for me too, but I still loved this place. Just being here listening to the ocean comforted me and gave me peace. I desperately needed that now.

I walked to the edge of the cliff, sat on a boulder and gazed out across the water that sparkled under a crescent moon. The tide was half out. Shale ledges and rocks the size of soccer balls glistened below, slick with the receding tide.

My dream was to rebuild here. I hadn't decided if it would be a simple cottage, like the one we'd lost, or a castle, like the ones I used to build in the patches of sand on the beach below. Maybe it would be a manor house, like the one my neighbours had built. I let my mind wander, imagining the possibilities.

Sadly, the future, even one with James, was more uncertain now than it had been when I woke this morning. Well, technically, yesterday morning. I checked the time. Nearly 4:00 a.m.

Cold crept into my bones. I stood and brushed off my pants. As much as I wished I could stay here forever, I couldn't put off contacting Sebastian much longer. He'd rain hell on me if he learned of the kidnapping's resolution from the CBC.

I inhaled one last breath of the briny air and said farewell to the patch of soil I still called home. With no one in sight, I flew up into the adjacent park's tree canopy. It was a straight shot north from where Sunset Park jutted into the ocean to my condo on the University Endowment Lands. I pulled my hair into a ponytail, snugged my Ryders in place and dove into the night.

Tankers and container ships bobbed below like toys in a bathtub. The ever-present log booms on the Fraser River waited, for what I don't know. Perhaps they partied with the booms anchored in the shallows near the university.

Soon enough, I landed on my building's roof, and when I'd caught my breath, I ghosted and made my way inside to my corner unit. I re-formed and turned off the motion sensors.

A 4:00 a.m. phone call to Sebastian. Joy, oh joy. I heeled off my shoes, walked to the kitchen and poured a snifter of Drambuie. That ought to help. I settled on the sofa and sent Sebastian a text, hoping he'd turned off his phone. I wasn't that lucky.

Five minutes later, my phone buzzed. Here we go, I thought, and picked it up.

"What is it?" Sebastian said.

"You were right to be suspicious of Cain." It couldn't hurt to start by stroking his ego. I then proceeded to tell him what we'd learned about the house on Spires, the recovery of the baby and Sam's conversation with General Cain.

The explosion I expected never happened. Instead, I got a simple, "I see."

I didn't trust it. It felt too much like a dud cherry bomb, a firecracker with a wonky wick ready to explode if I poked it. I kept quiet.

Eventually, he let me in on his thoughts. "Why would Cain jeopardize our contract with ICO? What changed? It had to be something significant enough to risk our cooperation. Any idea what that might be, Emelynn?"

Sam's advice sat in the forefront of my mind. I wouldn't sacrifice myself so easily. "Perhaps our six-week B&E spree got someone's attention?"

He paused long enough to convince me he was considering it. "Make certain the detective doesn't burn his bridges with Cain. We need that connection."

Sebastian must have thought we were morons. "He won't do that. Not until he has answers."

"Cain just pushed the detective in front of a locomotive. There's no room for doubt. Make certain."

I rolled my eyes. "All right."

"Good," Sebastian said, and promptly hung up on me.

Dick! I savoured another sip of Drambuie and debated if rude and arrogant were two sides of the same dick-headed coin.

My next call was to Mason. If I'd woken him, he hid it well.

"Emelynn. What is it?"

"I have an update."

"Make it quick. I'm on my way out."

At this hour? Where? I wondered, but he sounded impatient so I gave him an abbreviated version.

"Damn it to hell! The timing couldn't be worse. I'm in the middle of something I can't delegate. Sebastian is going to want to convene the Tribunal because of this and use it to extend his reign. This ICO business can't come to a head before I take over. I'm not ready. You need to stall him."

"Me? This is Sebastian you're talking about. How the hell am I supposed to do that?"

"Figure it out, Emelynn! I can't deal with this ICO shit right now."

And here I'd thought the fireworks would come from Sebastian. "Jesus, Mason."

"I'm sorry, but I'm hours away from bagging a Redeemer. I have to go. Keep me in the loop."

At least Mason said goodbye before he hung up.

I finished the Drambuie, brushed my teeth and crawled into bed. Maybe the world would come to an end before I woke and solve all my problems.

Sadly, that didn't happen. My phone woke me at 10:00 a.m. It was Colin at the front desk.

"Good morning, Ms. Taylor. You have a visitor. Laura Aberfoyle. Shall I send her up?"

Mom? What was she doing here already? "Yes, please. Thank you." She was supposed to be in a hotel in Ottawa tonight and arriving this time tomorrow. I jumped out of bed and rushed to the bathroom. Back in the bedroom, I yanked on last night's clothes and raced to the hall to turn off the alarm.

When I opened the door I heard the ding of the elevator. The doors rumbled open and my mother emerged. "Mom," I called. She turned to my voice and her face lit up.

"Hello, sweetheart," she said, wheeling her bag behind her.

"Come in." I stood back to let her pass and closed the door.

She settled her suitcase against the wall and turned around. My mother had never been overly demonstrative. In the years following Dad's death, we'd been unkind to one another, but we'd grown closer in the last year. We shared a warm embrace, and then she held me at arm's length and studied me, as I studied her. She stood a few inches shorter than I was. I'd inherited her green eyes, and wondered if mine looked as tired as hers.

"Your hair's grown," she said, touching the curling waves that fell loose to my elbows.

Her hair was a shade darker than mine, cut to her shoulders and threaded with grey.

"I didn't expect you until tomorrow."

"Couldn't stand another night in a hotel. Took an earlier flight. I didn't think you'd mind."

"Of course not. I'm glad you're here. Can I take your coat?"

I hung it in the closet. "Would you like a coffee or something to eat?"

"How about a cup of tea?"

I grabbed her bag and started down the hall to the spare room. "Did you get any sleep on the plane?" I asked.

"Not much. Hard to sleep on those things, isn't it?" My mother viewed flying as an unpleasant means to an end. How I wished I were in a position to change her mind.

"Here we are," I said, and lifted her bag to the tufted bench at the end of the bed. "Your bathroom's through there," I said, pointing. "Freshen up, and I'll put the kettle on."

When Mom joined me in the kitchen, she had a bit more colour in her face. "Dr. Coulter must be paying you very well to be able to afford the mortgage on this place," she said, looking around with admiration.

I handed her a cup of tea. "The insurance money helped." Our cottage had been one of the original Arts and Crafts–style homes built in Summerset, and well known in the heritage community. After the Redeemers burned it to the ground, Mom gave me the settlement money for a down payment. What my mother didn't know was that Mason and Stuart Reynolds had paid for the balance of the condo. They'd insisted, calling it reparation for the loss of the cottage at the hands of a madman they'd "failed to take care of," a euphemism for "failed to eradicate."

One more truth I kept from my mother. The lies and omissions required a sharp memory on my part, and conversations with her required my full attention. Growing up, I'd been glad for the days when her research kept her distracted. I hated to think how hurt she'd be if she ever learned the extent of my deception. If I could take back all the lies, from the day I'd met Jolene on the beach when I was twelve years old, I would do it in a heartbeat.

"Let me give you a tour of the rest of the condo." We took our teas down the hall and I opened the door to the small gym I'd set up. I showed her my bedroom and how to use the security system, and we wound our way back to the living room.

She stared at the fishing rods I'd mounted on the wall. "I love that you kept these," she said, and reached out to touch one. "Your father sure loved to fish." I'd rescued the rods from the garage, which survived the fire, and had cleaned them up. They were a perfect reminder of my father, and one of only two treasures that survived the fire, the other being a photograph of Dad my mom had taken before they had me.

"Do you feel safe here?" Mom asked, taking a seat beside me on the sofa. She'd asked this question months ago, after I'd moved in, but now I suspected she had a personal perspective on the issue.

"I do. I keep the perimeter alarm on when I'm home, and security at the front desk is really good. Everyone in the building has a video feed of the front doors and the parking garage. I wish you had the same, Mom."

"I've given some thought to moving."

"You have?" This was news.

"Can you believe I've lived in that apartment for more than ten years? I never really liked it."

Her comment dropped my jaw. "Why did we live there for so long?"

"Convenience, I suppose. It's close to the university. After your father died I couldn't bear to take on a house. I didn't want to deal with shovelling driveways and mowing lawns. Then, once we'd settled in, I couldn't move you. You'd had a tough enough time as it was." Her expression held not an ounce of blame.

She cradled her tea and settled into the sofa. "I had a lot of time to think when I was cleaning up after the break-in."

"About what?"

"Like the fact there's nothing in the apartment I truly care about. I could walk away from it tomorrow and not miss a thing. My research—my work—is my entire life. If I didn't have that I'd have nothing."

"Your work is important, Mom. Think of the countless people who've benefited from it. It's sparked conversations and further research. That's not nothing." She was one of the smartest people I knew.

"It's not a life. It's not enough anymore. Ten years from now I'll retire, maybe sooner, and I want to have something to look forward to."

The burglary had set my mother's emotions on the high-speed spin cycle. "This is the break-in speaking. You'll feel different in a few months."

"No. The break-in was the catalyst I needed to see the light and make some changes before it's too late." She snickered and a blush coloured her cheeks. "Remember Dr. Stein?"

"Edgar? I knew it!"

"It's not what you think. We went to dinner a few times after I offered him your father's research, but that's all. No man I meet ever compares to your father. I have to admit though, it felt good to have a man's attention. I hadn't let that happen for a very long time."

"Maybe it's time to let someone else in," I said.

She shrugged. "I've asked for a leave of absence from work. Six months, maybe longer. It's time I started living my life again. I'm not sure how to do that, but it starts today."

"I'm so proud of you, Mom." I gathered my hair and dropped it behind my shoulders. Mom glanced at my earlobes and smiled.

"I haven't seen those earrings before."

I lifted my fingers to the grey-green studs I rarely took off. "James gave them to me." They'd accompanied his marriage proposal. James slammed back into my thoughts. Had Sam heard back from Tim Beale yet, I wondered?

"They're exquisite. What's the gemstone?"

"I don't know."

"How is James?"

"He's been out of touch. Working." Mom knew he worked in the US as a private investigator, and I'd shared my dismay over his lack of communication before.

"I'm sure it's for the best, sweetheart," she said. Mom liked James. She credited him with finding me after I'd been kidnapped. In her mind, James could do no wrong. "How are things between you two?"

"Great," I said, but worry gnawed at my gut.

"You don't sound very convincing."

"Oh? No, we're good. It's just . . ." I waffled, searching for the right words. "I wish he'd call. Some days I swear it was easier being single."

"Ah," she said, as if she had the answer.

"'Ah' what?"

"I know you, Emelynn. Ever since you were a little girl, you've been content to be alone. You're independent. You get that from me." She took a sip of her tea. "And now you care about someone and it frightens you."

Loving James wasn't what frightened me, but bringing kids into this world took me into cold-sweat territory. Any child of mine would be born a Ghost and bear the burden of a bull's eye on his or her back. That wasn't anything I could explain to my mother. "I feel like I've barely lived a life. He's older. He's ready for more, and I don't think I am."

Mom patted my knee. "Perhaps not. Only you know for certain, but make sure you know why." I frowned, confused.

"Before I met your father, I was quite happy living by myself. No one was more surprised than I was when I fell for him, and that scared me. I thought he'd leave me and break my heart. It's why I insisted on keeping my own place even though he must have asked me a dozen times to move in with him." Her face softened into a wistful expression.

She shook herself out of her memories. "When I found out I was pregnant with you, I'd never been more frightened. I worried I'd be a terrible parent, worried my research would suffer, worried I'd lose my independence, my freedom."

She reached over and smoothed my hair. "I'm so glad I didn't let my fear stop me. Loving your father was a gift I treasure, and you are the best thing that's ever happened to me." Tears glistened in her eyes. "What I'm saying is . . . don't let fear turn you away from James."

She edged forward on the sofa. "Now, if you don't mind, I'm going to lie down for a half hour, and then how about I take you out to lunch?"

I blinked back my own tears and she slipped into her room, leaving me thinking about fear, and James. I headed to my bedroom to phone him and left yet another message. I stared at the phone. If we had a child and he abandoned me for weeks on end, I'd resent the hell out of him. I loved James, but kids were a no-go.

Next, I called Sam.

"Any word from James's handler?" I asked.

"No. I called Beale's office. He's out of town. They wouldn't say where. I asked them to get a message to him. We'll hear soon."

"I hope so. Any more news on Cain's contact in the department?"

"Nothing in the call logs. I'm feeding the photos of Smithford and his partner through facial- recognition software. It's probably futile, but I have to do something. Still no ID on the female kidnapper."

"By the way, I forgot to tell you my mom is here." Sam had met my mother during her last visit. We'd still had the cottage back then.

"How is she?"

"Her condo was broken into. She's talking about moving."

"I'm sorry to hear that. Give her my regards. I'll let you know if I learn anything new."

When Mom got up, we took Dad's old red MGB to a bistro on Dunbar Street. Mom drove, and it put a smile on her face that lasted right through our late lunch. Afterwards, we strolled the neighbourhood, poking into every shop. I couldn't remember the last time we'd whiled away a whole afternoon together.

Mom picked up a new scarf and sunglasses, threatening to take down the ragtop on the way home. Summer clothing lines hung in store windows—sandals and bikinis, shorts and capris—a promise of warmer weather to come. A mannequin in a gauzy summer dress caught Mom's eye. I followed her into the store. The tinkle of a bell announced our arrival.

She approached the mannequin and smoothed her hand over the fabric. "Linen's perfect for summer, don't you think?" she asked.

"It is," I said, and tucked my hands in my pockets. Thin straps and cutaway backs no longer had a place in my wardrobe. The scars Carson Manse had left on my back made sure of that. "Let's go to the market before it closes."

We crossed the street and loaded a basket with fruit and veggies and picked up fresh halibut from a small seafood shop. The sky clouded over, and distracting thoughts of James, Sebastian and ICO settled in my mind like earworms.

Mom's plans for the ragtop were thwarted by a light drizzle during our drive home. It was close to six o'clock when we parked underground. We stopped to check for mail and I introduced her as a colleague to Colin.

Once inside the condo, I turned to the security panel. The alarm had been turned off. My heart suddenly raced. I dropped the shopping bags and ran down the hall, leaving my mother looking equal parts surprised and confused.

"James!" I shouted. Reaching the living room, I scooted to a halt. Mason turned from the window clad in Flier black. His gloves lay on the coffee table, his coat draped over a chair.

"Sorry. Not James," Mason said.

"What are you doing here?" I asked. Mason's face froze as his attention moved from me to the space behind my shoulder.

A smile thawed his face. "Laura," he said, recovering his composure. He stepped forward and offered his hand. "Mason Reynolds. We met last year at the hospital." I sifted through my memory, trying to remember the story I'd told her. Mason saved me the trouble. "I'm a friend of James Moss."

"Yes, I remember," Mom said, shaking his hand. "Emelynn tells me you have a lovely home in Bodega Bay, though its name slips my mind." I'd visited Mason twice. The first time, he'd taken me to my half-brother's grave and taught me how to ghost. The second time, he'd provided a safe haven after the fire.

"Cairabrae," Mason said. "Been in the family for generations. Let me take that," he said, relieving my mother of the bags she'd picked up after I dropped them in the hall. "Kitchen?"

"Yes. Through there—but I guess you know that," she said, casting me a sideways glare before accompanying him to the kitchen. "It was very kind of you to invite Emelynn for a visit last fall."

Mason's voice faded as he walked away. "She's welcome back any-time. Dad and I enjoyed her company."

I dropped to the sofa with my head in my hands. How would I explain Mason's presence inside the condo to my mother? And what the hell could have happened to bring him here? The fridge opened and closed amid the soft rustle of bags.

"Sweetheart," my mother called out from the kitchen. "Would you like an iced tea?"

Her words flashed me back to the cottage: she stood on the deck shouting the same question to me on the beach below. "Yeah, Mom. Thanks."

Water sprayed in the kitchen sink and a cupboard door banged closed. Laughter bubbled out behind me. I felt desperate to learn what Mason's visit was about. I took a few deep breaths to calm my heart and then removed my coat.

When Mom returned, she set a glass of iced tea on the coffee table in front of me and a bowl of wet grapes beside it.

"I'm going to put my things away," Mom said. "I won't be long."

She had no idea how much I appreciated her gift of a few minutes' privacy. The moment she was around the corner, I turned to Mason. He put his finger to his lips and motioned me toward the door to the balcony. He closed it behind us. I wrapped my arms around my torso. The light drizzle hadn't let up and evening was settling in.

"My apologies," he said. "I didn't think she would be here until tomorrow."

"Neither did I," I said, dismissing his apology in favour of the question at hand. "What happened? Why are you here?" I turned so I could keep watch through the glass for my mom's return.

"We had a solid lead on a Redeemer in Portland. Turns out he's been hiding up here."

"Here? In Vancouver? I've got to warn Avery." I started for the door.

He shot his arm out to stop me. "There's no need. The Redeemer's incapacitated. We'll interrogate him when he's able to speak again." I fought off a chill. I'd sooner play patty cake with a cougar than be on the wrong end of a Tribunal interrogation. But as unsavoury as interrogations and punishments were, carrying them out was the duty of anyone who held a seat on the Tribunal, one of the "expectations" Sebastian predicted would tear me apart. I feared he was right.

"This Redeemer is a high-value target," Mason said. "He was inside at Cairabrae. We could use James's skill set to drill through his lies, but we've not been able to reach him. You were expecting him?"

"He's on a case. When I found the condo's alarm off... I just hoped."

"That's unfortunate. James has been quite cooperative, considering our history." For generations, James and his family had been indentured to the Tribunal. The males in James's family could read memories, a skill that made interrogations much less messy. Though James's freedom from that obligation was still fresh, he understood the severity of the threat the Redeemers posed.

"Perhaps I'll put in a call to James's father. He may be persuaded to lend his assistance. You don't by chance know Redmond, do you?"

"I don't." Even if I did, I wouldn't want to be the one to ask him. He'd been under the Tribunal's thumb his entire life. He might not be as accommodating as his son.

Mason stared down at his hands. "I was abrupt with you on the phone yesterday. I shouldn't have been."

Though not quite an apology, I appreciated it.

"The business with ICO is a bloody mess," he continued, rubbing his palms together. "But we have to keep it on the back burner until I get the names I need from this Redeemer. If we don't put the Redeemers out of business, they'll continue their reckless behaviour, killing Fliers, stealing gifts. They won't stop until they're strong enough to take another run at us." Mason shifted his weight and furrowed his brow. "If we're caught at the centre of another bloody massacre, ICO's game will be the least of our worries. Our freedom will be on the line."

It hardly felt like a game to me, but then again, I wasn't dealing with the Redeemer. "Cain lied to protect someone. We don't know who yet, or why, but it was obviously more important than our contract with them."

"Just keep playing along," Mason said. "Buy me some time. And for god's sake, keep Sebastian busy. I don't want him convening the Tribunal before I'm ready."

"Ugh. That man is impossible."

"Please try. With the Redeemers out of the way, we'll have a little more time to persuade the old guard of the need for change. Next time the Tribunal meets, I plan to show them exactly what we're up against. They can't keep ignoring the technology that will eventually expose us. It's inevitable." Mason and his father wanted to control that exposure, to make it an event as nonthreatening and favourable to Fliers as possible, but wealth and power blinded the Tribunal. They were the strongest of our kind, and they'd successfully countered every threat they'd ever faced. Most on the Tribunal saw no need for an irreversible change that would force them into the light.

"With us out in the open, ICO and whoever they're protecting will lose their leverage," Mason said. "And if we do it right, the public will be on our side." Mason jammed his hands in his pockets and stared past me to the overcast sky. "Think of the freedom, Emelynn. Never again would we have to worry about someone threatening to expose us. No more deception. No more hiding. Hell, we could fly anytime we liked, day or night."

As much as I loved the utopia he proposed, there were two flaws in his plan. One, no one could predict if governments would agree we posed no threat, and two, even if the last Redeemer was eliminated, the cause of their uprising—the fact that they had no voice in our world—would not rest unchallenged for long.

"I hope you're right, Mason."

"How did you leave things with Sebastian?"

"Let me see. Just before he hung up on me last time—"

"Emelynn," Mason said. The low rumble of his voice warned of his impatience.

"I don't *leave things* with Sebastian," I said. "He leaves them with me, and during our last conversation, he dumped a not-so-subtle accusation that I may have been responsible for ICO's change of behaviour. Then he told me to hold Sam's hand because apparently Sam and I are daft enough to cut ICO loose."

"I know he's difficult, but he's one of our best."

"Yeah, and he knows it, which adds to his arrogance quotient." I shifted my weight and rubbed my arms. "Though it annoys me to admit it, he's good. He suspected ICO before Sam or I did, and he came through for us when he found the drones tailing us."

"He's always put the Tribunal first. Get in touch with him. There have to be some loose ends on that case he can help with. Or you could restart the mentorship. Use whatever you can to keep him close."

"You will owe me so big when this is done." I looked up in time to see my mother approach.

The balcony door opened. "Aren't you two cold out here?" she said.

"It's refreshing," Mason said. "A nice change." I stepped ahead of him into the condo, happy for the warmth.

"You may have missed a call, Emelynn. Your phone vibrated a moment ago."

"Thanks, Mom," I said, and picked it up from the coffee table. Another call from California with no name and a 619 area code. I flipped through my call history. It was the same number as the last call from California. "Mason, does your dad have a phone with a 619 area code?"

"No, Bodega Bay is 707. I believe 619 is San Diego."

"They didn't leave a message."

"How long are you in Vancouver?" Mom asked Mason.

"I've got a couple of hours on my hands, but with any luck, I'll be able to wrap up my business later tonight."

"Then why don't you stay for dinner?" my mother said. I jerked my head up from my phone and darted a glance from my mother to Mason and back again. Had I entered the twilight zone?

Mom continued. "We picked up some fresh halibut this afternoon. There's plenty for another plate, and I'll make a salad, maybe some rice?"

"I'd like that," Mason said, and quickly followed up with, "That is, if Emelynn doesn't mind."

Way to go, Mason. They both looked at me as if I held the permission card. "No, I don't mind. Please, stay for dinner."

"Terrific. It's settled then," Mom said. I wondered if she'd still think it was terrific if she had any idea what *business* Mason was hoping to take care of later.

"If you'll excuse me," I said, "I have to make a phone call."

"We'll be fine. Take your time, sweetheart."

I wandered down the hall toward my bedroom. Was it my imagination or was my mother flirting with Mason?

Chapter Nine

I shut the bedroom door and dialled Sam. It went directly to voice mail. He must be on his phone, I thought. I left him a message and then scrolled down to the call I'd missed and tapped the call icon.

"You have reached Vector Labs. Our hours of operation are 8:00 a.m. until 6:00 p.m. Please leave a message, or visit us online at Vector dot com."

I disconnected and typed "Vector Labs" into Google. Their address was in San Diego, so Mason had been right about the area code. Vector Laboratories provided "highly specialized science and laboratory services." If you were in the energy, environmental, transportation or life sciences sector, they were your go-to lab. Why would someone at a lab-for-hire call me? Twice? I bookmarked the website and returned to Mom and Mason.

I found them in the kitchen, Mason with his sleeves pushed up to his elbows at the sink and Mom at the stove. Definitely the twilight zone. The oven beeped to announce it was up to temperature.

"Oh good, you're back," Mom said. "Mason needs your colander, and I can't find it." A bottle of red wine sat opened and waiting on the counter.

"Under the sink," I said. Mom stirred the rice and replaced its lid. The halibut, now in three pieces, lay on a cutting board ready for the cast-iron skillet. Mason bent to find the colander.

"Can I help?" I asked, feeling like an interloper in my own kitchen.

"How about you set the table?" Mom suggested.

I wandered in and out of the dining room with plates and cutlery and listened to Mom making good on her plan to change her life. The fact that Mason was at least five years her junior didn't seem to faze her. Maybe flirting was like riding a bicycle.

During dinner, I told them about Vector Labs in San Diego.

"You should call my friend Sebastian," Mason said. I nearly dropped my fork. "He has business interests in the area. He might know who they are." Mason's eyes sparkled with mischief. "You've met him, remember?"

I tucked my tongue in my cheek. "Small head, beady eyes?"

"Emelynn!" my mother said, casting me a look of admonishment I hadn't seen since high school. Mason broke into laughter.

"Don't worry, Mom. Mason knows full well that Sebastian isn't my favourite person."

"It's fine, Laura. Emelynn and I have an understanding where Sebastian is concerned. He's a colleague of mine, or, if you believe your daughter, a necessary evil." He looked back at me. "You should still call him. He knows San Diego." He smiled again with that mischievous grin. "I'll send you his number."

I gave him the deadpan stare he'd earned, and he laughed again. Mom watched our antics with amusement, and then warned Mason he'd get as good as he dished dealing with me. I puffed out my chest and resisted the urge to stick out my tongue at him.

Mom set down her cutlery and touched a napkin to the corner of her mouth. She'd focused on the wall behind me. Her amusement morphed into a frown. "Sweetheart, where did you get that painting?" The seascape Stuart had sent me as a housewarming gift had drawn her attention. A flush of adrenalin hit me. "It looks so much like the one from your father's study." She rose from the table to take a closer look.

"That's one of Jolene's," Mason said, gazing at the painting. I snapped my head in his direction and stopped breathing. His expression was one of pride, without a hint of guile or awareness of the bomb he'd just dropped.

I shot a glance at my mother. She'd stiffened; her shoulders were hunched. My heart fluttered into panic mode. Jolene's name had never crossed my lips in my mother's presence.

"Jolene." Mom repeated the name as if testing it on her tongue. She stood still as a corpse.

Mason, absorbed in his own memories, hadn't noticed. "She was my sister," he said, compounding what I sensed was colossal damage. "Unfortunately, she died a long time ago."

"Your sister?" Mom's voice sounded strained, her back rigid. That my mother didn't express her condolences told me all I needed to know. Jolene's name meant something to her, and it wasn't good.

Mason jerked and pulled his phone from his pocket. He gazed at the small screen briefly and tucked it away again. He scooted his chair back and stood. "I'm sorry, but I've got to go."

My mother turned from the painting. Her face had morphed into a polite smile mask. Mason didn't know her well enough to see it.

"Laura, dinner was delicious. Thank you." He turned to me. "Emelynn—" he started, and then the panic on my face registered. "Ah . . . don't forget to call Sebastian."

I threw down my napkin and jumped up. "I'll walk you out."

Mom remained rooted to the floor. Mason reached out to shake her hand. "Goodbye, Mason."

Confusion flitted across his face. My heart pounded. Somehow Mom knew Jolene's name. The possibilities dribbled out at a frustrating pace. Dad must have told her, but how much did she know?

I collected Mason's coat from the back of the chair in the living room and started down the hall. He hurried to catch up. "What did I say?" he said, furrowing his brow.

"Shit, Mason. How could you forget? *Jolene*?"

As the light dawned, his face fell. "Oh hell."

We'd reached the front door. I opened it.

"It'll blow over. Jolene and Brian lost a son. Your father would have told her that. Bit of a shock hearing her name is all it is."

"And how the hell do I explain you, Mason? What is Jolene's brother doing with a key to my condo?"

He clamped a hand on my shoulder and bent to my ear. "Get hold of yourself. If you can't cover your tracks, tell her. Laura is your mother. She falls within the permitted circle. She's strong. She can handle it."

"You think that's what I'm worried about? I've lied to her since I was a kid. Kept the most important part of my life from her. How do you think she'll handle that, Mason?"

He straightened. "I'm sorry. I've made a mess of things, but I've got to go."

Fucking hell! I closed the door behind him and walked a death march back to my mother.

She stood in the dining room staring at Jolene's painting again. "How long have you known?" she said, her voice a thread above a whisper.

I felt like I was defusing a bomb. "About Jolene?" I asked.

She nodded. "How did you find out?"

Thankfully, something I didn't have to lie about. "I found a letter from her to Dad. It was in a box in the attic."

Mom dragged her gaze from the painting to me, a look of expectation on her face.

"She'd been to the cottage. Knew you were pregnant."

Mom nodded. "I should have seen the resemblance. Mason and Jolene, the blond hair, pale-blue eyes."

"The letter was her goodbye to Dad."

"You know about their son?"

"She mentioned him in the letter."

Mom turned back to the painting, and I knew her mind was busy fitting a puzzle together. In moments like these, I wished she weren't so damn clever.

"Your father rarely spoke of the son they lost. I didn't judge him. I can't imagine the grief of losing a child. Maybe it was selfish, but I was grateful he never brought Jolene into our marriage."

"I'm sorry, Mom. I should have told you about the letter. I just figured you and Dad had your reasons for keeping that tragedy private."

Her gaze remained on the painting, but she didn't see it. "He did . . . have his reasons. He told me once that her family came from old money. That they had power and influence. I hadn't known she'd passed away. Was it an accident?"

"Suicide, I think."

She furrowed her brow. Her mind never stopped fitting and refitting the pieces, and she was dangerously close to solving the puzzle. "Tell me again how Mason and James know one another."

My phone buzzed, and I'd never been happier to be interrupted. "Hello, Detective Jordan," I answered, and walked away from my mother.

My formality didn't derail Sam. "I just got off the phone with Tim Beale. Moss isn't working an ICO case."

I stopped short. "What?"

"Beale was summoned to the FBI's field office in Dallas two weeks ago. He spent the last week in Germany. He hasn't been in touch with Moss."

I thought back to my last conversation with James. "I was certain James said Beale had pulled him in on another case. He must have picked up one from the local department in New Orleans."

"Beale says no. He thinks Moss took a private contract."

"He thinks or he knows?"

"Process of elimination."

"And we're taking his word for it? Do you trust him?"

"I wish I could, but no. He hasn't earned it yet." I liked that Sam didn't give automatic brownie points to his colleagues. "A private contract takes ICO out of the spotlight."

"That's convenient. We also have no direct line connecting ICO to our infant's kidnapping case. This doesn't feel right. We have to find James and warn him."

"I agree. Let me do some digging from this end. Why don't you touch base with his family? See if they know anything."

How do you touch base with a family you've never met and ask such personal questions? I'd be lucky if they spoke to me. Regardless, I agreed to call them, but I couldn't make the call from here. Not with my mother stepping up to the twenty-questions podium. I stuffed my phone away and walked back to the dining room. The table had been cleared and Mom was busying herself in the kitchen.

"I've got to go. Detective Jordan has a new lead. He wants me to meet him at the station." Mom believed Sam was still working on my kidnapping case.

She straightened, wiping her hands on a towel. "I'll come with you."

"Thanks, Mom, but it's not anything you can help with. Besides, you're still on Toronto time. You'd fall asleep on me." I turned for the door before she could protest and called over my shoulder. "I might be late. Don't wait up." I grabbed my coat and keys and bolted for the door, praying she didn't follow.

To avoid being trapped in the hallway waiting for the elevator, I jogged past it to the stairwell. When the heavy door closed behind me, I stopped and rested my back against the wall. I could throttle Mason. My mind raced. Just how much did my mother know? Would Dad have risked telling her about Fliers? Ghosts? Surely not. To do so when he was no longer a part of our world would have put Mom in the Tribunal's path. He wouldn't have done that.

I pushed off from the wall and walked down one floor then caught the elevator to the parking garage.

There was no way Mom knew about us, so I only had to work out two details: a plausible reason for me to have a painting of Jolene's, and an explanation for the impossible odds of Mason turning out to be Jolene's brother. Time travel would be easier to explain. I suppose I could have seen the painting when I visited Cairabrae. But a friend of James turning out to be Jolene's brother? That was too much of a coincidence. Mom was a scientist—she'd pretty much removed "coincidence" from her vocabulary. Sadly, that was all I had. The mortar was barely dry on the repairs Mom and I had made to our relationship. It upset me to think about putting it in jeopardy. I feared my lies would catch up with me one of these days, and break something I treasured.

I climbed into the MGB and drove toward the university. Soon after I turned onto Wesbrook Mall, I pulled over and parked. James had told me his father was a lawyer in New Orleans. I typed *Redmond Moss* into Google then scrolled through the ads, the *Redmond Moss is on Facebook* and *Redmond Moss on Twitter* links, and found his law firm. I dialled. Not that I expected to reach anyone after hours, but the firm might have a number for emergencies. An answering service picked up. They couldn't help me, or more accurately, they wouldn't help me, but they took my number and said they'd pass it on in the morning.

One more lead crossed my mind. Late last spring, James had mailed me a cheque from his father. It was the reward money their family had offered for the safe return of James's sister, Sandra, after she'd gone missing. I signed on to my bank account, hoping I could find a copy of the cheque I deposited. I flipped through last May's and June's records before I found it. Unfortunately, Redmond's number wasn't on it and the address was that of his law firm.

Crap. Mason would have the number, no doubt, but I'd sooner chew off an arm than interrupt what he was in the middle of. Unfortunately, that left Sebastian. Why did it always have to be Mason or Sebastian? My life would be so much easier if these Tribunal people had a phone directory like every other organization on the planet.

I let my head fall back against the headrest. At least involving Sebastian kept him busy. Mason should be happy about that. Where had I left things with Sebastian? Oh yes, he'd hung up on me. I suppose I could update him on Sam's discussion with Tim Beale. I lifted my phone and dialled.

Sebastian answered in a gruff voice. "What now?"

I took a calming breath. It didn't work. "Really?"

Sebastian didn't respond. Peeved, I barrelled ahead. "I need Redmond Moss's phone number."

"Why?"

I explained that Sam had learned from Tim Beale that James wasn't working on an ICO case.

"Is that right?" Sebastian said.

"It might be, but if it isn't, then ICO is playing games with him."

"We should have annihilated Cain when we had the chance."

Regardless, I thought, impatiently. "We need to warn James and he's not answering his phone."

"I'm not at liberty to give you Redmond Moss's phone number."

I clenched the phone in my hand, counted to three. "Sebastian, please."

"I'll call Redmond, explain the situation. Give him your contact information. If he chooses to, he'll contact you."

"Damn it, Sebastian."

"That's enough! Remember who you're talking to." As if I could forget that. "And FYI, it's the same answer Redmond would get if he wanted your contact information."

I paused, wondering if that was true. "All right. Be sure he knows he can call me night or day, will you?"

Sebastian sighed into the phone. Then I remembered something else. "Before you go, do you know a company called Vector Labs in San Diego?"

"Why?"

Indeed, why? Why couldn't he simply answer a question? "Someone from that number is trying to reach me."

"They have property in the north end of San Diego. Miramar, I believe. I'm not aware of any Flier connection, but perhaps that's changed. Leave it with me."

"You'll let me know what you learn?"

"I'll be in touch."

What the hell did that mean? The man was positively exhausting. "Fine. I'll wait to hear from Redmond." I disconnected and started the car, blasting the heater. It was too cold outside to hang around for a call that might not come. There was a Tim Hortons' on Broadway east of Oak that stayed open late. I texted Sam my destination, put the car in gear and drove.

Customers filled half the tables in the small coffee shop. Fearing a long night ahead, I ordered an Americano, grabbed a stale newspaper and settled in. When the phone finally vibrated to life, I jumped.

"Hello," I said, not even checking the display.

"Is this Emelynn Taylor?" The man's voice held a hint of an accent I couldn't immediately place.

I pulled the phone away from my ear. No number. "It is."

"This is Redmond Moss. I understand from Sebastian Kirk that you have information regarding my son."

He said Sebastian's name as if it were a curse. "Information?" I said, confused. "I think there's been some kind of misunderstanding." Even as I said it, I didn't believe it. Sebastian had deliberately misled him. "Do you remember my name?"

"Indeed, but I was not aware of your connection to Sebastian Kirk." The words were iced, but the accent was warm. Southern.

"I don't have a connection to Sebastian Kirk, but I know who he is. He bought a house here in Vancouver. He's joined my covey. I merely asked him for your number."

An awkward silence fell. Not knowing what Sebastian had told him left me blind. I continued. "I'm a friend of James's." Silence still. "Do you know who ICO is?"

"I do."

Thank god James had told him that much. "Then you know about their contract with the Tribunal."

"Yes."

Single syllable answers. He wasn't giving an inch. "That contract identified two Fliers to work with ICO. I'm the second one."

"Are you?"

I hung my head. "Please hear me out. A disturbing chain of events occurred here in Vancouver in connection with the last case I worked on. I'm worried there will be fallout for James and I can't reach him."

"If you know James, that shouldn't surprise you."

If I knew James? Had James not mentioned me to his father? A strap tightened around my chest. If Redmond didn't know about James and me, he had no reason to talk to me. Somehow I had to make him trust me.

"I tried to find you without Sebastian's help. I apologize if that was unpleasant, but your numbers are unlisted. Your answering service was no help. I care about James. I need to get a message to him. That's all. Can you do that for me?"

"You work for ICO. Ask them."

"ICO is the problem. They tell me James isn't working an ICO case, that he's working a private contract. I don't believe them."

"James doesn't discuss his work with me."

Redmond Moss was not a man to be moved, but I had to try. "All I need is for you to ask him to call me. That's all. Would you please do that for me?"

A shadow passed across the table and I looked up, startled to see Sam. He scraped the chair out from under the table and sat opposite. He'd been listening to my conversation.

"This one time, I will give James your message. But I will not entertain another call from Sebastian Kirk. Do you understand?"

"I do. Thank you." I disconnected and placed the phone on the table. Sam stared at me with expectation. "That was James's father, Redmond. He wasn't happy."

"He doesn't like your friend Sebastian."

"Friend? Really, Sam? For the record, I don't blame Redmond for not liking Sebastian. He has every right to that opinion."

"Oh?"

"Never mind. You heard what I learned. What did you find out?"

"James's phone isn't pinging anywhere, but that's not a surprise given James's IT skills. The local police report no activity near the home address in New Orleans we have on file for him, so no disturbances, shots fired, break-ins. No one's accessed his driver's licence, and there's no new activity on his credit report."

"So nothing helpful."

"Afraid not."

Which dumped us back into the waiting queue. "Then all we can do is hope Redmond can get a message to him."

CHAPTER TEN

S am and I were the last ones to leave Timmy's when it closed at two o'clock in the morning. James hadn't called. I promised Sam I'd get in touch with him the moment I heard anything, and we went our separate ways.

In the hallway outside my condo, I inserted my key with the utmost care, depressed the handle and quietly opened the door. I reset the alarm, tiptoed to my room and gently latched the door behind me.

After I finished in the bathroom, I crawled into bed and stared at the ceiling. I checked my phone one more time then fluffed my pillow and rolled over.

A soft knock on my door told me my efforts to be quiet had been wasted. Which meant Mom wasn't done with her questions. Crap. I reached over and turned on the bedside lamp. "Mom?"

She cracked open the door. "May I come in?"

"Sure," I said, and scooted up so my back was against the padded headboard. "You all right?"

"I'm fine. Detective Jordan kept you out quite late. What did he learn about your case?"

"It turned out to be nothing. We went for coffee. He sends his regards."

Mom nodded and sat on the edge of my bed. She'd changed into a nightie and had pulled on one of the guest robes. She looked to her lap, where her fingers smoothed the folds of her robe. "I need to ask you something."

Damn, here it comes. I steeled myself, barely listening as I tried to remember the threads of the lie I'd hoped to patch over Mason's blunder.

"We haven't always been close. Losing your father was hard on both of us, but I love you. You know that. You will never be too old for me to try to protect. I want what's best for you, and I'm worried. I need you to be honest with me." She bit her lower lip, and then straightened with resolve. "Are you involved in some kind of illegal activity?"

I shot her a quizzical one-eyed glare. She remained unaffected. I searched her face for the hint of a smile, but she was dead serious. "What are you talking about?"

"I promise not to judge."

Now I was really confused. "Judge what?"

"Sweetheart, I know what this condo is worth. I looked it up. Even with the insurance money from the fire, you wouldn't get a mortgage for the balance. Not on any salary Dr. Coulter could afford. Where are you getting the money to pay for it?"

"Mom!"

"It's a perfectly legitimate question."

"It's a perfectly personal question. One I would never ask you."

My mother moved closer and took my hand between hers. She met my gaze with fierce determination. "You are not my mother. If you are in some kind of trouble, I can help. I want to help. But I need to know—how are you paying for this condo?"

Words dried up in my throat. The puzzle she'd been working on wasn't the one I'd imagined. "I'm not involved in anything illegal, Mom. You didn't raise an idiot. I know how to get a mortgage."

"I'm happy to hear that, but you haven't answered my question."

I chewed on my answer, unsure how truthful I should be. At least she'd assumed I had a mortgage. Owning the condo outright would be so much harder to explain. I held my nose and spit out another lie. "Mason Reynolds holds my mortgage."

The hands that held mine stilled, and her features fell. I didn't understand her reaction. "Why would he do that? You hardly know him."

She was either angry or fearful, and I couldn't tell which. I felt a sudden compulsion to jump off this runaway sled I feared was heading for traffic at the bottom of the hill.

"Because of Dad," I said. She tipped her head, a question on her face. I continued. "When I was at Cairabrae after the cottage burned down, I saw that painting. And just like you did earlier tonight, I recognized its similarity to the seascape that hung in Dad's study. You can imagine how surprised we were to learn of the connection. Mason's father was so pleased I liked it, he sent it as a housewarming gift."

"That's remarkable," Mom said, barely disguising her skepticism.

"Yes, it is. And when Mason learned that I was Brian's daughter, he offered to help me find a new place to live. I thought it was kind of him."

Mom patted my hand. Her smile mask was back. "Yes, very kind of him. I'll have to thank him next time I see him. Well, it's late." She dropped my hand and stood. "I'll see you in the morning." She walked to the door and turned. "One more thing," she said. "You never did tell me, how does James know Mason?"

She was definitely working on something, and if I didn't figure it out, she would snare me. "I don't know, Mom. I never asked."

She nodded. "Good night, sweetheart."

"Night, Mom."

She left the door ajar and plodded back down the hall toward her room. I turned off the lamp and rolled onto my back. My answers hadn't disarmed her. She was headed down a rabbit hole and I didn't know how to stop her. Tomorrow I'd call Mason and warn him to be careful. I considered Mason's advice to tell Mom about the gift but couldn't think of a thing doing so would change. The truth would only destroy our newly repaired relationship.

Sleep took a while to find me. I only knew it had upon waking. The scent of coffee teased my eyes open. I replayed the last discussion I'd had with my mother. Had she honestly thought I'd been involved in something criminal? I prayed the Mason-holds-my-mortgage idea had jelled overnight.

I checked my phone. No messages, and it was almost nine o'clock. I rolled out of bed, used the washroom and slipped my phone into my housecoat's pocket. The walk to the kitchen to face my mother seemed particularly long and strewn with apprehension.

A clean mug had been set out. I poured a cup of coffee, splashed milk into it and wandered into the living room. Mom was dressed and sat in one of the club chairs. She lowered a newspaper as I arrived.

"Good morning. You been up long?" I asked.

"A couple of hours."

"Couldn't sleep?"

"Not very well," Mom said.

"I'm sorry. Where'd you get the paper?"

"Your front desk. I was heading out to the newspaper box and Colin offered me his copy. Said he was finished with it. Are you hungry?" Mom asked. "I can make you some oatmeal."

"I should be cooking for you, not the other way around. Have you eaten?"

Mom shook her head and stood. "It gives me something to do," she said, and started for the kitchen.

I followed her and took a seat at the island. She managed to find everything with minimal direction from me. My phone buzzed. I pulled it from my pocket and checked the screen. "It's the front desk," I said, and answered it.

"You have a visitor. Mason Reynolds. Shall I send him up?"

I lifted my hand to my forehead and closed my eyes. Why was he still in Vancouver? Damn it! I should have called him before I got out of bed. "Just a minute," I said. My mother faced me with a wooden spoon in her hand. "Mason is here."

"Good. I'd like to talk to him," she said, and turned back to her pot.

Oh crap. Nine o'clock and all was definitely not well. "Send him up, Colin. Thank you."

I hung up and stared at the phone. My mom . . . quizzing Mason. What could possibly go wrong? "What are you going to talk to him about?"

Mom rattled the spoon on the edge of the pot. "You'd better get dressed. I'll entertain Mason until you get back."

I filled my lungs and stood. "I'll let him in."

"No need," she said brightly, and started for the hall, intentionally thwarting my effort to intercede. Did all mothers have a magic wand to turn their offspring back into teenagers?

I quickened my pace and trailed behind her. She stopped at the front door and put one hand on the door lever and one eye to the peephole. I went into my room and closed the door. Once inside, I pulled out my phone and texted Mason. *I told Mom you hold my mortgage. She doesn't know about the gift.* I pressed send and prayed he'd get my message before he stepped off the elevator.

Mason's voice in the hall had me pressing my ear to my bedroom door. He and Mom were being cordial, for the time being.

Visions of Mason telling her about the gift fuelled my dressing regimen. I yanked on yoga pants and a hoodie. Commando. No socks. I showed my teeth the toothbrush, pulled my hair into a messy bun and raced for the bedroom door.

I scooted down the hallway and stopped shy of the kitchen doorway. Mason had his back to me, his hip resting against the counter. My mother was out of my sight line. Water splashed in the sink. My gaze gravitated to a large bouquet of flowers lying on the cold granite slab of the island.

"Remind me," my mother said. "How do you and James know one another?"

Her casual tone was anything but. I entered the kitchen and Mason looked over. "Hey, Emelynn," he said. I couldn't tell from his expression if he'd seen my message.

Mom turned from the sink with a crystal vase half full of water in her hands. She set it on the island. "Emelynn, do you have scissors I could cut these stems with?"

"Knives are in the sharps drawer."

"I'd prefer to use scissors. Do you have a pair?"

"Somewhere around here. I'll go find them." Her pasted-on smile had seemingly escaped Mason's notice, as had the fact she'd just gotten rid of me. Mason actually looked pleased with himself. I wanted to smack him.

As I turned to leave, Mom restated her question. "So, how do you know James?"

Their voices faded as I hurried down the hall to my bedroom. I prayed Mason's answer wouldn't spark new curiosity on my mother's part. Moments later, I returned. They had moved into the living room. I held the scissors and stilled to listen.

Mason's voice sounded defensive. "Because she'd been through hell. Knowing Emelynn is Brian's daughter makes her feel like a niece to me. That's as close as I'm ever going to get to being an uncle, but I can see how that might seem strange to you."

Damn it. I'd only been gone a few minutes. What had they gotten into? I moved closer until I could see their reflections in the oven door.

Mason fished in his pocket and produced a ring with two keys. He stepped directly in front of my mother, who'd crossed her arms, and coaxed one of her arms free. He pressed the keys into her palm. "These are my keys to this place. When you're convinced I'm not out to harm your daughter, you can return them."

Mom tried to give them back, but Mason stepped away.

"I'm sorry," Mom said. "I didn't mean to offend you."

"It's okay. I understand. You're her mother, and you don't know me. I hope one day we'll know each other better." My mother folded her fingers over the keys. She wouldn't be impressed if she knew the keys were just for show.

"Please say goodbye to Emelynn," he said, and then turned for the hall. I pressed my back against the end cupboard. The hall door opened and closed. I slunk out of the kitchen and back to my room. With the scissors still in my hand, I plunked down on the end of my bed.

Whatever was bothering Mom, Mason was part of it, and apparently flowers weren't going to appease her. My phone buzzed. I pulled it out of my pocket. No number. Please let it be James. "Hello."

"This is Redmond Moss." A voice I hadn't expected.

"Have you heard from James?"

"No. I've not been able to reach him. I'm at his place now." I imagined James and his father used randomly generated usernames and scrambled IP addresses in a way that was similar to the *Viagra* system James had put in place for Mom and me. "When was the last time you spoke to him?"

"Hold on a moment." I flipped back through my call log—one week, two weeks, and then I found it. "April 2. He said he was getting ready for another job."

"Do you know what it was about?"

"No."

"The last time James used his laptop he researched a company in San Diego."

I stilled. "Which one?"

"Vector Labs."

The oxygen level in the room bottomed out.

"Emelynn?"

"Someone's called me twice from that lab. Both times they hung up."

Now it was Redmond's turn to go silent. Eventually, he said, "I'll be in touch."

"Wait! What are you going to do? How can I reach you?"

"I'll call you," he said, and the phone went dead. It seemed trust was a rare commodity in my circle.

Were the phone calls from James? I needed to talk to Sam, but not here. I opened the bedroom door and nearly knocked my mother over.

A flush crawled up her neck. "I won't need those after all," she said, looking at the scissors in my hand. Had she been eavesdropping? "Mason left. He said to say goodbye."

"That was fast. He couldn't stay?"

"I guess not. Your breakfast is ready."

"I can't stay, Mom. I've got to go."

"Right now?" Her shoulders slumped, reminding me that she was my guest, and more importantly, my mother, who had come here because her home had been violated. And she'd just made me breakfast. I could wait another five minutes.

"Sorry," I said, shaking my head with an apologetic smile. "You're right. It can wait a bit." I started down the hall with her at my side.

When we arrived at the kitchen, Mom's gaze followed mine as I spotted Mason's keys on the counter. She stated the obvious. "Mason returned your keys."

"Why? Did you two argue?"

"No." Mom turned to the stove and dished oatmeal into two bowls. The flowers had been arranged in the vase. "I think he misunderstood my concern about the mortgage he holds on this condo."

"You said you were going to thank him, Mom, not interrogate him. What did you say?"

"I simply asked why he'd been so generous."

"I told you why."

"So you did. You'll forgive me if it seems odd considering I've only heard you mention his name once or twice. But I do hope I didn't offend him, and if I did, I'll apologize."

Mom set the bowls on the island, where the milk and brown sugar waited. I sat on one of the bar stools and pulled a bowl close, inhaling the sweet scent of vanilla and cinnamon. No matter how often I made this dish, hers always tasted better. "Thanks for breakfast, Mom." As I savoured a warm spoonful, for the very first time, I appreciated how much simpler my life had been in Toronto. Back then, the only thing I'd had to hide was my on-again, off-again relationship with gravity. Now, my lies were choking me.

"Where are you going this morning? Work?"

"Not today," I said, unwilling to tack on another lie. "I'll only be an hour or two. The keys for the MGB are on the hall table if you want to go out. Help yourself. I'll take the Volvo."

"Thank you, sweetheart. Perhaps I'll go downtown. Check out Nordstrom."

When we'd finished breakfast, I loaded the dishwasher and excused myself, grabbing the old Volvo's keys on my way out. I drove onto the university's campus in a direction opposite the one my mother would take, then pulled over and parked.

A grown woman reduced to sneaking around her mother as if she were a kid smoking pot. I shook my head. Sadly, as long as she remained in investigative mode, what choice did I have?

My first call was to Mason. It went to voice mail. Was he already on a flight back home? My list of questions for him was longer than my patience.

I hung up and dialled Sebastian. If he had information about Vector Labs, I needed it now, not at some obscure point in the future when it suited him. He answered with "Yes." Curt, but it was a step up from his usual rude.

"It's Emelynn."

"Indeed. Has Redmond contacted you?"

"Yes. Thank you." And given Redmond's glacial attitude toward Sebastian, the less Sebastian knew about our conversation, the better. "Did you learn anything more about Vector Labs?"

He exhaled loudly into the phone. "No Flier connection. They're legitimate. It's a publically traded company with a healthy balance sheet." His double standard regarding the timely passing on of information didn't go unnoticed. Then again, treating people as equals wasn't his strong suit. "What did you learn from Redmond?"

"He hasn't heard from James," I said.

"And you?"

"No word."

"So what aren't you telling me, Emelynn?" Man, he was a nosy SOB. And smart. Damn it.

"James researched Vector Labs before his last assignment."

"Have you had further contact from the lab?"

"No, and so far they haven't left a message."

"They don't need to. Their invitation is implicit."

"The calls might have come from James."

"My money's on ICO. Looks like it's time I paid Cain a visit. Until we learn more, stay away from that lab." He hung up on me. I stared at the little screen. Dick. Wad.

Frustrated, I made my last call. Sam was becoming my pressure-release valve. "Redmond called," I said. I told him that Redmond had been unable to reach James. "He says the last thing James researched was a company called Vector Labs."

"Who are they?" Sam asked.

"Some rent-a-lab in San Diego. I'll send you a link, but get this—I've had two hang-ups from that company's phone number in as many days."

"Doesn't sound like something James would do."

"No. I agree. I'm pretty sure Redmond is going to check it out, but I can't stop thinking—what if James is in trouble?"

The ensuing silence ended with Sam's outburst. "This is bullshit! First ICO locks us out and now some rent-a-lab is playing hard to get. What the fuck is going on? Pack a bag. We're going to San Diego."

Oh crap. "That could be a problem. I've been ordered to steer clear of Vector Labs."

"Ordered? By whom? Last I checked, you worked for me."

My relief was instantaneous. It was just what I needed to hear. "You're right, I do." And Sebastian could bite my ass because James was way higher on my list of priorities than an order from him.

"Glad you agree because I've never been very good at waiting around for answers. Meet me at the airport. I'll send you the details. And Emelynn? Use your alter ego's ID."

CHAPTER ELEVEN

Mom hadn't yet left the condo when I arrived back home in the late morning. I found her at the dining room table with a pen in her hand, scribbling on a notepad. She held her phone to her ear. "I'll call you right back," she said, and disconnected in an unnecessary rush.

"Sorry to interrupt," I said. "Thought you might have left already."

"Soon." She set her phone down and quickly flipped the page on her notepad. Was she hiding something? Not that I was in any position to speak. "You weren't gone long. Want to come to Nordstrom with me?"

"I can't, Mom. I know you've just arrived, and I'm the worst daughter in the world, but something's come up. I have to go to California with Detective Jordan."

"Oh? Is this to do with your case?"

I nodded, letting another lie slip by. How long would I be able to use Sam and the long-solved missing criminal excuse to hide my activities? "We have to leave right away. I'll probably be gone two or three days." Miss Manners would have kept me after class and had me write drills on the board: *A good hostess does not abandon a guest.* Given that said guest was also my mother, I'd probably earn a ruler over the knuckles as well.

"You tell Detective Jordan that I'm not happy with him. He can see you anytime."

I apologized again, but Mom dismissed my apology with a swipe of her hand. "Never mind. It'll give me time to get reacquainted with

Vancouver. Besides, my leave of absence has been arranged. I'll extend my visit so we can have more time together."

"I'd like that," I said, not liking it as much as I wished I could. It wasn't her fault, but hiding who I was and what I did had turned into a bigger complication than I'd anticipated.

I hurried to my bedroom and tossed clothes in a bag. Sam's email arrived along with a boarding pass. After packing, I hugged my mother goodbye. "I'll call if I can," I said.

"Travel safely, and hurry home." She pecked me on the cheek.

I shuffled through the airport's security line and joined the busy travellers slotting their way to designated gates. The departures board indicated our flight was on time and boarding at 12:30 p.m. I spotted Sam in the distance. He stood in front of a bank of windows looking out at the Air Canada jets lined up at the terminal. I'd never seen him dressed in a suit and tie. He looked pretty good.

My mother foremost on my mind, I bent to the phone, dialled Avery and tucked into a crack of privacy between a pillar and a garbage can. He answered immediately. "I'm sorry to dump this on you," I said, "but I've only got a minute." I then updated him on my mom's visit and told him what had happened with Mason, and Jolene's painting. Then, because bad news followed me like a stench, I warned him that my contract with ICO was on the rocks.

He assured me he'd put the covey on alert, and offered his help in our search for James. "I'll call your mother," he said. "Touch base, make sure she's okay while you're gone."

I thanked him and we disconnected. When I emerged from behind the pillar, Sam was staring out into the swarming crowd. Looking for me, I assumed. He caught my wave and his posture relaxed. The flight crew had started boarding the aircraft. We exchanged greetings and joined the queue of people waiting to head down the ramp to the plane.

"Las Vegas?" I asked, gesturing the boarding pass Sam had emailed me.

"I have a cousin who lives there. Can't think of a better place to spend my week's vacation." A carnival barker's grin crept across his face. It looked as if I wasn't the only one who'd picked up a few tips from James.

"Why did you want me to use Dana Christopher?" The fake ID was one James had set up for me a while back.

Sam checked for eavesdroppers. "I can't hide my movements—I'm travelling with my gun—but you can, and we need all the diversionary tactics we can get right now."

"But ICO knows about my alter ego. It was the name I was admitted under at the hospital, after the Cooper brothers' case."

"I know. I'm the one who gave them that name. The doctor who treated you, Penn, he knows you as Dana, and I'm sure a nurse or two, maybe the guards, but that was a while ago, and I kept Dana's name out of my reports." He exhaled a long, slow breath. "Dana's our best bet."

On board, we passed through the rarified section as we made our way along the narrow aisle to find our seats in economy. I swung into the window seat. Sam didn't quite manage to fold himself into the aisle chair. At six two and two hundred pounds, economy didn't quite cut it. I lifted the centre armrest to give him more room.

My phone buzzed as I straightened from tucking my bag under the seat in front. It was Mason. Crap! Not a conversation I wanted to have while trapped next to Sam. I turned into the window and answered. "Hey."

"You rang earlier. What's up?"

"What happened with you and Mom?"

"Not what I'd hoped. I wish you hadn't told her I held your mortgage."

"Yeah? Well not as much as I wish you hadn't mentioned Jolene."

"Touché. If it's any consolation, I stayed in town last night in case you ended up in a tough spot with your mom."

"I appreciate that, but I can't tell her what we are. She'd never forgive me."

"She's certainly not easily swayed."

"No. She's not." Sam unclipped his seat belt and stood to help an elderly man hoist his bag into the overhead bin. "How'd it go with your . . . work last night? Did you get what you needed?"

The ensuing dead air notched up my unease.

Finally, Mason said, "Listen Em, there's no easy way to tell you this, but the Redeemer I'm dealing with . . . he mentioned you by name."

"What!"

"You're the reason he was in Vancouver. He helped plan the newborn's kidnapping."

"Why?"

"The *why* is obvious—he saw you and the detective during the raid at Cairabrae. Knows who you are, what you are. He sold the intel to someone and had to prove it was worth the price. The newborn's kidnapping was his vehicle for proof. We won't know whether he was successful until we get him to give up who he sold the intel to."

"And you can do that? Find the buyer?"

"I can't, at least not quickly, but Redmond Moss can, and he's on his way as we speak. You can thank your pain-in-the-ass mentor for that. Sebastian's the one who convinced James's father to help us out."

"Sebastian! That prick. He didn't *convince* Redmond. No wonder Redmond would barely talk to me."

"I thought you didn't know Redmond Moss." Mason's voice had an edge to it I didn't like.

"I don't! I asked Sebastian for Redmond's number because I'm worried about James. I should have known Sebastian wouldn't pass on my message for free—you know, out of the goodness of a heart he clearly doesn't have."

"I didn't know. You should have asked me."

"You were a little busy."

"True, and I'm sorry about Sebastian, but hang in there. We'll have answers soon. Like I said, Redmond's on his way here."

"I wouldn't count on it."

"Oh? Why?"

"Redmond hasn't heard from James either, but he did learn that James researched Vector Labs before going off-line."

"Oh shit!"

"Yeah, exactly. And before you ask, yes, I told him about the hang-ups I received. I'd bet my front teeth that Redmond is on his way to San Diego, not Vancouver."

"Goddamnit! Time is not on our side here. I'll make some phone calls. You stay put. I don't want you going down to San Diego until we know more about that lab."

"Funny, that's exactly what Sebastian said. But I have no choice."

"What do you mean?" Mason said. Sam retook his seat and fumbled with the seat belt.

"I'm with Detective Jordan right now. We're on a plane headed there."

"Are you putting me on? Someone's trying to get you down there and you're playing into their hands?"

The announcement to turn off electronic devices crackled over the speakers. "Yeah, well hoping and praying those calls from Vector aren't from James isn't working for me. Someone's got to check it out. Might as well be us."

"I don't like this, Emelynn."

"I don't either, but I can't sit still and wait. And don't forget who's been training me. I won't do anything stupid."

"You be careful. Assume the worst and take every precaution. Sebastian has left for Ottawa and I can't get out of here right now so if you need help, call Dad. He's connected."

He didn't have to worry about me calling Sebastian again. Ever. "Thanks, I will," I said, and repeated Stuart's number aloud after Mason gave it to me, memorizing it before I ended the call.

I looked over at Sam. He nodded to my phone. "Take the battery out of that."

"Why? The GPS is disabled. It's not traceable—not even in the cloud."

"It *was* untraceable. If James has been compromised, we can't trust it. We'll pick up burner phones when we get to Vegas."

"But I need the phone numbers in here."

"Then copy them out," he said, reaching into his jacket pocket. He handed me his notepad and pen. "Quickly."

I pulled up my contact list and started jotting down numbers, beginning with Stuart's that I'd just memorized.

"Miss?" I looked up. A stewardess leaned over Sam. "You need to turn that off now."

I apologized. She hung around until she saw me turn it off, and then continued on her rounds. I tucked it back in my pocket. Sam glared at me and held out his hand. Reluctantly, I passed him my phone. He snapped it open, removed the battery and the SIM card and handed the pieces back to me unconcerned that he'd severed my safety line.

"Are you wearing your Garmin?" he asked.

Damn. I hadn't even considered that. I removed the GPS from my wrist and handed it to him. "You'd better not be counting on me to find our way. I'm hopeless without that."

He flicked off the back cover and popped out the battery. "'Bout time you learned how to use a map, isn't it?"

"I use maps just fine, thanks. They make terrific wrapping paper."

"That conversation you were having sounded heated. Is everything all right?"

"Yeah. Just one more person who doesn't want us to go to San Diego."

The flight to Las Vegas took just under three hours. "This is where you and I part ways," Sam said, as the plane taxied to our gate. "After we disembark, go to the ladies' room and change your clothes and hair. Take a cab to this address." He handed me a note. "Make sure you're not followed. I'll meet you there in an hour."

There turned out to be an In-N-Out Burger. No one followed. I ducked out of the late-afternoon sun at a picnic table under the shade of a bright red umbrella. When Sam pulled up, I did a double-take. Gone was the businessman and in his place was a soccer dad in a ball cap and blue jeans.

"You hungry?" he said, climbing out of a tired-looking pickup truck. Without waiting for an answer, he walked toward the restaurant and held the door open for me. An unwelcome blast of cool air hit me.

"Whose truck, Dad?" I asked, while we waited for our burgers.

Sam cocked an eyebrow. "My cousin's. And FYI? I'm not old enough to be your dad."

We escaped the air conditioning and took our burgers back to the picnic table. I peeled off the paper wrapping and separated the bun to take a look at the burger. A blob of salmon-coloured mayonnaise dropped on the table. "How far to San Diego from here?"

Sam swallowed a mouthful of burger and took a swig of Coke. "Five hours that way," he said, pointing.

"You sure our ride's gonna make it?"

"Nope." Sam finished his burger and watched me make a mess of mine while he polished off his French fries. When we were done, he took our trash to the receptacle and picked up my bag. He dropped it into the dusty bed of the truck and we clambered into the cab. He started the engine and pulled a map from the driver door's pocket. "See if you can find San Diego on that, would you?" he said, handing it to me. He donned a pair of aviators, did a shoulder check and backed out.

"You're a brave man, Mr. Jordan." I unfolded the tortuous thing, found Las Vegas and traced my finger south and west to San Diego. I reached into my handbag and pulled out a pen. "You mind?" I asked, showing Sam my intention.

"Do you really need to do that?" he said.

"Yes, I really do," I replied, and drew a line roughly along our route. We found our way to Highway 15 and settled in for the long drive.

The highway's asphalt lay like a ribbon across the desert floor. It ran flat for miles. Low buildings gave way to scrub brush tufting out from the sand. Mountain ranges lay ahead, and I couldn't yet see our path through them. In the oversized side mirror, downtown Las Vegas shrunk until it resembled a Barbie castle in a sandbox. We left the windows cracked to make up for the truck's lack of air conditioning.

"Have you always lived in Vancouver?" I asked, curious to learn more about Sam. In the almost six months since I'd been working with him, he'd never discussed his personal life.

"No. I was raised in Hamilton."

"In Ontario?"

"Yup. Steel town. Hamilton."

"What brought you to BC?"

"I was looking for some answers. Didn't find them. Ended up enlisting in the army."

"That explains the hair, but are you really going to leave it at 'looking for some answers'?"

Sam laughed. "My birth mother lived in Vancouver. She'd died by the time I tried to find her. Never did learn who my father was."

His visceral reaction to the abandoned baby made much more sense now. "That's rough."

"Nah. I have no complaints. Curiosity sent me searching is all."

"Why the army?"

"Wanted to travel the world. Learn to shoot."

"And did you?"

"Did four tours. Croatia, Sarajevo. Cured me."

"Of what? Wanting to travel?"

"No. Of the illusion of justice."

"And so you became a cop?"

He met my sarcasm with a chuckle. "Thought I'd work on eradicating the degenerates closer to home."

"You sure it's not because you like to shoot?"

"Maybe."

"Were you ever married?"

"What's with you and the questions today?"

"It's a long drive. And you know everything about me. I barely know anything about you."

He smiled without taking his eyes off the road. "Never married. Got close once."

"Ever think about having kids?"

"Kids need two parents. Maybe one day. How about you?"

"I've given it some thought." I pictured the delight on James's face whenever he interacted with kids. "Not sure I'm ready for that kind of responsibility." One of my running routes took me past a park with a set of monkey bars and some strap swings. On rain-free days kids were always there, charging around, squealing. "This job isn't exactly a good fit with motherhood."

Every few hundred yards, a Joshua tree sprouted from the sand. I soon learned that Sam's adoptive parents still lived in the Hamilton home where he'd been raised. He had no siblings but lots of cousins thanks to three aunts and two uncles.

Then Sam reached over and turned on some tunes, signalling the end of Question Period. He settled on a rock-and-roll station that played classics from the sixties.

We'd been driving for a little over an hour when Sam turned on the blinker. "Our limo's gas mileage appears to be in the lower single digits," he said, and pulled into an ARCO station outside a little town called Baker. While Sam filled up, I hit the restroom and returned to the truck with two disposable cellphones, a family-sized bag of Cheese Puffs and two iced teas. Towards the west, the sun was dropping behind the Sierra Nevada mountain range.

While Sam motored along, I made a valiant effort to open the cellphones' shell packs. After cutting my finger, I gave up and rifled through the glovebox looking for something sharp. The sealed packs should have come with the Jaws of Life, but I had to settle for rusty nail clippers. They left ragged edges, but at least I was able to set the phones free without spilling more blood. There was nothing to set up—just had to turn them on. I programmed each with the other's number and then turned my undivided attention to the Cheese Puffs.

Two hours later I looked at Sam and wrinkled my nose. "Do you smell that?" I asked.

Sam dropped his gaze to the dash. "Shit. It's overheating." He slowed to a crawl and pulled a U-turn.

"We passed a service station a few miles back. They'll have coolant."

A few miles back was Temecula, which, by my calculations, was still more than an hour shy of San Diego.

The news we received in Temecula wasn't welcome. A steady drip of fluorescent yellow made a puddle under the car. All the coolant in the world wouldn't fix a leaky radiator hose. And unfortunately, the shop's mechanic had left for the day. The gap-toothed after-hours attendant tried to be helpful. "There's a Motel 6 down the road. It's got a pool. I can call a cab and get you fixed up first thing tomorrow morning."

Sam rubbed the back of his neck and looked over at me. "Looks like we're spending the night."

I took a deep breath and exhaled my frustration. There was no other option. It wasn't as if I could fix the damn truck myself. Ugh! We'd lose an entire night.

"I need to check my phone. James could have called. Maybe Redmond. There's a chance we don't even need to go to San Diego."

"No! If Vector Labs turns out to be nothing, then have at it. But right now, we have to assume your phone's been compromised. Turning it on? You might as well lean on a horn. They may be expecting us, but I'll be damned if we're going to announce our arrival."

It wasn't that I didn't know all that—James had explained it enough times. But the phone in pieces at the bottom of my bag tempted me like a cigarette on quitting day for a smoker.

"The waiting never ends, does it?" I said.

"Look, it's late, we're both tired, both hungry," Sam said, sensing my frustration. "Better to case the lab in the morning and approach it fresh tomorrow night."

We used my ID to get adjacent rooms at the Motel 6, and after dropping our bags, we crossed the street and walked to a Thai restaurant recommended by the motel's night clerk. After dinner, we returned to the hotel, said our good nights and hit the sack early.

When the service station opened at 7:30 a.m., we were waiting. By 8:00 a.m. we were on the road again, with fresh coffee, stale muffins and an assortment of salty treats. I refolded the map to frame the last leg of our trip. An hour later, we hit our target.

"Look. San Diego!" I pointed to the proof on a road sign. "I found it," I said, giving a little fist pump.

Sam levelled a bored look my way. "Pretty cocky. Let's see how well you do finding Vector Labs."

"Is that a challenge, Detective?" I said, and opened the map to find the blow-up of Miramar and the north end of San Diego.

"Apparently," Sam said with an easy grin. "What's my exit?"

I'd already marked up the map so only had to orientate it to our direction of travel. "Mercy Road," I said, settling back to watch for it.

We exited the highway and drove west on Mercy Road, and then turned north and passed through a grid of residential neighbourhoods. The streets widened and low-rise industrial malls took over. Small industry gave way to large warehouses spaced between stretches of undeveloped land.

As we closed in on the lab's address, we slowed to a crawl. A manicured hedge ran along the property's frontage. Vector Lab's well-kept sign was made to be seen from a distance and sat to one side of a long, paved driveway. The single-storey structure was set back on the property. It had a strip of parking across the front and a larger lot off to one side.

We drove past and took the next left down a gravel side road. Dust billowed up behind us. The first turn off the road led to a delivery entrance at the back of the lab. We carried on and dragged our dust ball along a road with mailboxes posted at the ends of long rural driveways. The truck fit right in.

A few miles on, Sam pulled to the side of the road and stopped. "I suggest we backtrack a ways, pull off the road and hike in. We can set up in the bush beside the lab. Should be able to get a good view of the entrance and the parking lot from there."

"Sounds good to me."

Sam restarted the truck and we turned around. A few minutes later, he pulled off the gravel into tall grass and parked. We grabbed our bags and set out through clumps of black sage on a gently rolling landscape. Cover wasn't continuous, but aspen and cottonwood trees grew tall at regular intervals, providing a modicum of camouflage.

"There," Sam said, pointing to the lab's roof in the distance. He pulled a pair of binoculars from his bag and scanned the horizon. We continued along and got within a hundred yards of the parking lot's asphalt, and then we crouched at the base of a large laurel oak. I shielded my eyes against the sunshine. Out came the binoculars again and when Sam was done, he handed them to me.

Security cameras jutted out from under the building's eaves at each of the two visible corners. I imagined the other corners had the same setup. The front end of a UPS truck jutted out from a loading bay at the back of the building. Thirty or so cars filled parking slots.

"Now what?" I asked.

"Now we make ourselves comfortable and do some good old-fashioned surveillance."

"Tell you what," I said, checking our surroundings. "You get a start on that 'sitting on your derrière' routine. There's next to no wind. I'm going to get a closer look."

"All right. But don't go in. I want to watch for a while, see what we can learn from out here."

I left my bag on the ground, squeezed my crystal and blinked out of sight. Wasting no time, I flew over the parking lot toward the side of the building, heading directly for the security cameras. They were functioning but stationary and without zoom capability.

I dropped down to the employee-entrance door. A black access control plate mounted to its right meant a security card was needed to get inside. Large darkened windows were set in the wall at regular intervals on either side of the door.

I cruised around to the rear of the building. There were no windows. The back end of the UPS truck was snugged up to a receiving door. A second receiving door gaped open. I peeked inside the open bay door. Empty pallets lay stacked against one wall. Beyond the loading bay, sturdy steel shelving housed shrink-wrapped supplies. I spotted the UPS driver walking across the concrete loading-bay floor. He closed the truck's rear rolling door and exited the receiving bay by a side door. He paused on the landing and punched something into a hand-held computer. Behind him, fastened to the wall, a ladder provided access to the roof. The UPS driver finished up then hurried down a set of concrete steps back to his truck.

I continued on to the far side of the building and confirmed the two cameras there were functioning. I found no door, but the windows toward the front of the building weren't darkened. Looking inside, I could tell from the furniture and the suits that these were offices. My circuit of the building ended at the main entrance. On a glass panel to the left of the entrance were the names and logos of a dozen companies, presumably each of which either hired the lab or rented lab space within. They were the same companies touted on Vector Labs's website.

Inside the heavy glass door, a woman no older than I was occupied a single chair behind a curved reception counter. To her right, generous leather chairs and low tables awaited visitors. On her left, an oval conference table sat in a glass-fronted room. Solid wood doors were set into the wall behind her. The security cameras in the reception area were mounted under darkened domes, which could house anything. Infrared receptors at knee level on either side of the exterior and the interior doors meant someone was monitoring the comings and goings after hours.

Finally, I drifted up to the flat rooftop. The usual ventilation and air-conditioning units cluttered the centre of the space. The roofing membrane was covered with a thick coat of what I suspected was road dust. Looking over the raised lip of the roof, I spotted large uplighting fixtures hidden in the shrubs at the front of the building and on both sides of the employee door but nothing on the other side, or at the back. I watched the UPS truck pull away from the building and drive toward the service road.

With my inspection complete, I returned to Sam. He had his back to the tree and his binoculars trained on the building. I re-formed beside him. He jerked and his elbow slipped from his bent knee. His notepad lay open beside him.

"Sorry," I said. "Didn't mean to startle you."

He shot me a dubious glare. "What'd you learn?"

"Security's low key, basic," I said, and filled him in on the exterior cameras, the reception area and the building's layout. "How about you? Learn anything?"

"Parking up front is for visitors. It's empty. Side parking is for employees, and the decals on the cars are colour coded. Looks like a local company does the landscaping." Sam had jotted down a raft of licence plate numbers. He reached into his bag and pulled out a camera with a lengthy zoom lens. He handed me the binoculars. "See for yourself." He resumed his vigil. "What does James drive?"

"He doesn't own a car," I said. Sam pulled back from the camera and swung his head in my direction. I shrugged. "Maybe he owns a motorcycle or rents something when he needs it?" A twinge of embarrassment coloured my face. What kind of girlfriend didn't know this basic detail about her boyfriend?

Sam returned to his camera lens. I focused on the employee entrance and swept the binoculars to the left, toward the main entrance. A grey sedan rolled up and turned into the visitors' parking lot. Moments later, the driver door opened. The man who emerged wore a tailored suit and brushed a hand through dark hair as he stood in the shelter of his door. Sam's camera whirred and clicked off a series of photos. The way the man surveyed the surroundings suggested he'd not been here before. He closed the sedan's door and scanned the building as he walked around to the passenger side of his car. I lost sight of him as he opened the passenger door and reached inside. When he emerged from the far side of the car, a ribbed aluminum briefcase, the likes of which I'd only ever seen in the movies, dangled from one hand. With a chuckle, I asked Sam, "Is that handcuffed to his wrist?" Sam chuffed and the man disappeared into the building.

"Rental car," Sam said, and jotted down the details in his notepad. A green National sticker had been applied carelessly askew on the lip of the trunk.

The man was inside for almost two hours, and during that time, four cars left the employee parking lot—two of them returned—and a FedEx van made a delivery. Sam took photos of everyone. I polished off the pepperoni sticks we'd bought that morning. When the man in the suit left, Sam's camera whirred and clicked again. The man repeated his observation routine and returned his briefcase to the passenger seat before strolling back to the driver door. He ran his hand through that thick hair again and then ducked inside. Moments later, the car pulled out and retraced the route it had taken in.

By the third hour, I feared I'd drop dead from boredom. "Is all surveillance this dry?" I asked.

"Yup. Not quite the thrilling life most people associate with being a detective, is it? No getting around it though. Observe, collect data, analyze, make connections, find another angle and repeat. You don't always see the value of what you're doing when you're in the field with ants crawling up your pant leg and mosquitoes treating you like a smorg, but I can tell you, it's the small details that break cases wide open. Always."

"I thought you hated waiting," I said.

"This isn't waiting. It's observation. There's a difference."

Personally, I couldn't see the fine line between the two. How many years had it taken Sam to hone his patience, I wondered? Every thirty minutes, I stood and changed position. I opened the last bag of chips. Sam got up only once, and that was to relieve himself one tree over.

By late afternoon, the growling in my stomach was loud enough to give our position away. "I need some real food. Let's go get a bite to eat and come back after dark," I suggested.

"Nah. You go ahead. Bring me something. I want to be here with my camera locked on the employee exit when the lab closes."

I checked the time. "You sure?" There was plenty of time to do both.

"Yeah. Go, and be quick about it. I'm hungry."

Chapter Twelve

My skills wouldn't add much to Sam's surveillance until after dark anyway, I rationalized, and feeling useless felt like another form of waiting. I left and hiked my way back to his cousin's truck.

It was exactly as we'd left it—dusty on the outside with the heat of Hades lying in wait inside. I climbed into the cab, turned the key in the ignition and opened the windows wide. If Sam hadn't disabled my GPS, finding dinner would have been as easy as punching in a few buttons. Instead, I played spectator at a tennis match as I retraced our route, swinging my head left and right in search of a towering red-and-yellow sign. Whether that led to McDonald's or In-N-Out Burger didn't matter.

When I hit Mercy Road and still hadn't found the arches or the arrow, I turned around and headed back to the only establishment offering food I'd seen along the way—a Tex-Mex-style bar with neon signs promising *cold cerveza* and *Jose Cuervo*. I parked and took a moment to reassess. *Inviting* wasn't exactly the word I'd use to describe the place. Iron bars on too-small windows and a row of ragtag motorcycles parked to the side of the entrance gave me pause, but my mouth watered at the heavy scent of grease.

I jumped out of the truck and walked across the crumbling asphalt. Tepid air reeking of spilled beer gushed out when I opened the door. Voices hushed, and it took a moment for my eyes to adjust to the dim interior. I ignored the stares of the men who'd suspended their pool game to check out the new arrival. A hard-living woman in day-old makeup slid off the lap of a man whose girth would test the suspension on any of the bikes out front.

"What can I getcha?" she said, stepping behind the bar.

"Do you have a menu?" I asked.

She tapped a chipped fingernail on a laminated menu taped to the bar.

I gave it a quick scan. "Two burgers with fries," I said. "To go."

"Somethin' to drink?"

"Two Cokes."

She sauntered the length of the bar and swung her hips through a hinged door at the end. I turned around and took in the dingy interior. The clack of balls told me the pool game had resumed, but more than one player kept me in his sights.

Their scrutiny made me uneasy. I walked in the opposite direction and slipped into a seat at a table as far from the game as possible. The six or so men hanging around the pool table were the only people in the place. Keeping a low profile would have been so much easier at a drive-through window.

Five minutes passed and the bartender didn't reappear, which told me she doubled as the cook, at least in daytime hours.

Laughter and back slaps from the biker gene pool preceded a hush and then steady, heavy footfalls coming in my direction. The man who'd drawn the short straw planted his Icon boots beside me. Shit. Anonymity just said goodbye.

"Haven't seen you before. Where you from?"

I stopped my fidgeting and looked up. The man's hair fell from a widow's peak to his shoulders. A broad chest challenged the stretch of his T-shirt. He looked like a complication best avoided. "Nowhere special."

"Huh, don't know that place. What's your name?"

"I don't mean to be rude—"

"Just asking your name, honey. Being friendly's all."

Funny, it didn't feel friendly, but something told me answering him would be easier than getting him to leave. "Dana."

"You wanna come meet the boys, Dana? Play some pool?"

"Thanks, but I'm just going to grab my food and go."

"We're harmless, promise."

I offered him a smile, hoping he'd take it and leave.

"Mind if I sit?" he said, as he pulled out the chair on the other side of the table and plunked down.

I raised my eyebrows, straightening in my seat. "I'm not staying."

"Here, or in town?"

Damn. With each question, my hope of remaining faceless dissipated. "Both. I'm leaving as soon as my food order is ready."

He leaned in. "You ordered for two. Who you travelling with?"

With my palms on the edge of the table, I pushed back. It was time to check on that order. "My husband."

His gaze dropped to my left hand. "You sure?"

I took a long, steady breath. Did he really think I'd be flattered by his attention? Sitting down had been presumptuous, but he'd just stepped into pushy territory. "No disrespect, but I'm not interested."

He straightened one leg and made a show of relaxing back in his chair. "Your order's not gonna be up for another ten or fifteen. We don't get many strays in here, 'specially pretty ones. Set awhile."

Ten or fifteen minutes of talk would only encourage him. More footfalls approached. I stood and started to step away, but one of his stout pals came up behind me and bounced his chest into my back, forcing me to take a step forward toward the table. "Please don't touch me," I said.

Stout guy didn't acknowledge me. He stood firm and too close. "You scaring her away?" he said to the man with the widow's peak.

A third man, taller and wider than his buddies, joined the fun. "Where you going, little lady?"

I crossed my arms and turned to look at each of them. "Are you boys going to make me regret coming in here?"

"Don't be like that," the tall one said, and then he made the mistake of putting his arm around my shoulder. My elbow shot back of its own accord and nailed him in the ribs. He grunted in surprise and I ducked out of his reach.

My gaze flipped from the man I'd elbowed to the loud thump that was Widow's Peak's chair tipping backwards in his haste to stand. "You're being disrespectful to my friends," he said.

The stout man stepped into my personal space again, but my attention was back on the tall man I'd elbowed. His wide-eyed surprise had disappeared under a heavy brow and a whole lot of pissed off. Shit!

I deked to the right in another effort to get away from them. Widow's Peak stepped out from the table, leaving nothing but air between the three of them and me. I shook my head. I should have searched longer for a drive-through.

"I'd like to leave now," I said, but they stood between the door and me and weren't budging. The three of them exchanged glances as if they were reaching an accord, and I had the impression it wasn't *How 'bout we let the little lady get on her way*. Terrific! Three against one, and their backup crew was mere steps away across the room.

I didn't like their odds.

With any luck, I'd only have to cripple one of them. Tall Guy stepped up to volunteer. I switched my full attention to him and gathered the strength of my crystal into a low-voltage jolt. Painful but not deadly. With a swing of my head, I hurled it at him. His head snapped back and his chest followed. The soles of his boots made an appearance and then his back hit the floor with a resounding thud.

"What the..." Widow's Peak darted a glance at me and then scurried to his buddy's side. Stout Guy did the same. I backed away as they took turns slapping Tall Guy's face and calling his name. His pool-playing buddies stampeded toward us. I slunk away from the milieu keeping my back to the wall.

Last to the party was the bartender-cook, who'd come around the end of the bar with a paper bag in one hand and two cans of Coke in the other. She jerked to a stop, but the moment she processed the huddle of bodies on the floor, she abandoned the bag and sodas on the bar and rushed in to help. The Neanderthal would live, but he'd have one hell of a headache when he woke up.

No one noticed me scoop the bag and cans from the bar. I dropped a twenty in their place and slipped outside. With the sun blinding me, I ran flat out for the truck. I tossed my order in the open window, jumped in and had the engine racing before my door was closed. I hammered on the gas pedal with my heart banging in my chest.

After a few blocks, I checked my speed, slowed the truck and caught my breath. My hands were shaking. Damnit! I should have left the bar at the first sign of trouble. Hell, if I'd listened to my instincts, I wouldn't have gone inside at all. It had been reckless, but it was unlikely the bikers would connect me to what had happened to the Neanderthal. Too bad in a way—they could use a lesson in manners. A little part of me hoped the biker boys would give Neanderthal man a hard time for fainting.

By the time I pulled off the gravel road and parked the truck in the tall grass again, I'd stopped shaking. I grabbed the bag of grub, locked up and hiked back to Sam.

He sat in the same position I'd left him in—his back to the tree, the long lens of the camera in the cradle of his hand, his elbow below supported on a bent knee. "What took you so long? You get lost?"

"You don't want to know."

He looked away from the lens and up to me. "Oh?"

I shook my head and dropped to the ground beside him. "Never mind. I couldn't find the golden arches, so you'll have to choke down a greasy bar burger instead." He set the camera down as I opened the bag and handed him a burger and a can of Coke. I ripped open the bag and made a tablecloth of it for the fries, and then unwrapped my own burger. "What'd I miss?" The burger wasn't bad. Fries were soggy. None of it was hot enough.

Sam chewed a mouthful and swallowed. "A semi came in. Backed up to the receiving dock. Six cars with yellow parking decals left." He took another bite. Chewed. "What time did you say the lab closes?"

"Six o'clock, at least according to the announcement on their answering machine." I checked the time. It was five thirty. Lots of vehicles were still in the employee lot. We finished eating and washed everything down with the Cokes.

I took up the binoculars and trained them on the employee entrance. After six o'clock, another clutch of employees left. Half wore lab coats, half of the remainder dressed in business clothes and the rest wore casual attire. Absently, I assigned them roles: janitor, sales exec, secretary, scientist.

"That's five blue decals and another yellow," Sam said, noting the times beside the corresponding licence plate numbers on his notepad.

At half past six, another handful of employees left. The transport truck was still plugged into the receiving dock. I counted fifteen cars still in the lot.

"I'll bet you some of those labs work around the clock," Sam said, as a new car entered the lot and parked. "You'll have some stragglers to contend with when you get inside."

Sunset was still two hours away, and I'd grown restless again. "I'm going to change," I said, and collected my pack. I took cover behind Sam's tree and traded my shorts for black yoga pants, my T-shirt for a black turtleneck and my Eccos for black Nikes. I pulled my hair back, secured it into a bun and grabbed my Ryders. Last, I hiked off a distance with a tissue and relieved my bladder.

"The wind's come up," Sam said, when I returned.

Months ago, when I'd been new to ghosting, a breeze would have scattered me, but Sebastian had insisted I learn to push against the elements. I was stronger now. "I can handle it."

"Okay. What's the plan?"

I dropped the pack beside him. "From what I could see earlier, getting inside won't be a problem. I'll do a room-by-room search. If James is in there, I'll find him and ghost him out."

"You need to do more than that. We need information, names. This may be our only shot at finding out who's screwing with us. James is the priority, but keep your eyes open for laptops, backup drives or anything else they're using to store data."

He pulled his bag onto his lap and rummaged through it, producing a mesh knapsack. "Use this. Bring me everything you can carry. Search the executive suites. The CEO's name is Holden. CFO is Garcia. Keep your phone on vibrate. I'll warn you if I see trouble out here."

"I like that you're not a stickler for the law, Sam. Takes the stress out of working with a cop on my criminal activities."

"My crayon may cross the line from time to time, but I think ICO is behind this. That makes them corrupt, so the law is really a moot point. ICO doesn't play by anyone's rules but their own, and that makes them very dangerous."

"Even if I find James in there and get him out, what comes next is more than colouring outside of the lines. You know that."

"I knew it the minute I realized Cain had hung us out to dry, but I'd already picked a side. I did it months ago, when I signed up for this ICO gig and withheld critical information."

"Information about me being a Ghost?"

Sam didn't respond, just raised his camera and continued his vigil.

I settled in to wait for full dark. Another two hours crawled by while I wondered what I'd find inside. I tried not to imagine the worst, but it was difficult considering how long James had been gone. Was he being held captive? Was someone using him to reel me in? James had researched Vector Labs, but for all I knew, Vector could have been a minor player in whatever new case he'd taken on. A player he'd dismissed weeks ago.

Man, he and I were going to have one serious-ass talk about communication when this was over.

As darkness crept in around us, Sam pulled a nightscope from his pack. I picked up the binoculars, made one final sweep of the grounds and building and stopped short.

"Shit! Someone's on the roof," I said. "Northwest corner. Lying on his stomach. Definitely not from the maintenance department."

Sam moved his scope a few inches to the right. "He wasn't there ten minutes ago, unless he's been hiding in the lee of the HVAC equipment."

"His hands are in front of his face. Holding binoculars, I think."

Sam swung his head away from his scope. "Even for you, that's impressive without a nightscope."

I had Jolene to thank for the perfect night vision. I shrugged. All Fliers had it. "He's wearing a black beanie, black shirt. Could be one of us. James's father is a good bet."

"Your kind doesn't have a corner on the black-clothing market. Every criminal worth his night job has duds just like those."

I set the binoculars on Sam's pack. "If it's Redmond, he might be able to help. If it's someone else, I'll make sure he doesn't interfere."

Sam grunted his approval. I liked that he didn't question my competence.

I pulled out my burner phone and double-checked it. The sound was muted and I had full bars. "All set."

Sam looked at his cellphone. "It's eight forty-five. I want a text from you every ten minutes. If you don't check in, I'm calling Stuart."

"How did you—"

"Cop, remember," he said, pointing at himself. I didn't think he'd been paying me any mind on the plane when I'd repeated Stuart's number out loud. Guess I wasn't the only one who'd memorized it. I smiled and Sam settled back in and resumed his surveillance. "Be careful. I'll be watching."

With a squeeze of my crystal, I ghosted and flew straight for the rooftop. The breeze was light, barely a challenge after all my practice. I hovered above the man who lay prone in the thick dust. He'd set his binoculars down and was concentrating on the tablet he held, tapping and then swiping across the face of it. I dipped down closer to get a look at the creased piece of paper on the rooftop in front of him. It was a floor plan with Vector Labs's logo on it. To his right, a small black nylon pack lay half open. The handle grip of what looked an awful lot like a handgun protruded. He'd likely made sure it was within reach, something I needed to take care of before I confronted whoever this was. I reached for it, solidified my hand to get a hold of it and then backed away.

I re-formed to his left and established a block to protect myself from his jolt if he turned out to be a Flier. Only then did I speak. "You planning on breaking in?"

He jerked but didn't lose his composure. His head moved ever so slightly to the right, looking for the gun, no doubt, then slowly turned in my direction. In no particular rush, he squinted and examined every inch of me, assessing, gauging. His gaze finally landed on the weapon I held pointed down by my thigh.

"That's mine," he said, looking at my prize.

"Was yours," I said, "and you didn't answer my question."

He set the tablet down and rolled his left shoulder in a preamble to getting up. I raised his gun. "Stay where you are. Answer my question."

"What's your name?" He spoke with an accent.

"That's not how this works. I'm the one with the gun. Shall I call the police or do you want to tell me why you're here on this rooftop?"

"You're not going to discharge that weapon, nor are you going to call the authorities," he said, as he followed through with standing up, ignoring the weapon pointed at him. Did he have a death wish? I wondered, backing away from him. I'd heard that accent before.

"Shooting me would draw attention I don't think you want, given that you are not an employee of Vector Labs."

Maybe not so much a death wish—more like he'd taken a calculated risk. He wasn't stupid. I solidified my stance, legs shoulder-width apart, gun gripped firmly in both hands. "You sound pretty sure of yourself."

He dusted off his slacks and then straightened, resting his hands on his hips. He studied me a moment and then exhaled, reached up, pulled off the beanie and ran a hand through his hair.

I recognized him. "You were here this afternoon. Drove a rental car, carried a silver briefcase."

"And apparently you were watching."

I tipped my head. "You're Redmond Moss."

"And you, I believe, are Emelynn Taylor."

I lowered the gun. "That was a dangerous game you were playing just now."

"You wouldn't have shot me."

"No. I'd have done something a lot worse." I stepped forward and returned his gun. "You haven't heard from James?"

"No. You?"

"No."

Redmond's gaze slid from my face to one earring and then the other, as if he recognized James's gift. He frowned.

"What?" I asked, fingering one of the offending earrings.

He shook his head and looked away.

"What were you doing at the lab today?" I asked.

Redmond's gaze settled on his feet. "I met with a man named Garcia. Told him I represented a high-profile client in need of confidentiality and specialized equipment."

"Garcia is the CFO. What did you see when you shook his hand?"

Redmond snapped his head up. He narrowed his eyes.

"We don't have time for this, Redmond. I know James reads memories. I know you do, too."

"Precious few know that detail. It's not information we share."

"I know, and I would never tell anyone." Redmond crossed his arms, closing himself off. I tried again. "How about we work together?"

"Work together? Would that be me and you, or me and the Tribunal?"

I'd have to remember to thank Sebastian for tainting my relationship with this man before I'd even met him. "I'm sorry. I didn't know Sebastian would use me to get something from you. The man has no conscience. If Mason hadn't told me what Sebastian had done, I still wouldn't know."

"Mason Reynolds? Stuart Reynolds's son?"

"Yes."

He nodded, barely hiding a sneer. "Another founding family. What's your connection to them?"

"James didn't tell you?"

"James is a very private man. More private than I knew." Again, he looked at my earlobes.

"Stuart had a daughter," I said. "Mason's sister. Her name was Jolene. She gifted me when I was twelve years old."

"So you're not *born*?" The tone of his voice was familiar. Gifted Fliers were second class.

"No."

"But you are Tribunal, nonetheless."

"I am not Tribunal. Jolene wasn't in her right mind when she gifted me. I had no connection to her."

He tilted his head in disbelief. "Regardless of what you say or think, you are Tribunal. I don't work with the Tribunal." Redmond turned away from me and bent to tuck the gun back into his pack.

"I know what the Tribunal did to your family, Redmond. It was wrong. I can't change that or fix it. What I can do is find James. And I will find him, with or without you. But I'd prefer to do it with you."

With his back to me, he stilled. "I don't know you. Why would I trust you?"

"Because I love your son. I want him back as much as you do."

Redmond turned around and studied me. He remained utterly unreadable until he spoke. "I saw James, but it wasn't through Garcia. It was a man named Fuente, who oversees the labs. When I shook his hand, I held on as I mentioned the controversial nature of the experiments my client wanted to conduct. Fuente envisioned James behind glass in a narrow room. My son was wearing a hospital gown and had an IV in his arm."

My hand sprang to my mouth, but anger quickly took the place of horror. "Where?"

"I couldn't tell. My first guess was here at the lab, but we can't get in. The exterior cameras cover every inch of the building, all 360 degrees, and they're monitored remotely. I've been trying to tap into the feed, but it's heavily encrypted. Would take hours. Garcia assured me a generator kicks in if the power is cut. So we're not getting inside."

At least he'd said *we*. "I can get in."

He cocked an eyebrow.

"You aren't the only one with talents you'd prefer to keep to yourself." It wasn't as if Redmond didn't know about Ghosts—every member of the Tribunal who'd coerced him to use his memory-reading ability was a Ghost. To say he didn't like them was probably a gross understatement, and revealing myself as one of them would likely condemn me in his eyes—but James was my priority.

I pulled out my phone and dialled Sam. "I'm going in," I said.

"I take it that's Redmond?" Sam said.

"Yes. I'll check in again in ten." I disconnected and returned the phone to my pocket.

"Who's that?" Redmond asked.

"My handler. You don't know him."

"Where is he?" I didn't feel compelled to answer that one. Not yet anyway.

Redmond took the hint and moved on. "Does your handler know me?"

"He knows James. He knows you're his father and he knows about Fliers, but he doesn't know your family's secret. He does, however, know mine." I reached up and tightened the band that kept my hair in check, and then I pulled on the black gloves Mason had given me. "We have a pickup truck parked off the side road immediately west of here. If I find James, that's where I'll take him."

"Give me your phone," Redmond said, holding out his hand.

I pulled it from my pocket and handed it over. He punched a number into it and handed it back. "That's my number. I'd appreciate you keeping me apprised."

I nodded and turned toward the front of the building. When I got to the lip, I squeezed my crystal, clearing up any questions Redmond might have had, and drifted down to Vector Labs's glass entrance.

CHAPTER THIRTEEN

I breezed through the front door. I hadn't realized how warm it was outside until the chill of air-conditioning hit me. Light from the visitors' parking lot reached inside and washed the floor in dim shadows. The glass-walled meeting room lay to my right, visitor seating to my left and reception straight ahead. A phone console's lights blinked behind the curved reception counter. Two Bluetooth headsets sat idly beside it.

I carried on and sifted through the crack between the heavy wood doors behind the counter into a carpeted anteroom. It too was dark, except for the light that filtered in through frosted-glass doors at the far end of the room. Infrared trip sensors were now active, and criss-crossed the floor at knee level. Directly in front of me stood another abandoned reception desk, and on either side of it, more visitor seating. Offices lined the walls on the left and right. Four of them had name plaques: Holden, Garcia, Fuente and Sanders. Nice of them to help me out. I'd return after I searched for James.

The frosted-glass double doors led deeper into the building. I ghosted through them and stopped at the head of a well-lit, wide hallway that ran straight to the back of the building. Undoubtedly, I'd found the labs behind the darkened windows. Industrial linoleum covered the floor and reached six inches up the walls. Baseball-sized domes affixed to the ceiling housed security cameras, but there were no infrared trip sensors, which made sense if some labs had employees on site at all hours.

I started down the hall. Glass doors fronted each lab and thin black rectangles mounted on the walls beside them provided controlled access. Some of the doors were blacked out, others frosted; a smattering had lights on inside. I decided to search the labs on the left side first and come back up searching the ones on the right.

I blew through the first lab door. The only light in the room came from the hallway. No one was inside and there were no security cameras. Microscopes stood on stainless-steel counters beside test tube rockers and a centrifuge. Could the built-in refrigerators conceal a hidden room? I wondered. I pulled back on my ghosted form and opened one of the refrigerators. Light spilled out and illuminated rows of sealed test tubes and stacks of carefully labelled Petri dishes. The contents of the second refrigerator looked much the same. Neither concealed a hidden room. I checked the lab's floor for a hidden hatch. Found nothing. The blackened windows on the outside wall also functioned as emergency exits. They were secured and alarmed.

I headed down the hall to the next lab, where a crack of light escaped from under the blackened door. Inside, a lone woman had her hands plugged into gloves that were attached to a chemical hood. Her concentration was commendable. At the far end of the room, a computer screen glowed. I drifted around to look at it. Hieroglyphics would have been easier to understand. I approached the stainless-steel island in the middle of the room and took in an autoclave sterilizer and row upon row of jugs, some plastic, some glass, some opaque, some brown. The refrigerators weren't built-in so had nothing to hide—not that I could open them without startling the woman at the chemical hood. Against one wall, glass tanks green with algae were supported at chest height on steel legs. Beside them sat stainless-steel sinks as deep and wide as those in a morgue.

The four remaining labs presented similar stainless-steel counters, appliances and equipment, some of which I couldn't identify. I found no hidden rooms, no sign of James. Guessing it had been ten minutes, I texted Sam a thumbs-up and returned to the hallway.

A steel door to the receiving dock marked the end of the hall. There was little chance of finding James there: the second loading-bay door had been open most of the day. I continued up the other side of the hall. These labs were considerably larger. After I searched the first two, I came across the hallway that led to the employee exit and parking lot. Down that hallway were washrooms and a janitor's room that revealed nothing. I texted Sam again. The remaining labs turned up more employees, more equipment, more chemicals, but no space where they might have hidden James. Where the hell was he?

Disappointed, I slipped back through the frosted doors into the carpeted anteroom with the executives' offices. Then I ducked into a washroom and called Sam. "He's not here," I said, when he answered.

"Is there a basement?"

"Not that I could see, and I checked every door. I'm back in the executive suite now. Redmond told me Fuente might know something. I'll start with his office and check in with you in another ten."

I hung up and exited the washroom. If Redmond was right, Fuente knew where James was being held. I breached Fuente's private space. It was palatial. There were no security cameras and no motion sensors. His desk was glass and clear of paper. Three meticulously aligned Montblanc pens and a colourfully painted Day of the Dead skull paperweight were the only items on its surface. Behind the desk, a sleek black leather chair sat half turned toward a large window, which looked onto a green lawn. The windows were alarmed.

There wasn't a computer in sight, but the built-in pale maple cabinetry offered fingerholds of hope. I re-formed and pulled open the first lateral filing cabinet's drawer and flipped through it. Inside were contracts with suppliers, the same names I'd seen affixed to the lab equipment. Another file drawer contained more contracts with suppliers for a laundry list of specialized glassware, chemicals and lab consumables.

Further searching turned up a file with names and contact details for maintenance personnel. Not exactly the treasure trove of nefarious Vector employees I'd hoped for, but I took a photo of it anyway and sent it to Sam. When I'd finished rifling through the last cabinet with no further intel, I slammed it closed. Damnit!

I ghosted and moved on to Holden's office. It too was free of cameras and sensors. I guessed the cameras in the hall and the window alarms provided enough security that they felt no need for further measures in their private office spaces. That thinking might change after tonight. I re-formed to conserve energy and texted Sam once more.

Holden's desk was dark wood, mahogany perhaps, or cherry. The walls were covered with early-twentieth-century black-and-white photos. Most were of men in lab coats posing with equipment or in huddles around microscopes. Important moments in science, no doubt.

Instead of file cabinets, Holden's office had glass-fronted display cases which housed antique lab equipment. The only space for files in his office was in his desk, and it was locked. I ghosted my arm, reached inside the deepest drawer, grabbed hold of the first few files and pulled them out. They materialized when I dropped them on the desktop. I flipped through a folder with employee evaluations: a couple of analysts, a bookkeeper and a secretary. The positions were low level. I took photos of them anyway and sent them on to Sam. I returned the first group of files. A second handful of folders provided nothing useful. My third dip in produced signed contracts. Some were performance contracts, but most were employee contracts. Again, I snapped photos and sent them to Sam, but I'd yet to uncover anything I could connect to James or ICO or any government-sanctioned operation.

I texted Sam then headed to Garcia's office which, like Holden's, turned up nothing condemning. Saunders, who turned out to be the VP of operations, used his office as a home away from home. I had to push aside golf clubs and gym bags to get to his files and found nothing of value inside.

There had to be something here. Even if Vector wasn't involved, Fuente definitely was. Maybe none of the other executives knew what Fuente was up to? Could be that Fuente was operating a lucrative side business off-site. What I needed was Fuente's home address so we could take our interrogation to his front door.

I texted another thumbs-up to Sam then ghosted and returned to the executive reception area. I paused near Fuente's office. Whoever sat at the reception desk would have contact information for everyone, surely. I gazed up to the domed security camera. That would have to be taken care of. I drifted up to the ceiling and partially re-formed my gloved hand exactly as Sebastian had taught me. In it, I cradled a collapsible cone, standard burglar gear according to Sebastian. I slipped the cone over the dome. Anyone observing the cover-up would see a steady uniform blackout, and without a visible source, they'd assume a malfunction. At least as long as I remembered to remove the cone before I left.

I dove down to the desk, ensured I was out of the infrared sensors' zones, and re-formed. I rifled through the desk's unlocked drawers. Not only did I find a listing of the lab employees and their contact numbers—I also found a separate listing of the executives' home addresses and phone numbers. Solid gold! I laid it all out on the desktop and snapped photos of every sheet. I double-checked the photos for clarity before I sent them to Sam and put the items back to where I'd found them.

Finally! I'd found something useful. I exhaled my relief and returned to the ceiling. I ghosted all but my hand and reached up to the cone I'd used to cover the camera. With a swift twist, I released the collapsible cone and slowly withdrew it before ghosting it and my hand.

I slipped inside the washroom and this time dialled Redmond. I told him what I'd found and promised to call him again after I was safely away from the building. Next, I called Sam. "You got the photos?"

"Sure did. Good work. No sign of James?"

"No. I'll check Fuente's office again in case I missed something and then I'm out of here."

After I hung up, I stared at the phone. It was ten thirty. Where are you, James? I stuffed the phone into my pocket and rubbed the back of my neck. I recalled Redmond's description of James's cell: a narrow room. I hadn't searched the semi parked at the back of the building. It was the right size. A long shot, perhaps, but I had to check it.

I ghosted again and headed through the frosted-glass doors to the labs. A door on the right opened and I floated up to the ceiling to avoid the man in a white lab coat who emerged. I continued down the brightly lit corridor, past the employee exit hall, and stopped at the steel door marked Receiving at the end of the hall.

I took a deep breath, crossed my mental fingers and pushed my ghosted form through the steel door to the darkened loading bay. Heated air smelling of diesel exhaust hit me like a foam bat. Another domed camera on the ceiling meant I'd be staying in ghosted form awhile longer. I ignored the assault on my senses and took a tour of the dock.

The transport truck filled one loading bay, and the second bay's door had been rolled down and locked. I checked behind the stacked pallets and examined the area around the steel shelving. I found nothing. The door to a small windowless office was open. Inside, a soiled office chair sat behind a battered table. A water cooler stood to one side. I caught the scent of burnt coffee and spotted a coffee pot that made me want to gag. I glanced at the clipboard sitting atop an in-tray. It held receiving reports. Looked like more of the same in the tray below.

I returned to the loading bay and the one last place I could search. The back end of the truck was tucked tight against the padded door frame. The truck's double doors were secured—vertical steel rods held them in place and padlocks added an additional layer of security. I imagined shrink-wrapped pallets of supplies and equipment stacked inside the truck.

I blasted through the truck's back door and instead of pallets, I found one large crate and a forklift. Beyond the forklift, vertical slats of what looked like heavy rubber acted as a curtain. I floated above the forklift, and when I got to the rubber slats, I forced my way through and into the dark space behind.

In the pitch-black interior, I found James.

He was just as Redmond had described. He lay unconscious on a cot behind a glass wall with an IV buried in the crook of his arm. His bare feet and naked legs jutted out from the bottom of a hospital gown. My thoughts splintered in a hundred horrific directions. What had they done to him?

I whipped to the glass wall and stopped short. A sliding door provided access. Praying the door wasn't airtight, I flung my ghosted form at it and, thankfully, slipped inside. With my heart racing, I rushed to James's side. He was breathing, thank god. I re-formed and pulled the IV from his arm. He didn't stir. I cradled his face in my hands. He hadn't shaved in days. "James." He didn't respond. "I'm going to get you out of here." I yanked out my phone. *No service*! Something or someone had jammed the signal.

At the sound of a suctioning slurp, I snapped my head around. A diesel engine fired up and the floor lurched beneath my feet. I tumbled, landing on my butt beside James's cot. The truck was moving. Alarm sent my adrenal glands into overdrive. On the far side of the rubber curtain, a light came on and flared across the roof. A hand reached through and parted the slats and a man in a white coat entered. His nose and mouth were covered with a surgical mask. Steely eyes peered out below wiry, unkempt eyebrows. A cap covered his hair. He stood with his head on a tilt, staring at me as if I were an animal in a zoo.

I gathered the strength of my crystal and formed a powerful jolt—a killing jolt. The moment it reached its white-hot peak, I whirled it at him. The glass spider-webbed. The man's eyes bulged, but he didn't go down. Why? I'd jolted through glass many times before. If the man had been hit, he'd be dead. Instead, he fumbled for a phone he had in his pocket and jabbed at the screen.

Immediately, I grasped for James's arm and ghosted, taking him with me. I drove us into the spider-webbed glass wall. Wisps of our ghosted forms flattened out on the inside of the glass, going nowhere. With a firm grip on James, I lunged again, this time at the ceiling. When that didn't work, I tried the other walls, all unsuccessfully. The cube had been sealed. We were trapped.

A snick I could barely hear over the diesel engine grabbed my attention like a knife to my throat. I jerked my head in its direction. A hiss registered above the crunch of gravel under the truck's wheels. Something was seeping in through a small valve. With James in tow, I punched up and pushed into the valve, trying to get through, but couldn't make headway against the pressure of the incoming air. But . . . it wasn't air.

I drifted down to the floor in pieces, releasing my hold on James. Terror spread through my mind like a gas slick on water, morphing and re-forming. A pair of shiny black shoes planted themselves in front of the glass wall. They were the last thing I saw before my world went black.

Gauzy dreams haunted me. A blinding light, a cold table. The clack of metal. A man in a surgical mask, startled to meet my gaze. And then nothing.

The incessant dripping of water woke me. How annoying, I thought, and rolled over. My stomach lurched. Saliva filled my mouth and I pried my eyes open. I was going to be sick. I tried to sit but was overcome with dizziness and flopped back onto my side on the mattress. I opened my mouth and retched. Bile burned the back of my throat. I swallowed, swallowed again and then carefully rolled onto my back. A sprinkler head protruded from a stippled ceiling.

Where the hell was I? I fought the fog in my head, grasping for answers. I'd been searching Vector Labs. I was supposed to meet Sam. What had happened?

I blinked until my vision fully cleared and then rolled my head to the left. Weak light bled around the edges of heavy curtains, masking the time of day. To the right of the window stood a dark brown door. Its brass latch wasn't engaged. A framed notice was affixed to the door. I was in a hotel.

A notepad and pen lay alongside a phone on the bedside table. I reached for the notepad and froze. A bandage lay across the back of my hand. I pulled my hand back and tore off the bandage. My breath hitched at the sight of the puncture wound underneath.

Images of an operating room and a man in a surgical mask flared in my mind. Panic tore a chunk out of my sanity. I couldn't gulp enough air. Heat rushed out of my body. Sweat leaked from every pore. With frantic swats, I patted my body for sore spots, stitches, missing parts.

A vision of Avery's face pushed through my panic. *Breathe*, he said. *Just breathe.*

What had they done to me? *Breathe.*

Where was James? *Breathe.*

Was he still alive? *Breathe.*

Tears welled then overflowed. *Breathe.*

I'd found him. He'd been warm and breathing. I'd held him, and then I'd let him go. I should never have let go. I'd lost him. Racked with guilt, I rolled onto my side and let the tears rain. I lay there forever, feeling wretched, useless. A steady drip of water was the only sound, and each drip echoed in my ears as if it were a marble dropping instead.

It wasn't until I acknowledged feeling violated that I regained control. They'd knocked me unconscious for a reason. What had they done to me? What had they done to James? Who the fuck were these people? I vowed to hunt them down. They'd better pray that James was alive.

With renewed vigour, I pushed myself up and planted my feet on the floor. My head spun. I closed my eyes and pressed my hands into the mattress, willing my stomach to stay put. When the nausea abated, I noticed a pinching sensation in the crook of my left arm. With a pull of my sleeve, another bandage emerged. Another puncture mark. Bastards! They'd pay for whatever they'd done to me and to James.

On the table beside the bed, a clock blinked 12:00. I reached for the notepad. Best Western Seven Seas. Never heard of it. But if they'd dumped me here, maybe James was here too. My phone was gone, I had no watch, no idea what time it was or how long I'd been out of it.

Cautiously, I stood. My abdomen protested with a sharp cramp. It passed. I looked down. My clothes were right, or at least they were mine, as were my shoes.

I took baby steps toward the curtain and squinted against the light I anticipated as I pulled the edge back. I was on the ground floor. It was dusk. What day, I wondered?

Steadying myself against the wall, I made my way past the bed toward the sound of the dripping water. A red stain marked the porcelain beneath the tub's spigot. I returned to the door and read the address off the notice on the back of it. 411 Hotel Circle South, San Diego.

A tourist map and breakfast menu were tucked inside a faux leather portfolio on the TV stand, which was opposite the bed. I snagged the map and a bottle of water and dropped to the end of the bed.

I found Vector Labs on the map and traced my finger south toward 411 Hotel Circle South, in the heart of San Diego. Fifteen miles. Would Sam still be waiting for me? Redmond probably assumed I'd ditched him.

I twisted the cap off the bottle of water and took a few cautious sips. When I was convinced it would stay down, I drank half of it. As I lowered the bottle, a wave of panic hit. My gift! I called to my crystal. Immediately I felt its warmth. Relief overwhelmed me. My crystal was intact, emitting pulses of power beneath my skin; each one strengthened me.

The hotel phone taunted me, but I didn't dare use it. They could be monitoring it as well as watching the room. I wouldn't make it easy for them to follow me and find more of our kind. If James was here at the hotel, I'd find him and take him with me before whoever "they" were knew I was gone.

Though still unsteady, with a squeeze of my crystal, I ghosted. I wouldn't be able to remain in this form very long. I wasn't strong enough. With that in mind, I pushed outside through the door frame's cracks. Full dark was close. I squeezed through the door into the next room. It was empty. I continued along the building, checking each room. A clock in the lobby finally told me the time. 8:12 p.m. I still didn't know which day it was.

The one-storey hotel had two wings. I found James in the last room of the second wing. He was still unconscious but breathing. Relief came mixed with terror. Had he been sedated all this time? What the hell had they given him? He wore the same hospital gown and didn't react when I called his name.

I re-formed to rest and sat on the bed beside him, smoothing my hand down his stubbly cheek. Had he lost weight? I leaned down and brushed my lips against his. Sadly, this wasn't a Disney movie. He didn't wake.

I rested my head on his chest. The steady thump of his heart brought tears. "I love you," I whispered. How could I have ever questioned marrying this man? All the time I'd spent considering the obstacles James and I had to face, and I'd never once considered what it would be like to live my life without him. Thinking of it now crippled me.

I held him tight, but the ragged thought that I was wasting precious time forced me into action. I sat up and got back to the basic training James had instilled in me. Standing, I walked a quick circuit around the bedroom and bathroom, checking the closet and all the drawers. Like my room, his was also empty.

I looked back to James's still form on the bed. Months ago, I'd ghosted him out of a ship in a boatyard on Granville Island. We'd been caught in the wrong place and I'd had no choice. He'd asked me then to never do it again. Ghosting turned him into the form he associated with the Tribunal, which, like his father, he loathed. And here I was—about to do it again. But it wasn't as if I could carry him out.

"Forgive me, James," I said, even though I knew he couldn't hear me. I reached for his hand and laced my fingers through his. I applied steady pressure to my crystal until it melted into my soul. My body faded and I watched as James's body vanished with mine. He became light as air and drifted up off the bed with me.

Where to? Sam's cousin's truck was closest if it was still parked near Vector Labs. If it wasn't there, I'd figure something else out. I pushed us out through the loose-fitting door. Full dark had set in. I turned north searching for a safe place to re-form—I'd never make it the fifteen miles to the truck in ghosted form. Flying with James wasn't the issue. He was a Flier; the moment he was airborne he shed gravity. It was ghosting that drained me, and it had already started.

Drifting high above the busy street, I searched for a dark corner. I found it on the roof of a mid-rise apartment building ten minutes north. A caged light bulb hanging above the rooftop access door painted a circle of light. I skirted around behind it, dropped James's hand and drifted away from him to re-form. Sitting on the roof with my knees pulled into my chest, I watched James's body once again become whole.

He remained unconscious, and looking at his pale visage, it was clear I couldn't fly with him as he was now. He'd be a bloody beacon in the sky with his light-blue hospital gown and chalk-white skin. After resting a few more minutes, I ghosted again and drifted down the face of the apartment building. I pushed into the first darkened unit I found, praying the tenants weren't home.

After searching it, and another unit, it dawned on me that dark clothing wouldn't be in abundance in closets in San Diego, where it was perpetually summer. But I did find a navy bedsheet. I hoped the tenants weren't particularly attached to it.

Back on the roof, I wrapped the sheet around James, covering him from head to foot, and then sat back on my heels. Another cramp in my lower abdomen caused me to pause. Just what I needed. It was the wrong time of the month for my period, which meant I'd probably strained something.

When the cramping passed, I found myself once again apologizing to James. I didn't have the strength to lift him off the rooftop—ghosting him was the only way to release his gravity. I took his hand and squeezed my crystal. Three feet above the roof, I let go and we both hovered. I re-formed mid-air, and the moment James became fully corporeal, I pulled him close, fitted the sheet snugly around his body and dragged him flying with me into the night.

Without my GPS, I had only the streetlights to guide me. I followed the northerly course I'd traced my finger along on the tourist map, but it wasn't until we flew over the Tex-Mex bar that I felt sure of my route.

When we arrived at the patch of long grass where the truck had been parked, my heart sank. The truck was gone and I was exhausted. I landed us as gently as my fatigue allowed and lay flat on my back staring up at the stars in the cloudless sky. At least it wasn't cold. The world was silent except for a squawking bird that didn't seem to notice it was dark and that it should be sleeping.

I turned to James. He looked so peaceful. Then his eyelids fluttered. I shot upright, calling his name as I scrambled to my knees. "James!" More fluttering. "James!"

But the fluttering stopped. The small flare of hope extinguished. At least his pulse remained strong and his heartbeat was steady.

It was probably nine o'clock. Maybe later. I considered our options. No phones, no IDs, no cash, no credit cards. The cramps started up again and I cursed. "I am not camping in the fucking woods," I said, hugging my midsection. "No way!"

After five more minutes of cursing, I made a decision. Exhausted or not, I'd go back as far as the Motel 6 in Temecula, where Sam and I had stayed. If Sam wasn't there, I'd ghost us into an empty suite so we could rest up. If James hadn't regained consciousness by the time we got there, I'd call 911 to get him the medical attention I feared he needed.

Anger and worry fuelled my flight. Forty-five minutes in, James stirred. He remained unconscious, but he struggled briefly and moaned. I carried on with renewed hope that he was coming out of it. It took every ounce of my flagging energy and two gruelling hours to get to the motel. At the two-storey Motel 6, I settled James on the roof and took a moment to collect myself.

After I caught my breath, I dropped off the roof into the shadows behind the building and walked into the well-lit parking lot. I rounded the palm trees at the entrance and caught sight of Sam's cousin's truck. I covered my face with my hands and allowed myself a moment's relief. It was short-lived—a glance back at the hotel's facade made me want to scream in frustration. So many rooms! How the hell would I find Sam without announcing my presence?

I had not an ounce of finesse left in me. I'd hit the wall and it was made of concrete. Knowing it went against everything I'd been taught, I marched straight into the lobby, picked up a house phone and waited for the operator. Sam wouldn't have used his own name. I followed a hunch. "Can you connect me to Dana Christopher's room, please?"

"I'm sorry, we don't have a guest by that name."

I hung my head. I'd been so sure. "Thank you," I said, and disconnected.

Where to now? I wandered back to the parking lot in a cloud of confusion. Could Sam have left the truck here for me? I approached the truck with a level of caution generally reserved for approaching suspected car bombs. I glanced inside at the ignition. No key. I tested the door handle. Locked. I crouched and checked for a key on top of the tires and under both bumpers and came up empty.

Too late, I looked up at the light standard ten feet away. With a shake of my head, I closed my eyes. A camera had caught me doing exactly what every carjacker does. How long until hotel security sent someone out? Or called the police? A low chuckle escaped—resignation from a madwoman. It was one thing to get caught stealing a Jag or a Porsche, maybe a Beemer in a pinch, but a twenty-year-old beater pickup?

Backing away from the truck, I turned and jogged down the row of vehicles, aiming for the shadows beyond the hotel. But as I passed the last vehicle, I stopped dead and turned around. The grey sedan had a green National sticker, stuck on at an angle. Redmond!

I ran full tilt for the front door, whipped around the inside corner and once again picked up the house phone. "Redmond Moss," I said, breathing heavily.

"One moment, please. I'll connect you to his room."

I held the phone in a death grip. One ring. Two. "Hello."

"I have him," I said. "I have James."

Chapter Fourteen

B ring him to me," Redmond said. "I'm in the north wing, facing the road, room 224. It's the last room on the second floor."

"Where's Sam?" I asked.

"I'll ask him to join us. Hurry."

I hung up and beat feet out of the lobby and down to the back of the parking lot, into the shadows.

Up on the roof, I approached James. "One last time," I said, and grasped his hand. I ghosted with him and drifted up and over the edge of the roof. I found Redmond's room and breezed in through the window cracks. Arms crossed, Redmond stood staring out the window near the foot of one of the two beds. His expression gave nothing away—a lawyerly tool, no doubt. I couldn't see Sam.

I placed James on the bed closest to the window and then drifted away. Redmond's attention snapped to his son as James re-formed. This time I had no problem interpreting Redmond's expression: horror.

Redmond twisted his head back and forth, searching the room. I'd re-formed on the far side of the second bed. When he found me I had no time to react. He hit me with a jolt that knocked me two feet back and into the bedside table. My body wiped it clean with a loud thud that sent a lamp and clock crashing to the floor.

"How dare you turn my son into one your kind!"

Redmond ran to James and ripped the sheet away. As he leaned over him, I crumpled to the floor. I didn't lose consciousness—my bones simply melted under the weight of me. The blood vessels in my brain pulsed and my eyes refused to focus.

Ten minutes might have passed, maybe thirty. Angry voices sharpened my attention. A hand landed on my shoulder. I heard a grunt as I was manhandled and lifted from the floor and placed on the bed.

Sam's voice came to me with soft words of apology, and then I heard him mutter, "If she's hurt, I'll fucking kill you, you son of a bitch."

I peeled open my eyes. Sam sat on the bed beside me and picked the hair from my face with the dexterity of a blind mime. I lifted a hand and laid it over his, stopping him before he poked an eye out.

"Thanks," I said, and Sam shifted to give me more room. James lay motionless on the bed beside me. Redmond leaned against the wall farthest from me, with his arms crossed again. Sam had placed himself between Redmond and me. Gallant but reckless.

"Are you okay?" Sam asked.

I rubbed my forehead to ease the dull throb. "I'll be fine."

Sam grabbed my hand and examined the puncture wound. "Shit!"

"Tell me about it. There's a matching one on my other arm," I said. "How long was I gone?"

"Twenty-four long fucking hours," Sam said, releasing my hand.

I sensed Redmond moving and shot him a warning. "Don't come near me!"

He teetered on the balls of his feet then settled back against the wall.

Sam braced himself on the heels of his hands. "Tell us what happened."

"James was in the transport truck," I said, and then told them everything I could remember.

Sam explained to me that by the time I'd missed my ten-minute check-in, the truck was long gone. He immediately suspected his phone had been compromised and destroyed it. Thankfully, he'd been able to save the photos I'd sent him, but we'd made a mistake not having a backup cellphone.

Redmond figured I'd screwed him over. He'd spotted Sam and confronted him before Sam made it back to his cousin's truck.

I looked at Sam. "Did you call Stuart?"

"No!" Redmond barked, and stepped forward against my glare. "And he's not going to. The Tribunal will not use my son as a bargaining chip. Never again!"

A moan from James drew our attention.

"He's coming around," I said, and struggled to sit up. "We need to get him to a doctor."

Redmond pulled out his phone. "I've got a charter on standby. I'm taking him to New Orleans."

James rolled his head toward me. His eyes opened and closed. I leapt from the bed and dropped to the floor on my knees beside him. "James!" He reached for me and again opened his eyes, trying to focus them, as though he were a drunk on a bender.

I latched onto his hand and looked up at Redmond. "New Orleans is five, maybe six hours away," I said. "Let me see if I can find someone closer."

James rolled his head toward his father. "Not New Orleans," he said, his voice a rasp. "Bugged."

Bugged?

"What are you saying, son?"

He closed his eyes. "I'm bugged. Can't go home."

Redmond slid his gaze from James to me, as if I were the one responsible. I squared my shoulders and pretended not to feel the weight of his silent accusation.

"If that's true," Sam said, placing a hand on my shoulder, "there's a very good chance you are too."

A lump threatened to choke me. I swallowed. "Redmond, let me call Stuart. I won't mention your name or James's. You know he has the connections."

"Call," James whispered. I squeezed his hand in reassurance and looked again to Redmond.

Redmond white-knuckled his phone. The muscles along his jaw popped out, just like James's did when he tried to control his anger. "Call him."

Sam passed me a phone. I took it and stood, dialling as I paced a line back toward the door.

It went to voice mail. No surprise. Stuart wouldn't have recognized the number. I left him a message and the number Sam gave me then hung up and continued to pace while I waited. Sam's phone rang a moment later.

I answered. "Stuart?"

"Tell me you're okay," he said.

"I am," I said, "but I need your help."

Promising I'd fill in the details later, I asked him to find me somewhere I could go to get checked for an implanted tracking device. Good as his word, he didn't ask questions. Sam handed me his notepad and a pen and I jotted down an address in San Francisco.

"I'll set it up," Stuart said. "Use Jolene's name. The doctor is one of us. He'll be expecting you."

I hung up and addressed Redmond. "Can your charter get us to San Francisco?"

Redmond didn't answer, but he made the call.

James struggled into some of Redmond's clothes and then Redmond and Sam helped James into his father's rental.

I rode with Sam in his cousin's truck and dug through my pack to retrieve the cash I'd stashed. My hand landed on my fake ID. Had using it been the trigger? Sam hadn't thought ICO would draw the connection between Dana and me, but maybe they had. Maybe they'd been tracking Dana all along.

"I need new ID," I said.

"I'll work with James. Get you another one. There's a phone for you in the glovebox. My number's in it."

We met up with James and Redmond at the Riverside Municipal Airport, a thirty-minute drive south.

On board the small jet, James took a seat opposite his father, and a row away from me. They spoke in low tones, and not once did a smile cross James's lips. I wanted to go to him, to ask him a thousand questions, to touch him, but understood this father-son time was important. They were close. I hadn't known that, but I could see it now in their body language. Their shared history of the Tribunal forcing them to read memories was the glue that bound them. Such a sad legacy. I wanted to offer James the warmth of a smile, but he avoided looking my way.

Ninety minutes later, we landed in San Francisco. The colour had returned to James's face, but all he'd managed to drink was a small glass of ginger ale. He walked off the jet under his own steam and a limo met us.

The address Stuart had given us was that of a walk-in clinic in a low-rent district. The time on my new burner phone read 1:57 a.m. Definitely after hours. We were met at the front door by a security guard and a man who fit the description Stuart had given me. After I introduced myself as Jolene, the doctor took us in without further questions. The security guard locked the doors behind us.

"I'm Dr. Mills. Come this way," the doctor said. He guided us down a hallway to his office and opened the door.

"Gentlemen," he said, addressing the men. "You can wait in here. This will take a half hour."

"You have two patients," I said. "I hope that's not a problem."

"Not at all," he said with a frown. "But I can only do one at a time. Who's first?"

"Take him," I said, indicating James. "He's been sedated for hours, maybe days. We don't know with what."

"I'll need to draw blood."

James nodded.

"How will you find the implant?" I asked.

"MRI," Dr. Mills said. "We'll see anything that shouldn't be there."

"Unassuming place to have an MRI scanner," Sam said.

It occurred to me that Dr. Mills didn't realize Sam wasn't one of us. "Exactly. And we'd like to keep that fact under the radar."

Sam raised his hands in surrender. "Won't hear it from me."

"Shall we?" Dr. Mills said, addressing James. They left and then the waiting began. The wait felt excruciatingly long.

When James returned, he had a fresh bandage on his arm. Dr. Mills addressed all of us, stomping all over doctor-patient confidentiality. "It's impossible to tell what he's been sedated with or for how long. All anaesthetics are a cocktail of barbiturates. He may suffer some memory loss, general anxiety, trouble sleeping, but without knowing exactly what he's been dosed with, and for how long, it's hard to know."

"And the tracker?" Sam said.

"Indeed, he had one. Underside of his left wrist. I've removed it."

"It's an RF transmitter," James said, holding up a small vial. Inside was a tiny tube four millimetres long—the size of a large grain of rice.

"Will they know it's been removed?" I asked.

"Not from the procedure and not by visiting here. This is a walk-in clinic. Makes sense you'd both check in with a doctor after your ordeal. Our MRI scanner and OR aren't public knowledge."

I stole a glance at James. He seemed distant, almost as if he were avoiding me.

"Are you ready?" Dr. Mills asked, addressing me.

I nodded and followed him.

He took three vials of blood before instructing me to lie down on the MRI table. After he'd set up the equipment, the table slid inside the large white doughnut. When the loud whirring noises stopped and the table slid back out, he told me he'd found a tracker, but it wasn't in my wrist—it was in my forearm.

And it wasn't new.

I left the small OR with the tiny tracker in a vial and a smouldering knot of rage and fear in my chest. ICO didn't know it yet, but they'd just lost the game of deadly deception they'd started.

Back in his office, Dr. Mills reported to the group. "The tissue around her tracker was completely healed. Likely been in there two or three months."

I knew exactly when it had been implanted and by whom, and if the flare of Sam's nostrils was a gauge, he knew as well. He'd been there.

"May I see it?" James asked, holding out his hand. I handed him the vial. He examined it up close and returned it without saying a word. I stuffed it in my pocket.

"We need to go," I said. Dr. Mills might believe our visit wasn't putting him in danger, but I wasn't so sure.

"Security will escort you out," Dr. Mills said. "I'll send the blood-test results to Stuart Reynolds."

"Thank you, Doctor," I said, and offered my hand.

"My pleasure. Anything for friends of the Reynolds family. We appreciate your service."

Our service? Stuart must have told him we worked for the Tribunal. His gratitude would sting like vinegar in Redmond's festering wounds. I didn't dare look at him.

The security guard approached. "Follow me. Mr. Reynolds is waiting outside."

Redmond grabbed his son's shoulder. "You have no obligation to see Stuart."

"I know," James said, laying his hand over his father's. "More importantly, he knows."

We followed the security guard back to the entrance.

Stuart leaned against the driver door of a black Escalade. He put me in mind of Sam Elliott but without the moustache and cowboy hat, though the hat was probably inside the SUV. The limo was gone. Stuart stepped away from the SUV as we approached. The deep lines between his gnarly eyebrows faded as we approached and he met my gaze. I walked into his arms and took comfort in his embrace. In that moment, I felt like his granddaughter, like family.

With an arm still around me, Stuart shook hands with Sam. "Good to see you again, Detective."

"James," Stuart said, shaking James's hand next.

Redmond kept his distance.

"Thank you," Stuart said, addressing Redmond.

Redmond offered a tight nod but not his hand, though something told me Stuart hadn't expected anything different.

"Where's the limo?" Redmond asked.

Stuart checked his watch. "It'll be back any minute. We need to talk."

"About what?" Redmond said.

"What happened at Vector Labs."

I gave him an abbreviated version and then turned to Redmond. "Your phone is compromised."

"It's disposable," he said.

James looked pointedly at Sam. "I want copies of the images Emelynn sent you." He then pulled the vial with the transmitter from his pocket and held it out for Stuart to see. "Emelynn had one as well. They're identical and they're still active. They'll know where we are."

"ICO is responsible, I presume?" Stuart said. When no one answered, a murderous smile crept onto his face, a harbinger of what lay ahead. "Well, that changes everything, doesn't it?"

"ICO isn't aware that we know they're behind this," I said. "If they knew, James and I wouldn't be here."

"What's the plan?" Sam said.

"We lie low until we identify the players," James said.

Sam nodded. "So, business as usual?"

"Status quo until we're ready to take them out." James turned to his father. "ICO has been looking for my family. I can't be anywhere near you or Mom until this is over. It's too dangerous. You need to keep Mom and Sandra safe. I'll set up a new protocol as soon as I can."

"We can come to you, son," Redmond said.

"And if they're watching?" James said.

The limo returned and parked next to the Escalade. Redmond looked up to the heavens for an answer that wasn't there.

"Go home, Dad. Please. Tell Mom I'm fine and give Sandra a hug."

"The rest of you can come with me," Stuart offered. "ICO already knows about Cairabrae. You can rest up a few days."

"Before you do," Sam said, "we need to report to ICO, tell them what happened. It's what we'd do if we didn't know they were behind it. It goes without saying we don't tell them about finding their trackers."

"You're right," James said. "I'll call Beale."

"I'll deal with Cain," Sam said. "And then I'm returning my cousin's truck. I'll see you back in Vancouver," he said, addressing me. He leaned in and brushed a kiss on my cheek. "Get some sleep."

With sad resolve, Redmond approached James and pulled him into an embrace. "Be careful, son. If I can help, call." When they separated, Redmond handed him a credit card and a roll of bills.

Sam and Redmond settled in the limo for the drive back to the Riverside Airport. When the limo was out of sight, James turned to Stuart. "Thanks for the offer, but I'm not going to Cairabrae."

"Why!" I said.

"You know why," James said.

"It's the safest place for both of you right now," Stuart said.

"He's right. It's four in the morning. Where else would we go? Please come," I said, unconcerned that I sounded desperate. In truth, I was—desperate to talk to him, to hold him. To know what had happened to him.

"No."

"Then give me your transmitters," Stuart said. "I'll take them to Cairabrae and you two can catch your breath."

"You'd do that for us?" I said.

Stuart pulled my hands into his. "Without question. And in the days to come, I'm going to do a lot worse. We all are."

"I know, and I'm sorry."

"Not your fault."

Maybe not all of it, but I'd made enough mistakes to bear some of the blame. I gave his hands a squeeze and let go.

I turned to James with my hand out. He hesitated for only a moment before dropping his transmitter in it. I added mine and handed them both to Stuart. "Thank you."

Stuart addressed me. "You've been working with the detective for a while now. Do you trust him?"

"With my life. He's a good man."

"What about you, James?"

"Jordan's not an ICO asset. They only tagged him because he was already exposed."

"You didn't answer my question."

James levelled a cutting glare at Stuart. "Jordan lied to protect *her*," he said, tossing his head in my direction. "ICO knows it. You can trust him."

Stuart slowly nodded his head considering James's words. "All right. I'll call Sebastian. The Tribunal will convene. Make a plan."

"We've already made a plan," James said.

"Yes. And it's sound. But you can't do it alone."

When James offered no reaction, Stuart asked if he could drop us somewhere.

We got out of Stuart's Escalade at a stoplight on Market Street in downtown San Francisco. When the Escalade was out of sight, James hailed a cab. "The Marriott," he said, and settled in. It was a ten-minute drive, but we didn't stay. We entered the deserted lobby, grabbed a visitor guide to San Francisco and made a show of studying it until the cab cleared out and then headed out again. The next cab was from a different company.

Barely a word passed between us as we hopscotched cabs all the way to Half Moon Bay. James's reticence felt like an accusation. The last cabbie let us out with a shake of his head and a shrug near the Half Moon Bay Airport. He'd warned us the airport was closed and there were no other buildings nearby.

"Hotel's this way," James said, striding away from me.

"James! Stop," I called, racing after him.

He didn't even slow down. "What?" he shouted, over his shoulder.

"Slow down! Talk to me." When he did neither, I halted, refusing to chase him like a dog.

James stopped and fisted his hands by his side. When he turned, his expression was stone cold. "You should have gone to Cairabrae."

"Are you angry with me?"

"This isn't about you!" He clamped his jaw shut and stared out to the horizon. "I wish it was just anger in here," he said, punching his chest. "It's not. It's rage. It's fury so fucking hot I'm afraid of how it's going to play out."

"I'm sorry."

"Stop saying that! I'm not Stuart. I'm not going to tell you it's not your fault!"

"And what about you?"

"Me?" he said. "You think I had something to do with this?"

"You could have picked up a goddamn phone. Answered a fucking message. I called you a dozen times. Tried to warn you."

He spun away from me and kicked his shoe into the gravel at the side of the road, spewing stones. He shouted profanities into the night and kicked the gravel again and again until I thought he'd break his foot.

When he'd dulled the edge of his temper, he turned back. "They weren't after me. They were after you. I was just a fucking lure." Resentment leaked out in his tone, in his narrowed glare. He branded me with it.

I creased my forehead. "How do you know that?"

He braced his hands on his hips. "They told me you had special skills. And when I told them they were misinformed, they showed me film . . . of you . . . of you and Sebastian Kirk. You and the detective. You gave them quite a show."

It took a moment for his revelation to sink in. Sebastian would blame me, no doubt. I wouldn't rush to tell him, but it explained how Cain knew Sam had been keeping secrets, why Cain had frozen Sam out. But James was conveniently forgetting his own missteps.

"And what about the show you've been giving authorities for years? Do you not remember your special contribution to the New Orleans Police Department? Reading memories to find missing kids and murderers then pawning off your *special skills* as psychic abilities in the hopes no one would take you seriously? Maybe someone finally took you seriously."

"Do you not think I'd know if that's what they were after? They wanted to bag a Ghost, and they already had you tagged."

I couldn't meet James's glare and hung my head. "I didn't know. ICO implanted the tracker when I was in the hospital after that case with the Cooper brothers." It could only have been ICO. I'd been under the care of their doctor, Dr. Penn. Not only had they sedated me, they'd also stuck me with multiple IV lines to accommodate a dialysis unit, which cleaned my blood. Slipping in a tracker would have been easy. "That was two months ago."

"Yeah. It's someone in ICO. They'd been watching you for weeks. Knew all about ghosting, but that's not what they call it. *Vaporizing* is their name for what you do."

"What you do" came out like an indictment. I chose to chalk it up to his outrage. He was lashing out. I understood that.

"Mason tracked a Redeemer to Vancouver a few days ago," I said.

"Said he was a key player. Told me the guy had been at Cairabrae on the night of the massacre. The man sold information about me but Mason didn't know who bought it." Silence stretched between us again. "Is Stuart safe with our trackers on him?"

"Stuart can take care of himself," James said, spitting the words out.

I glowered at him. "And he just took care of us. Is he safe?"

James caught himself and paused. "The transmitters are harmless, and you know as well as I do that Stuart has capable security in place should anyone unexpected show up."

I was beginning to think James was right. I should have gone to Cairabrae. His mood was volatile.

"If I could change what happened, I would."

"You can't. What's done is done." He dropped his hands to his side.

"Tell me, James, what is it that's been done?" My guilt had a crushing weight to it.

He looked to the ground. I feared whatever it was he'd experienced.

"Tell me," I said. "How did they get you? When? What did they do to you?"

He swung his head back and forth and finally looked up from under a heavy brow. "Come on. Let's get a room. Get some sleep." He offered me a hand, but not out of affection; it was a tool to get me moving. I took it because he needed me to. He needed me not to ask questions about what had happened to him.

We started walking, but the silence between us felt like trouble brewing. "How do those trackers work?" I asked, filling the void.

"They're RF transmitters. They send out a radio signal that can be picked up if you know which frequency to tune in to."

"What's their range?"

"Hard to know. The technology is improving all the time. Maybe half a mile."

ICO didn't need the range. They knew where I lived, which cases I worked. Same with James.

Thirty minutes later, we arrived at the Seal Cove Inn. A night bell brought out the desk clerk, and we were soon given an elegantly appointed room with a private garden view.

I walked into the bathroom and immediately plugged the tub and started a bath. My clothes needed to be laundered. I wished we'd been able to stop and buy something fresh to wear. I stripped and pulled on one of the hotel's bathrobes.

James wandered in, splendidly naked, his shoulder-length hair loose. He walked into the shower stall ten feet away without even looking in my direction. His estrangement hurt. But I took comfort in his naked body, not because it was beautiful, but because I saw no marks. He hadn't been tortured, at least physically. He reached his face to the spray of water and slicked back his dark hair. The muscles in his arms and shoulders rippled. Water dripped in rivulets down his back and crawled over his perfect ass.

I'd have jumped his bones right there if he hadn't made it clear he needed distance. I could give him that, but having him naked and so close was too much. I left him in the bathroom and picked up my phone.

My call to Mason didn't require a lot of detail. He'd already heard the story from his father. Mason was concerned about me, which was touching, and a stark contrast to the man in the shower. "I'm still in Vancouver," Mason said. "The Redeemer has been persuaded to set up another meet with the buyer. We'll unravel their network and make them regret the day they crossed us."

"Good."

"You sure you're okay?"

"I don't know what they did to me, Mason. That scares the crap out of me, but the doctor didn't find anything except the transmitter. He took some blood. I'm tired, but I feel fine."

I wasn't fine. I'd been through this trauma before, when Carson Manse abducted me. I knew what lay ahead—the restless nights, the paranoia, the hopelessness. Maybe it wouldn't be as bad this time.

"And James?"

"I don't know. He hasn't talked about what happened. Not to me, anyway. Physically, he seems sound, but he's angry like I've never seen before. I'm worried about him."

"I'd be angry too. A man like James? He'll want to get even. You should probably stay out of his way. Give him some space."

"Yeah. I'm getting that impression."

"When you get home, we need to talk about your mother."

"Why?"

"She's hired a PI. He's digging into shit he has no business in."

"Damn! I knew she wasn't going to let the whole Jolene thing go. I'll talk to her."

James walked out of the bathroom with a towel around his waist and another draped around his shoulders.

"I've got to go, Mason. I'll keep in touch."

James sat on the other side of the bed and bent to rub his hair with the towel.

I walked into the bathroom and closed the door behind me. I reached to turn the water off and sat on the edge of the tub swirling my fingers through the warm water. I missed James. I longed to hold him, to make love to him, to talk to him. If things were right between us, we'd be in the shower together finding alternate uses for lather. Whatever had happened to him, whatever he was going through, I prayed we'd be able to sort it out before it broke us.

Chapter Fifteen

I dropped the robe in a heap at my feet and stepped into the tub. The warm water soothed my tired body but didn't quiet my mind. James's voice seeped in from the other room. Talking with Beale? I wondered. I sunk deeper into the water then dipped my head below the surface. The world grew quiet. If I could breathe underwater, I'd stay in the warm cocoon for days.

When I surfaced, I scrubbed myself and rested against the sloped back. The tracker had been in my arm when Avery invited me over to announce his engagement. Who else had I exposed? I retraced my steps through the past two months.

The bath water grew cold. I knew I was avoiding James, but I didn't know how to deal with his anger, the coldness in him. His behaviour reminded me of when I first met him. He was aloof then, too. Angry and bitter, though back then I didn't know it was due to his family's history with the Tribunal. James's father had pegged me as one of them. Had Redmond convinced James that was true? That I was the enemy?

Stepping from the tub, I snagged a towel, dried off, then wrapped another towel around my hair and pulled on the robe. James had gone quiet in the other room. I tried not to think about what was going on in his mind while I brushed my teeth and finger combed my tangles. Why was he withholding what had happened to him? Was it horrific or did he not remember? My mind spun with every possible scenario, and each one frightened me.

When I finally cracked the bathroom door, I saw James lying in the bed with the covers pulled over his shoulder. He was on his side, facing the window. I didn't think he was asleep, but it didn't take an expert in body language to tell me he didn't want my company. Unfortunately, there was only one bed.

I crawled in beside him, close yet miles away. Given the distance, it seemed inconceivable that James had asked me to marry him. I rolled away from him. Perhaps he'd changed his mind. I closed my eyes and fought against the ache in my chest as tears fell silently to my pillow.

It was still dark when I woke, and it took my mind a moment to catch up and remember where I was. I rolled onto my back and jerked. James stared down at me, propped up on his elbow. His jaw was set in a hard line, his eyes narrowed. He reached for the sheet that covered me and pulled it down to my thighs. Had James returned? I wondered, feeling the heat of his gaze slide down my body like a caress.

I lifted a hand to his chest but didn't reach it. He shook his head as he grabbed my hand and pressed it into the pillow above my head.

"James?"

"Shh," he said, releasing my hand to cup my breast. He rubbed his thumb across my nipple then leaned down and flicked his tongue over the hardened nub. I arched, wanting more, buoyed by the hope that we'd moved past the anger that lay between us. His hand wandered down my stomach and over my hip.

"Open," he said. I nearly cried with relief. James was indeed back—and bossy James was one of my favourite bedmates. I opened my legs. His hand immediately dropped between them, and he wasted no time sliding first one finger inside then three, pushing, stretching. I whispered his name, feeling my world right itself.

I reached for James's erection but he twisted his torso and intercepted my hand. He shoved it back over my head and then pressed a thumb to my clitoris, that most sensitive knot of nerves. I inhaled on a hiss. Punishment for moving my hand? James searched my face, satisfied, then bent his head to my breast and sucked a nipple into his mouth—hard enough to make me cry out.

James's sexuality had an edge to it at times. He pushed me to the point of discomfort, enjoying my reaction to the small pains he inflicted and wanting the same in return. James knew me well, knew my limits, knew I didn't connect the pain and pleasure dots like he did, but he kept testing, pushing his fingers deeper and adding pressure to his thumb. I squirmed to find some relief, hesitant to stop him, not knowing what was driving him. He leaned over and captured my nipple in his mouth again, and sucked harder than before.

"Stop!" I said, and pushed against his shoulders with a scowl. He stilled and lifted his head, but where I'd usually find a sly smile, I found a frown. He'd blown past discomfort directly to pain, barrelling through my limits as if he didn't know I had any. He'd never done that before.

Whatever have they done to you? I thought. With my hands still on his shoulders, he crawled between my legs. He dragged the swollen tip of his erection from the heat of my core to the tip of my cleft. I sagged, my scowl softened and I dropped my head back to the pillow. He blazed the same slow trail again, knowing I couldn't resist.

I exhaled with a low hiss. "Yes," I said. Once again, he pressed his erection against my core and this time he slammed inside, sheathing himself to the hilt in one powerful push.

I loved it and I hated it and I couldn't get enough of him and his anger that ratcheted up my lust with each punch of his pelvis. This wasn't lovemaking—this was him working something out, and my hips met every thrust, taking everything he gave me and wanting more, needing this release like I needed air.

When James stopped, I shouted, "No!" He liked that.

He flipped me over and slammed back in from behind. Each penetration hit the sweet spot inside, the one he'd finger until I came undone. His thrusts were relentless. He brought on an orgasm I thought would kill us both.

I'm not sure it even registered with him. He didn't even slow down. With his weight on his arms, he swung his hips like a piston, pounding like his life depended on it. I wasn't complaining. I could feel another orgasm building and prayed he wouldn't stop before it hit.

When it did, I fell apart, and all of my pent-up anger and frustration released in ugly groans and murderous cries. When it was done, I couldn't be sure he'd finished and didn't care. I disintegrated, curled into a ball and cried. James said nothing, but I suppose there was nothing to say. Before I drifted off to oblivion I remember thinking it strange that we still hadn't kissed.

When next I woke, daylight knifed across the floor, jutting from a gap in the drapes. James stood in silhouette at the crack, naked, looking outside. The image was straight out of a book of artistic black-and-white photographs, the kind you'd display on a coffee table.

I was burning the image into my retinas when James turned around. And that image was even better. The corners of my mouth lifted. I couldn't help it. He was gorgeous.

But the scathing expression on his face doused my libido. Instantly, I plunged back a day, to our arguing, the finger pointing, the angry sex.

I pulled the sheet to my chest and sat up. "You're angry again. Please don't be angry."

"Don't tell me what to feel."

"Talk to me, James."

"You won't like what I have to say."

"Probably not. But keeping it inside is going to be the end of us."

He crossed his arms, each hand fisting a bicep, and looked right through me. "Beale was dragging his ass. Said he couldn't assign me a case because he'd been called out of town. Then I get a phone call from an inspector at the FDA. Said Beale recommended me so I took the case. The FDA suspected a company called Quantum Genetics was using private labs to conduct illegal experiments. I found three labs Quantum used regularly. Vector was one of them. I cased the place, went in as a sales rep. Fuente played along, but now I know . . . he'd been expecting me. I took the coffee he offered. Drank it and woke up in that cell."

"How long?"

"Six days from what I can piece together."

A dozen questions danced on my tongue, but I held it.

"The first time they provoked me I jolted their glass wall. It shattered, but I didn't make it very far. When I woke again, they'd replaced the glass. The next time they provoked me, I didn't fall for it. They were testing their materials, and I wasn't about to help them any further."

He dropped his gaze to the floor. "When I wouldn't play their little game, they knocked me out. I have no idea what they did to me when I was unconscious. But . . ."

His pause stretched on. Emotions flashed across his face, as if he were fighting some inner demon. And when he finally spoke, he looked beaten. "They took my sperm. Not once. Not twice. Three times. Enough to make a whole lot of babies."

My thoughts fragmented like conversations at a party. My attention flitted among them. One conversation was working on the how of it, picturing the requisite beautiful woman on her knees, or taking him in hand and putting that look on his face, the lusty one he got just before he came. Another conversation was about a row of bassinets with swaddled babies reaching to infinity. And then I remembered the abdominal cramps I'd experienced after waking up in that motel.

The noise in my head stopped.

I pressed a hand to my lower belly and gazed up at James. I'd missed part of what he'd said. ". . . guinea pigs for them to experiment—"

"I think they took my eggs," I said, interrupting.

James snapped his mouth closed and stared at me.

"I felt cramping earlier. Thought I'd pulled a muscle, but now I don't think that's what it was."

James dropped his arms to his side. His face distorted.

I picked up my phone and dialled Avery. Our conversation was painful and punctuated with silence, as if every phrase I spoke ruptured the landline.

He reminded me a woman is born with all the eggs she'll ever have, and then he explained the extraction procedure. It would have involved a needle through the top of the vaginal wall to get to the ovaries.

"Eggs have to be mature to be fertilized. Without putting you through days of fertility treatments, they might have gotten one egg, two at most, but chances of successful fertilization are slim."

"What about immature eggs, or an ovary?"

"If they'd taken even one of your ovaries, you'd be in a lot more pain, and Stuart's doctor would certainly have noticed when he examined you."

"And immature eggs?"

Avery didn't answer, and his silence frightened me. "Avery?"

"Possibly. There's been some research on incubating immature eggs. Growing them to maturity in a lab. Mostly for young cancer patients. I'll look it up. When are you coming home?"

"I don't know yet. I have to see Stuart. Pick up the tracker . . . the tracker. Shit. I meant to tell you. It was in my arm the night I came to visit you and Victoria."

"ICO already knew about me."

"They didn't know you were one of us. They'll have seen the X on your roof. They know now."

"They probably suspected anyway. Listen, what's done is done. Ask Stuart to get in touch with the walk-in clinic. I'd like to see your MRI scans, and I'd like the clinic's doctor to take a closer look at your ovaries on these scans. Come see me as soon as you're home. I'll have some answers for you then."

I hit end and set the phone down.

"What'd he say?" James asked.

"He'll know more in a few days." I swung my feet off the side of the bed with my back to James. "I'm leaving. Going to Cairabrae." I stood and made my way to the bathroom. James didn't follow, didn't say a word. I closed the bathroom door and got in the shower.

Had they stolen my eggs? Each time my thoughts waded into the dark depths of that possibility, I forcibly turned away, afraid of where those thoughts would lead. I had no memory of it, so maybe it hadn't happened. It was so much better when all I imagined they'd taken was blood and X-rays and tissue samples too small to require stitches.

With nothing else to wear, I donned the dirty clothes I now imagined some stranger's groping hands had re-dressed me in.

When I emerged from the bathroom, James was wearing his father's clothes. He'd been pacing and stopped. "I've talked to the front desk, arranged for a rental car. I'll drive you to Cairabrae."

"No. You've made it clear how you feel about that place. Stuart can send someone down here with your tracker." Alone in a car with James and his seething bitterness didn't sound like a whole lot of fun. I'd rather be on my own.

"I'd like to drive you," James said.

"Why?"

"Because you're distracted. You shouldn't be driving."

"I don't need to be looked after, James, and I don't want to deal with your anger right now. I have enough of my own to deal with." I collected my phone and checked the time before tucking it in my bag. It was noon. Bodega Bay was a two-and-a-half-hour drive away.

James approached me with caution, standing on the edge of my personal space. "This thing with ICO, it's fucking with my head. I can think of only one thing they have planned for my sperm." His fists clenched and unclenched by his sides. "Children I won't know, who won't know me. Kids they'll treat like lab animals, experiment on. It's making me crazy. I have to stop them. If it kills me, I have to stop them."

Though I wasn't sure this was the root of James's anger, I didn't doubt the veracity of his words. James's paternal instincts had been awakened in the months since his family was released from indentured service to the Tribunal. His longing for children had been the biggest stumbling block to my agreeing to marry him. I wasn't ready for that responsibility.

I'd thought I had all the time in the world to have kids. Now I wasn't so sure.

But of one thing I was dead certain: ICO would not play God with a child of mine. It struck me then how having something stolen from you made you want it back, even if you weren't sure you'd wanted it before.

"I'll help you stop them," I said, and closed the distance between us, reaching my lips to his—the first kiss we'd shared since our ordeal began.

He wrapped his arms around me and I melted into him. Finally, he'd let me in. It took all my control not to sob. We were miles away from healed, but we could start the journey together on our way to Cairabrae.

I drove. It was important to me. In San Francisco, we bought clothes, cut the tags off and wore them out of the store. It felt good, as though we'd chalked up our first victory. Around the corner, we found a diner and had coffee and eggs from the all-day breakfast menu.

I drove in the curb lane and stayed under the speed limit. I knew James would bolt when we got to Cairabrae, and I wanted this time to reconnect with him. I wanted to tell him that I'd marry him, but ICO had taken that option from me, too. A *yes* right now would feel forced, a Hail Mary pass to glue our relationship back together.

Northeast of San Francisco, at the sign for Oakland, I decided to visit my half-brother's grave at Turner Acres. I hadn't been there since Mason's mother, Jeannette, had been laid to rest beside him.

We picked up flowers along the way, and after we parked, James walked with me to the black granite tombstone. Though it had stood there for more than twenty years, its polished surface gleamed in the sun as if it were brand new.

"Someone else has been visiting," James said, as we came around to the front of the stones. A desiccated rose lay atop Jeannette's headstone. Beside it, at the foot of my half-brother's stone, rested a plush blue teddy bear. I bent down and picked it up. It still felt soft, new.

The inscription was branded deep into the stone: *Andrew Reynolds Taylor, Beloved, March 2, 1986 ~ April 13, 1986*. Someone else had remembered his birthday or the anniversary of his death.

"Probably Stuart," I said, "Or Mason."

I set the teddy bear back down and left him sunflowers. They felt playful, happy—like the man I imagined he would have grown into.

Jeannette's tombstone was similarly simple. The only thing on it was her name, the phrase *Loving Wife and Mother* and the requisite dates. How could it have been only six months ago? I knelt and arranged a bouquet of white roses, the same as Stuart had laid her to rest with. Her favourite, or so I assumed. The same as the dried rose above.

"When we buried Jeannette I remember thinking that life couldn't get worse," I said. "I should have touched wood."

At Petaluma, we exited Highway 101 and headed west until we hit the Shoreline Highway at Bodega Bay, where we turned north. The narrow highway twisted and turned around high cliffs and wind-carved bonsai trees that framed vistas of the vast Pacific, which lay dark blue under a clear sky.

We took a right off the highway, climbed a slope and arrived at the black iron gates to Cairabrae in the late afternoon. The Reynolds's crest split in two and the gates opened: Stuart was expecting us. We drove another five minutes past tufted clumps of grass and sagebrush and stands of eucalyptus that huddled in groups like cliques at a garden party. We crested the final rise and below us, Cairabrae presented herself, her grey stone wings stretching out behind a columned facade fronted by formal gardens. Despite what had happened here, Cairabrae stood proud and regal.

But I could still picture the Redeemer snipers on the rooftop. I took my foot from the gas and slowed to a crawl. "Seems unreal, doesn't it? The place looks untouched." I pulled under the porte cochère and parked. When I cut the engine, I heard the water trickling from vases on the delicate shoulders of the Greek-inspired statuary of the fountain, the formal garden's focal point.

Ryan bolted from the front door and jogged over to open my door. "Emelynn," he said, his smile threatening to eclipse his face. I took the hand he offered and climbed out of the car. His hug was a bit of a surprise, but I went along with it. It had been a while since I'd seen him. He'd worked security for the Reynolds family for years, and had helped protect the Reynoldses and their Tribunal guests the night of the Redeemer attack. If it weren't for the fact that he was as fit as an athlete and the size of a pro wrestler, he might not have survived the tranquilizers the Redeemers had shot into him.

"Is Debbie here?" I asked.

"She's coming up from her quarters now. She's anxious to see you." Debbie also worked security. She'd been assigned as my personal body-guard for a time—an intrusion I'd hated, but we'd become friends.

She'd been grievously injured in the attack. Like Ryan, she was ex-military, and her conditioning had aided in her recovery.

Ryan spotted James, who'd exited the car on the passenger side. James had worked security with Ryan that horrible night and in the days leading up to it. They respected one another professionally, but James had always been considered an outsider. "James," Ryan said in greeting. "Can I get your luggage?"

"We don't have luggage," he said.

Ryan looked at me and frowned. "You're not staying?"

"We'll play it by ear," I said, knowing full well James wouldn't stay, even if I wanted him to.

Stuart stepped out the front door and called my name. I dropped my keys into Ryan's outstretched hand and walked into Stuart's embrace.

"Welcome home," he said. Stuart had always made me feel at home here, and he'd never once blamed me for his daughter's death. "How was the drive?"

"Good. We stopped at Turner Acres. Left some roses for Jeannette. Sunflowers for Andrew."

"They'd like that," he said.

"Someone else had been there. They left a rose for Jeannette and a blue teddy bear for Andrew."

Stuart frowned.

"It wasn't you?" I asked.

"No. Probably Mason." He turned to James, who stood behind me. "Good to see you, James." They shook hands—a small gesture Mason had difficulty with when it came to James. I was glad Mason wasn't here. "Welcome. Come inside."

Stuart ushered me ahead of him into the grand marble entrance. The wide staircase set back on the left curled up to a second floor. An enormous vase of fresh flowers rested on the claw-foot table in the centre of a foyer that never failed to put me in mind of a hotel lobby.

We rounded the flowers and I stopped short at the top of the steps down to the formal living room. Carson Manse had stood in this very spot. He'd had James on his knees beside him with a gun to his head. He'd threatened James's life to get me into the room. And when I'd stepped inside, Carson had shot James. I closed my eyes, but I could still see the crimson puddle growing beneath him, could still feel the terror of losing him. I took a breath and opened my eyes. James rolled his shoulder, the one that Carson's bullet had shattered. He looked away and started down the stairs. Thank god Carson was a lousy shot.

The living room had been redecorated since I'd last seen it. Not a surprise. Bloodstains and bullet holes weren't conducive to healing, even if they'd been scrubbed clean and repaired. A fresh start was much better.

"I'm sorry about Jeannette's piano," I said. The red-lacquered grand piano had been the focal point in the room. I motioned to the gilded harp that now stood in its place. "Does anyone play it?"

"No, but no one played the piano anymore either. Come out back. We'll have refreshments and catch up."

James followed us across the living room and out the floor-to-ceiling folding glass doors that made up the entire back wall. On the patio, a tray had been set on one of the low tables under cover. I gazed to the left, where the pool sparkled in the late-afternoon sun. Stuart showed me to a seat then he and James joined me.

"Iced tea?" Stuart said, reaching for a jug frosted with condensation. He began filling the glasses without waiting for replies, a small reminder of how presumptuous he could be. It amused me now, no longer annoyed me.

The pastures were greener than they'd been the last time I was here. Horses wandered far in the distance, grazing against the backdrop of outbuildings and barns.

As Stuart set the jug of iced tea down, Debbie emerged from inside the house. Her gait was strong and steady. "You look terrific," I said, jumping up to greet her. She'd been shot in the abdomen during the raid. She'd lost her spleen, a kidney and several feet of large bowel, but no one would know it to see her now, in form-fitting clothes.

She stood a bit taller than I was and returned my hug but didn't linger. She was an employee and always mindful of her position. I'd observed that same professional distance in all the staff.

"I'm happy to go running with you while you're here, or to the shooting range," she said. "Whatever you'd like."

"Thanks. Not sure how long we're staying, though."

She said hello to James then disappeared back into the house.

"What did the Tribunal have to say?" I asked.

"They haven't convened yet. Sebastian will organize it from Ottawa. He's still there unravelling General Cain's chain of command."

"Have you received the blood results yet from Dr. Mills?" I asked.

"No. I'll forward them on to each of you as soon as I do."

"Thank you. And if you don't mind, Avery Coulter wants to see my MRI scan. Would you ask Dr. Mills to send it to him?"

"I will," Stuart said. "Right away. Is Dr. Coulter concerned about something in particular?"

I hesitated, but only because I struggled to find the right words to tell Stuart what I suspected had happened. "He'd like Dr. Mills to take a closer look at my ovaries."

Stuart knitted his brows. "Whatever for?"

"I've had some unexpected cramping."

Stuart's puckered brows lifted in surprise, and he moved to the edge of his seat. "You're pregnant?"

"No."

Disappointment slipped in under Stuart's careful expression. "Then what's going on?"

"There's a possibility that ICO has taken my eggs." I left out what had happened to James. That was his detail to share if he chose.

Stuart froze in place. Neither James nor I moved until he did. When he settled back in his chair, his face was set in hard lines. "Your eggs carry my daughter's gift. Sebastian was right. We should have eliminated the leak right here."

"You couldn't have," James said. "It was too big a mess. You needed Cain and his American counterparts to cover it up. They did a solid job, buried what happened here so deep no one will be able to dig up the truth. Not that they'd believe it if they did."

"I believe you have some digging of your own to do with your handler, Tim Beale?" Stuart said.

"Yes," James said. "I'm making it a priority."

"I'd like to help."

James stumbled over his words. "Ah, yeah. Thanks. But no."

Stuart looked away, nodding. "Did you know I worked with your father? Back in the sixties?"

James recovered his composure quickly. "I doubt my father would agree with your verb choice."

Stuart smiled and allowed James his gibe. "Indeed. What the Tribunal imposed upon him, on you. It was wrong. I'm sorry for the role I played in it."

"And you think helping me with Beale will erase it?"

"No. Nothing will change the past. But I know how much you

mean to Emelynn, and I'd like to think we can forge something better going forward."

Phillip chose that inopportune moment to arrive. He was a fixture at Cairabrae, having managed the Reynoldses' household for fifteen years. He nodded to Stuart and then addressed me. "Hello, Emelynn. Welcome back."

He set down a charcuterie tray on the table in front of us. "Compliments of Consuela," he said. "Dinner will be ready in an hour. May I get you an aperitif?" I'd never seen Phillip anything but perfectly polite, never ruffled. He'd taken some time off after the massacre, but he'd returned and hired a new cook, and it looked as if he was back to his normal, and very formal, self.

"The usual for me," Stuart said, and turned to James. "James?" he asked.

"Scotch," James replied. "With a splash of water."

Phillip nodded.

"And you, Emelynn?" Stuart asked.

"I'll have what you're having," I said, and bit back a grin. I'm not sure Stuart had ever actually asked me what I wanted to drink. He normally presumed and ordered for me.

Phillip disappeared with our drink orders and Stuart resumed where he'd left off. "As I said, James, I'm at your disposal. I mean that. I want to help if you'll let me."

"I'll think about it," James said, which was an improvement over the flat-out no Stuart had gotten on his first attempt.

After that, I steered our conversation into shallow waters and asked about their new cook. No one mentioned Maria, the former cook who'd been like family and had been killed by the Redeemers. We finished our drinks and headed in for dinner. Consuela had prepared perfectly grilled lamb chops with a mint and pea salad, roasted potatoes and mustard beans. Dessert was a fruit flan.

"I hope Consuela never leaves," I said, and stifled a yawn. "That was delicious. Thank you, Stuart."

"You're welcome, my dear. I hope I don't have to beg you to stay the night?"

I kept my gaze on the table. I felt bone tired, and falling into bed upstairs in Jolene's old room would have been an easy ending to a difficult day—but not for James. Cairabrae was the last place James would choose to spend a night.

"James," Stuart said, standing. "Take Emelynn upstairs, would you? She looks dead on her feet. I'll see you two in the morning." Stuart breezed out of the room before James could muster up another no.

Stuart had once again taken top honours in the manipulation game. I'd have to thank him if it worked.

"What do you say?" I asked James.

"Maybe it's time." He stood and nodded toward the dining room door. "Lead the way."

Though I didn't entirely trust his sudden change of attitude, I smiled and took his hand.

CHAPTER SIXTEEN

At the foot of the curved staircase, I squeezed his hand. "You sure?" James's memories of Cairabrae didn't include exhilarating horseback rides or refreshing laps in the pool; he'd been forced to read memories for the Tribunal here.

"Yeah."

One word, and yet it held the promise of another victory: healing an old wound and moving forward.

We turned left at the top of the stairs and carried on down the hall to Jolene's suite of rooms. When Debbie had been assigned to watch over me, she'd moved into the suite across the hall. Was she there now, I wondered?

James walked in behind me and stopped where the hallway spilled into the sitting room. I crossed to the balcony door and opened it to a cool night breeze.

"The bedroom and bathroom are through there," I said, nodding toward the French doors. James stalked the room's perimeter, his gaze taking in every detail.

I set my bag on the coffee table and dug out my phone. "Mom's probably wondering where I am."

"I'm going to look around," James said, and slipped into an adjoining room. He wouldn't feel comfortable until he'd checked every inch of the place and had an escape plan mapped out.

I sent my mother a Viagra message and then called her. She answered the phone repeating my name like a question, as if my call had surprised her.

"I hope I haven't woken you."

I hadn't, but the number I'd called from had surprised her. "I lost my phone in San Francisco," I said, but didn't mention Cairabrae. I didn't want her to ask me about Mason. I told her my work with Sam was finished and I'd be home as soon as I could organize a flight.

"No rush, sweetheart. I'm making out fine on my own."

If she was telling me to take my time, could it be that her PI hadn't yet found whatever he was looking for? That would make Mason happy. We said our good nights and I took the phone to the bedroom and set it on the bedside table.

James emerged from the dressing room with a scowl on his face. "It looks like you live here."

He wasn't going to stay. I could feel it.

"They went a little overboard with the clothes. It was after the fire." Mason had sent Debbie shopping to replace what I'd lost to the flames that destroyed my home. He and Stuart blamed themselves for allowing the man responsible for the arson to escape.

"You live on Jolene's inheritance. You have an entire suite here," he said, sweeping his hands around the room, "and they paid for your condo in Vancouver. You're beholden to them."

His anger shocked me. "They're family. It's not the same."

"They own you."

"And that wad of money you took from your father? His clothes that you were wearing?" I took a breath and tamped down my emotions. "They don't own me—it's what a good family does, and I'm not having this discussion with you again."

James raised his hands in surrender, but he wasn't done. I cut him off. "I know you're angry, James. I'm angry too, but lashing out at me isn't going to help."

His anger simmered behind narrowed eyes. "You know, when I woke up the first time in that glass cell, I couldn't figure out how I'd gotten caught. I'd walked straight into their trap. People like me don't get caught. People like me do the catching, the interrogating, not the other way around. We sure as hell don't get rescued by our girlfriends."

I nearly choked on my surprise. "That's what's bothering you?"

"I'm better than that! I should have known. Been more observant. And getting caught wasn't the worst of it: they didn't want me. They toyed with me while they bided their time waiting for you. I wasn't a big enough prize for them."

"Wow. First a misogynist and now you're shouldering the biggest fucking ego I've ever seen. Do you hear yourself?"

He looked up from under a heavy brow. Confusion clouded his features.

"This isn't you, James. And this shit about me and this place—it's not what you're angry about."

"How the fuck would you know!"

"You were raped, James! Raped! What you're feeling is violation. You're angry because they forcibly took something from you and you were helpless to stop them."

James froze. He glared at me and one side of his mouth twitched. James rarely let his temper get the best of him. He was a plotter, a thinker. He preferred to be in control. I could see the struggle on his face as he considered what I'd said. I wished I hadn't used the word *helpless*. Eventually, his gaze dropped to the floor and with it, the bulk of his energy. He exhaled a long breath.

"I'm sorry," he said. His arms fell to his sides, his fists unclenched.

"I know." I also knew he was terrified and that for months to come, he would check shadows, start at unexpected noises and be unable to sleep through the night. But that wasn't what any man wanted to hear, and certainly not James.

"I was trained. In the military . . . trained to withstand pain, terror. Thought I'd been through it all, but this. This I . . . this is . . . I don't know. I'm going to hunt them down. Kill every one of them."

"You don't have to do it alone."

He raised his head and looked at me.

"You have one of the most powerful allies in our world in this house and offering to help you. Be smart. Use him."

"You've changed," James said. It didn't sound like a compliment. But it was the truth. Kill or be killed: Carson Manse had taught me that and ICO had just reinforced it. This was the world I lived in, and I no longer had qualms about my preference to stay on the adapt side of the adapt-or-perish equation.

James walked to the sofa and sat. He massaged his temples and eventually dropped his head back, exposing his Adam's apple. "Do you have anything to drink up here?"

I picked up the house phone and for the first time ever, pushed the pound key and then one. "Phillip, would you mind bringing me a bottle of Scotch?"

Phillip didn't mind. He arrived with a bottle of The Macallan Gold, two rocks glasses and a bucket of ice.

James and I sat on the sofa, sipping the fine Scotch. I curled my feet up. He stared into some middle distance. How long had he endured their manipulations, suppressing his body's impulse? It must have been awful for him in the end, knowing he couldn't help himself.

When I breached the silence, he came back from wherever he'd gone. "How many people do you think are involved?" I asked.

"Maybe six in the US, including Beale. Probably similar numbers in Canada."

"I would have thought more."

James shook his head. "Credible knowledge of our kind won't exist outside of a small circle within ICO. Governments keep units like ICO funded so they can reap the benefits of unsanctioned black ops and paranormal day trips without ever having to admit they're party to it. They lean on plausible deniability until the work produces a strategic advantage."

In the quiet evening, over the tinkle of ice cubes, I told James about the case of the kidnapped baby that wasn't, about the drones in Vancouver and about the insider rivalry Sam had told me existed between military and civilian intelligence. James told me Canada didn't have a unique claim on that rivalry.

James swirled his Scotch, spiriting a small ice cube around the second shot, and mapped out the people who needed to be interrogated and the locations that needed to be torn apart to find our reproductive material. He stood and stretched then wandered to the balcony door and leaned against its frame. "I don't trust the Tribunal. I know them too well."

"Stuart's not on the Tribunal."

"He's one of the founding families. Their only loyalty is to the Tribunal."

"It's not their only loyalty. Stuart is loyal to Mason. And to me."

"Maybe, but I've seen things that would test that theory—unpleasant things that unfolded right here in this house."

James's disapproval hovered, threatening to descend and smother us both. I didn't want that. Not tonight. He'd agreed to stay, which signalled a monumental shift in his attitude. To make that shift permanent, he had to make new memories in this house: memories strong enough to overpower the negative ones.

I stood and sauntered into his path. James watched me, his expression resolute. I reached my arms around his neck and dragged his mouth down to my kiss. He kept his hands by his side, holding on to his negativity. This would never do. I tugged his hands around to rest on my butt. That helped.

"Want to see how big the hot water tank is?" I asked.

That helped a lot.

"Are you trying to distract me?" he asked.

"I am ever so hopeful." I kissed him again and walked backwards, pulling him with me into the bathroom, tugging his shirt out of his jeans along the way. We stopped at the glass doors to the walk-in shower. He reached inside to turn on the water and every one of the spray heads. Then he yanked his shirt over his head and tossed it. The button and fly of his jeans were open, and he looked delicious standing there in bare feet.

A seductive smile crept onto his face. "Take off your clothes," he said, as he stepped back and crossed his arms.

"Such a romantic," I said, rolling my eyes, even though I loved it. Bossy James could convince me to do things I'd never have the nerve to do otherwise.

As steam billowed out of the shower, I gave him the show he was looking for. When I stood naked before him, he called me to him with a curl of his finger. "Now me," he said, "but no touching." I obliged and tugged off his jeans. He'd gone commando, as was his habit—one I liked and one I'd found convenient more than once. When I'd finished the unwrapping, I stood and unwound the tie from his hair. He drew me close and ground his erection against my stomach.

"I hope this no-touching policy is temporary," I said, pouting. "I don't like it."

He cracked a smile and opened the door to the oversized shower. With a hand on my ass, he urged me inside. He turned my back to the spray, pressed in close and opened my lips with his tongue. Water rained down, pelted us from the front, the back and overhead. I struggled to breathe without getting water up my nose. James took it as a challenge and devoured my mouth, cutting off one of my airways.

He marched me back to the end of the shower with the slatted cedar bench and sat, dragging me down to my knees. I bit my lip watching him sprawl. A devil's grin lit up his face. "Now you can touch, but only with your mouth."

This was the James I loved, the one who could make me wet with his words, the man I couldn't get enough of. I knelt before him, propped my hands on the bench either side of his thighs and eagerly bent to the chore. I started with my teeth, a gentle nip just to remind him I knew who he was. He hissed and I gazed up at him with a knowing leer. The next time I bent to him, he got my tongue, my lips and my soul.

Perhaps I shouldn't have been so eager. He finished and left me with an ache between my legs.

But James was nothing if not thorough. "Lie down."

"Here? On the floor?"

He nodded. "On your back."

I did as he asked and stretched out on the hard marble.

"Right to the end," he said.

I wormed up until my head was inches from the other end. Warm rain pelted down on me. I closed my eyes and gave in to the sensation. His fingers started their caress at my throat, smoothed my collarbone, massaged my shoulders, cupped my breasts and pawed my stomach. I kept my eyes closed as he coaxed my legs apart.

"Please," I whispered, begging for his touch.

He settled between my legs. "Watch me."

I opened my eyes and lifted my head. He darted his tongue to my clitoris and pulled a groan out of me. His fingers pushed inside and I dropped my head.

"Open your eyes. Look at me."

I did as he asked, but found it increasingly difficult as he worked his mouth on that little knot of nerves he commanded with each lick. When he finally took me over the edge, I dug my heels into his back and called his name to the shower-head gods.

He didn't wait for me to recover; he crawled up my torso like a predator and buried himself in me, banging my ass into the stone. I didn't care and he didn't stop. The second time always took longer. We shifted position. He sat with his back to the wall and I straddled him. He kept his gaze on my breasts as I rode him. I watched his face get that look, the one of pure ecstasy, and then he stiffened beneath me. I slowed and stretched it out, and when his clever fingers once again found that heavenly knot of nerves, I found my own finish.

I dropped my head to the wall beside his. We hadn't killed the hot water.

"I'm so glad you stayed," I said.

One of the good things about sex in the shower was the cleanup. Suds and a gentle massage were the perfect end to our lovemaking, and this time, that's what it had been. We crawled into bed with wet hair and sated smiles.

Sometime in the night, he found me again and we made languid love, spooning. He stayed inside me and we fell back asleep.

James didn't stir when I woke. Light spilled into the room through the French doors to the sitting room. I slipped out of bed leaving James to his slumber. I used the washroom, dressed and then tiptoed back to the bedroom. James hadn't moved. Perhaps I'll bring him a coffee, I thought, and left quietly.

From outside the swinging kitchen door, I heard a woman humming. The door squeaked when I pushed it open; nice to see not everything had changed. The heavyset woman in the kitchen turned. A shy smile crept onto her round face. Stuart sat at the old kitchen table and lowered his newspaper at my arrival. Something smelled delicious.

I turned to the woman. "Hi," I said, and offered my hand. "I'm Emelynn."

"My name is Consuela," she said, in a thick Spanish accent. "Pleased to meet you."

"You as well. Dinner last night was *muy bien*," I said, dusting off the little bit of Spanish I knew.

"*Gracias. Café?*

"*Si, Señora. Gracias.*" She poured me a cup, set it on the table with a spoon, and refilled Stuart's cup.

"Good morning," I said, taking a seat. I poured a splash of milk in my coffee. Consuela replaced the carafe and left us alone in the kitchen.

"Where's James?"

"Still upstairs. Thank you for inviting him to stay."

"He takes good care of you. I like that."

Stuart's old-fashioned notions didn't quite fit me. "I don't need to be taken care of, Stuart."

He folded his newspaper and set it to his right. "Everyone needs to be taken care of, dear."

I smiled despite my annoyance because I knew he believed it. If only it were true. How I wished that I could hand someone else the reins sometimes: when I was exhausted, when I was out of my depth or when I was beyond my ability to cope.

Perhaps James and I could be that for each other.

Stuart tipped his head in question and I realized I'd settled into a contented smile.

"He's asked me to marry him."

"Has he?" Stuart said. He didn't return my smile. "Have you said yes?"

"Not yet. But I'm going to."

"Then he will be a part of our family. I'm happy for you. That's wonderful news. I hope he accepts my offer of assistance."

"Me too. Don't let on about the proposal, though. You're the only one I've told."

"I'm flattered, and don't worry—I won't spoil your news. Speaking of unexpected surprises, Mason tells me your mother's investigator has been checking into our financials. Yours, too. Do you know what that's about?"

"Mason told you about the investigator but not the why?" I shook my head. "Figures. Mom and I came home to find Mason in the living room. We really do need to start using doors and knocking like regular people. I made up a story to cover his presence but then he went and told Mom that Jolene was the artist of that painting you sent me."

"Your mother knew Jolene?"

"No. She knew her name—met her once, briefly. She knew who Jolene was and that she and Dad lost a son."

"So what's the problem? Why the investigator?"

"Mom's having a hard time with the coincidences: James and Mason being acquainted, Mason being Jolene's brother. I'd hoped she'd drop the inquisition, but instead, she started probing from a different angle: my condo in Vancouver. She pieced together enough to know I couldn't manage a mortgage for that place on Dr. Coulter's salary."

"Smart woman. I'm looking forward to meeting her."

"When she pressed me, I told her Mason held the mortgage. It was a mistake but I figured she'd never believe the truth. So now, even though Mason backed me up, she's questioning why he would offer me a mortgage. Doesn't think my being Brian's daughter is a big enough incentive."

The kitchen door squeaked open and James walked in with a man I recognized.

"Coffee's hot, lads. Help yourselves," Stuart said, and turned back to me. "You remember Derek Lamb?"

"Yes. Good morning, Derek. James. Guess I'm too late to bring you coffee." I studied James's face looking for some hint that last night's magic had stuck with him, but he'd donned his professional face—frustratingly neutral.

James came to sit beside me, and I pressed my thigh against his. I wished I'd stayed with him until he woke. We could have added another good memory to help wipe out the bad.

Derek sat between James and Stuart.

"I talked Derek into a full-time contract," Stuart said. "He, Ryan and Debbie have Cairabrae covered."

Consuela returned with a handful of fresh herbs and set to chopping them. She added parsley and chives to a bowl of cherry tomatoes. Then she donned oven mitts and opened one of the ovens to remove a savoury pie of some sort. My stomach rumbled as I watched her plate our breakfast.

"You're going to love Consuela's frittata," Stuart said. The compliment put a smile on her face.

The frittata disappeared in record time. Afterwards, Derek excused himself.

"James and I are leaving today," I said. "I'm catching a flight home this afternoon."

"So soon?" Stuart said.

"As much as I'd like to stay, I've got to see Avery and work on diverting Mom's attention. My life is complicated enough without the addition of whatever she digs up."

"And I've got some payback to organize," James said. "I'll be in touch, Stuart. About your offer."

"Good. I'll be ready and waiting."

"As long as you understand that this is my gig. I make the decisions."

"Understood," Stuart said. I wondered if Stuart's understanding included the level of rage that coursed through James. And more importantly, could Stuart temper it?

Chapter Seventeen

T hree days had passed since I left Vancouver. It felt like three months. Back at the condo, I found Mom in the living room. She had the Rolling Stones on the stereo and didn't hear me come in.

"Hi, Mom," I said.

She looked up, startled, from an iPad I hadn't seen before and quickly closed its cover. "Sweetheart! You should have called. I would have picked you up at the airport." She set the tablet on the sofa beside her and jumped up to give me a hug.

"How was your trip?"

I removed my jacket, draped it over the back of the sofa and sat down. "Productive. What did you get up to while I was gone?"

"Let me see." Mom rounded the sofa and started for the kitchen. "I'm going to make a cup of tea. Would you like one?" Classic avoidance, and I was certain I knew why.

"No thanks. You were telling me what you got up to while I was gone."

"Nothing important, sweetheart. Just this and that. Kept myself busy." She disappeared into the kitchen and I heard the kettle filling.

I waited until the water stopped running. "Busy? As in hiring a private investigator to poke into Mason Reynolds's finances?"

The air in the condo grew heavy with quiet unease. Mom stalked back to the living room. She stood in front of me, all pretense of cheery "welcome home" gone. She wasn't smiling.

"Someday, when you're a mother, you'll understand what I did. If you'd been honest with me, I wouldn't have had to hire someone to tell me the truth."

"What exactly have I been dishonest about?"

"Jolene's painting." When I offered her nothing but a blank stare, she continued. "You told me Mason's father was so pleased you liked the painting that he sent it to you as a gift. But on the morning Mason returned your keys, he told me his father was happy to learn you liked the painting . . . *after* you'd received it."

Oh crap. "I think you're taking his words too literally, Mom. Of course I was happy to receive Stuart's gift. I called him to thank him. Told him *again* how much I liked that painting. You're reading something into this that isn't there."

Mom was unmoved. "Perhaps. But how do you explain this job you have with Dr. Coulter when he's not paid wages to anyone in the last three years?"

Apparently Mom and her PI weren't limiting themselves to the Reynoldses' finances. "Dr. Coulter pays me cash. Under the table."

"I don't believe for a minute that Avery Coulter pays you under the table." Mom crossed her arms, undeterred. "But then again, he doesn't have to pay you at all. I know for a fact there is no mortgage on this condo. It's owned outright."

My mind raced for a new lie to shore up the old one. "It's a private mortgage."

Now she was moved. "You're going to sit there and tell me Mason Reynolds loaned you the money for this place without registering the condo as collateral?"

"This is insane, Mom! Stop it."

"I won't. You're not being honest with me. I want to know why. What are you involved in?"

She wouldn't let it go. I hung my head. "You're right. I don't have a mortgage on this place but it's not because I'm running drugs or working for the mob or whatever else you imagine. The Reynoldses gave me the money for the condo. No strings attached. I own it." There. It was out. One less lie to maintain.

Mom dropped to the sofa. "Why would they do that?"

"They were being kind—in remembrance of Dad."

"And Mason went along with the mortgage lie?"

"I asked him to. I'm sorry. I didn't think you'd understand."

"I don't. Did it not give you pause? That they would buy this for you?" Her gaze skated around the room. "What's it worth? A million and a half? More?"

"Wealth is relative, Mom. A couple million is pocket change for the Reynoldses, but I expect your investigator told you as much. They donate more than that to charity every year."

"You're hardly a charity case, and I doubt you gave them a tax receipt for their efforts. What did they expect to gain from their generosity?"

"A relationship with me. They felt like they'd lost a son and brother when they learned Dad had died. I'm their connection to him."

Mom looked away, shook her head. "I can understand their surprise, maybe even their grief, at learning of your father's death, but their connection to your father ended with the death of his son more than twenty years ago."

"That's not how they feel about it. They treat me like a niece, a granddaughter."

She snapped her head back to me. "They are not your blood. You have no connection to those people. And buying this condo for you? It's wildly out of proportion to any reasonable grief they might feel. It's irrational, and I know they aren't that, so there has to be another reason."

That other reason was banging at the back of my head, screaming to be let out. I couldn't let that happen. Not now. My lies aside, if Mom found out about our world, her hatred for the Reynoldses would only be compounded.

"Save yourself some money, Mom. Call off your investigator. Your PI won't get any more information now that the Reynoldses know about him, and Mason's pissed about it."

"I don't care if Mason is pissed about it."

"Mason is not your enemy, Mom, and neither is his father. Blame me. I'm the one who lied to you, not them. They were being kind and generous and this PI business is making me look like an ingrate. It's embarrassing and humiliating. Please call him off."

Mom tilted her head, studying my face with narrowed eyes. Did she believe me? It was hard to tell. The kettle shrieked. She stood. "Would you like a cup of tea?"

It wasn't a yes but it wasn't a no. Maybe she needed time to think about it. "In a few minutes. I'm going to unpack."

I dropped my clothes in the laundry bin and changed into running gear. It was the one daytime activity sure to set my mind to rest. Mason's patience was limited and Mom's PI was testing it. Talk about poking a bear.

After an uncomfortable cup of tea, I excused myself. I warmed up on the lawn and set out without a destination. It was sloppy, but I was distracted. I had too many plates in the air and not enough hands to keep them spinning. Muscle memory took over, and my training kicked in. I stepped into observation gear and plotted my route.

At the twenty-minute mark, I jogged into one of my regular change alleys to turn my jacket inside out. But the sleeve got caught on the cheap bracelet I'd picked up at the airport to hold the tracker. I stopped mid-tug and stared at the locket. ICO had been watching this routine for months. They'd know all my tricks—might even have a drone overhead right now. My quick-change efforts might fool a bloody Redeemer lurking out there, but it was just a show for ICO now. One I had to keep up unless I wanted them to think I was on to them. Damn it.

I carried on with my well-rehearsed routine and doubled back looking like a different jogger. When I returned to the condo, I went straight to the shower. After towelling off, I called Sam to learn what I'd missed since we parted in San Francisco.

"I'm glad you called," Sam said. After I insisted that I was fine, at least physically, he told me he'd gotten an unexpected reaction from Cain.

"He's either a very good actor, or he was genuinely shaken to hear that you and James had been abducted. He offered to relocate you. I couldn't chance that it was a ploy so declined. He came right back with an offer of a security detail."

"No way."

"I know. I told him you'd hate it. I don't think Cain suspects we're on to him, but he's pushing me to find a new case. Something low key that will keep you close to home. Says staying busy is the best way for you to get over what happened. I don't know. He's hard to read. Could be he wants to test our loyalty."

"I think I should take some time off, Sam. Any chance you can stall him?"

"You just assured me you were okay. What's going on?"

A maniacal laugh bubbled out. "How much time is on this burner phone?"

"Sounds like not enough. How about we meet?"

An hour later, I sat in Denny's on Broadway waiting for Sam. As usual, he wandered in fifteen minutes after I did, scouring the room for anything or anyone out of place.

He took the seat beside me with the emergency exit to his left. "All right. Talk to me."

It's strange how time changes everything. Months ago, when Sam was investigating me, he would have been the last person on the list of people I trusted. Now he was at the top of that list, and I needed to let go of a spinning plate or two.

For the first time, I let Sam into our world. It was forbidden—against the rules. He wasn't one of us, but he'd protected our secret and me. He'd risked his job and his freedom for us. He deserved to know what and whom he was dealing with. Most of what I said about the Tribunal and how it functioned was met with a nod, as if he were checking off a box he already had on a list.

I told him everything that had happened, starting with the moment Mom and I found Mason in the living room and ending with my suspicion that ICO had taken my eggs. It was that last detail that enraged him the most. The only detail I held back was what they'd taken from James.

"Thank you for telling me," he said. Sam wasn't often at a loss for words. He was now. He didn't taste the coffee in front of him but gave the mug a quarter turn at regular intervals.

Eventually, he broke the silence. "When are you meeting with Coulter about, you know . . ." He nodded in the general direction of my torso.

"Soon. I need to call him."

"I'll try to hold Cain off, but be prepared. He won't like me stalling."

When I arrived home, I found Mom in the kitchen. She glanced up from her chopping board then carefully arranged thin lemon slices on top of a slab of salmon.

"I'm sorry about earlier," she said. "How you paid for this condo is really none of my business."

"I'm sorry, too. I shouldn't have lied, even if I didn't think you'd understand."

Mom offered a smile. "Thank you for that. Do you think we can move on? Forget about our little spat?"

Little? It felt colossal to me. I pulled her into an embrace, struggling to hold back tears. "I love you."

"I love you, too, sweetheart."

She put the salmon in the oven and we shared a bottle of wine. Our post-spat dinner was sprinkled with awkward conversation and lengthy quiet interludes. It was a relief to go to bed.

In the morning, I called Avery. He'd been waiting to hear from me. My stomach felt sick; I skipped breakfast. I dropped ICO's tracker on my bedside table. ICO might know about Avery, but I couldn't risk their snooping around his records right now. I left Mom a note and slipped out of the condo before she was up.

I drove to Avery's on autopilot, rehashing yesterday's argument with my mother. It had shaken me, but whatever awaited me at Avery's scared me more.

Outside Avery's house, I parked and turned off the engine. What horrific news would he have for me? Had ICO taken from me any chance I had of having children? My outrage had dulled, leaving me numb. Maintaining that level of anger took energy I no longer had. There were only so many battles one person could fight, so many fronts one person could defend simultaneously. So many spinning plates.

My phone rang, startling me. "Are you going to stay out there all day, or are you coming in?" Avery said. I turned in my seat. He stood in the doorway to his home office with his phone to his ear. He started walking toward my car.

"I was waiting for the valet."

Avery chuckled. "You must be lost then. Valet service is at the clinic on Granville."

"Ah, that explains the wait."

Avery opened my door and I hung up. "Hi."

He offered me his hand and I took it. "I have good news for you," he said, and closed my door. "Come inside."

"Victoria is upstairs," he said, assuring me of our privacy as we took seats at his kitchen table. "I've spoken with Dr. Mills from the clinic in San Francisco. He sees no evidence of swelling or bleeding in your ovaries, and I concur."

"Thank god," I said, but Avery put his hand up, halting my premature relief.

"Doesn't mean they didn't extract some eggs—they just didn't damage your ovaries in the process. The literature I reviewed isn't conclusive. There has been some success maturing eggs outside of the body, but the fertilization rates are extremely low."

"What about the one or two mature eggs you thought they might have extracted?"

He pinched his lips and took a breath. Not a good sign. "Did you have sexual intercourse before the MRI?"

"No."

"The one time I'd hoped you had," he said, managing a smile. "There's evidence of blood at the top of your vaginal wall."

"So they got mature eggs."

"It's a possibility. One or two, but again, the odds of them successfully fertilizing those eggs are minuscule."

"Isn't that what fertility clinics do every day? Seems to me they have a lot of success."

"Not exactly. Live birth rates from IVF are 50 percent, give or take, but only under ideal conditions. That's why they dose the egg donors with high levels of fertility drugs. They try to get eight to ten mature eggs in the hopes of increasing their odds. With only one or two eggs to work with, the odds drop dramatically. I'd say there's less than a 25 percent chance your eggs will produce a viable embryo outside the womb."

"Twenty-five percent."

"Probably lower." He clasped his hands and stared at them for a long time. "Are you still experiencing cramps?" he finally asked.

"No. Not since the day I called you. Did you get the blood-test results?"

"They were negative for barbiturates, no elevated hormone levels. Red and white blood cells were normal."

"And James?"

"James isn't my patient."

I nodded. "Of course."

"Less than 25 percent is very low, Emelynn."

"It's not zero."

"What happened? You never told me."

And so I did, swearing him to secrecy when I got to what they'd done to James. When I'd finished the story, he was furious. "What's the Tribunal going to do about ICO?"

"I don't know yet, but I can guess. Sebastian's in Ottawa identifying Cain's network. James is going after Beale's. After everyone who betrayed us is identified, I expect the Tribunal will behave true to form and orchestrate a series of really bad days for them."

Avery's anger dissipated with an exhale that puffed his cheeks.

"First the Redeemers and now ICO." He didn't add *where's it going to end*, but he was probably thinking it. I know I was.

"And your eggs?"

"I don't know, but I can't abandon them despite the low odds. I couldn't bear for a child of mine to be out in the world without any support. That's how I grew up and it was terrifying."

"I know. You were lucky to have survived." He opened his laptop. "If a surrogate isn't involved, your eggs will have been frozen and placed in cryogenic storage. Let me show you what to look for."

After he'd found several examples, he closed his laptop, I thanked him and checked my watch.

"Do you have to go?"

"Mom was sleeping when I left. She'll be worried about me after our argument yesterday."

"Argument? What about?"

"Jolene. Ever since Mason mentioned the name, Mom's been on some kind of mission. Initially, she was subtle about it, but when I was in California, she hired a private investigator to dig a little deeper. Mason discovered that her PI was nosing into his family's finances. He's *thrilled* about it, as you can imagine."

"No doubt. I would be too."

"Then you're not going to like what comes next. Her PI learned that you haven't paid wages in three years. I tried to tell her you paid me cash to get her off the trail."

"What the hell?"

"She didn't believe me. I'm sorry. It's the damn condo. She knows what it's worth. She's having difficulty believing the Reynoldses would buy it for me out of some distant connection to my father."

"No one can accuse her of being naive. What are you going to do?"

"I asked her to call off her PI. Told her Mason knew she'd hired him. That it was humiliating. I'm hoping she listens."

"Whether or not she does, I'll be bringing someone in to reinforce my privacy."

"I'm sorry," I repeated, and wondered if humiliating was the right word. Mortified fit better.

I took a long route home, putting off as long as I could the coming conversation with my mother. She was ensconced in a tub chair, turned toward the Pacific, when I walked in. "Hi," I said.

"Hi. I didn't hear you leave this morning. How's Dr. Coulter?"

"He's fine. I told him about your PI. Sorry, but he needed to know."

"I assumed as much when I read your note."

I barely had time to revel in her nonreaction when a knock at the door made me jump and sent my heart racing. "Are you expecting someone?"

"No."

"I'll get it," I said, and marched down the hall. Anger crawled up my neck. If it was Sebastian or Mason, this would be the last time either of them would be showing up without first checking in downstairs. But then my steps faltered. If it wasn't them, whoever it was had skirted security. I called on my crystal and formed a jolt aimed to stun.

I peeked through the viewer. It was Colin from the front desk. I sighed with relief and recognized my reaction for what it was—one of the repercussions of being abducted. Again. Damn.

When I opened the door, Colin held out a package. A bomb? I hesitated.

"It's marked urgent. I saw you come in the underground. I tried calling, but your phone's out of service."

My worry eased when I read the return address: Jay Em, from Cairabrae. I took the package. "Thanks, Colin." Jay Em. James Moss. Clever, though I was certain James hadn't sent it from Cairabrae. I had the package open before I reached the kitchen. He'd sent me two new phones. Identical.

"Who was it?" my mother asked.

"A package. James sent us new phones."

"Why? Mine's working perfectly."

"I lost mine, and yours and mine are paired. Here," I said, handing her the one with her name on a sticky. "We'll both have new numbers."

She grumbled about it until I reminded her James was keeping us safe. Regardless of Mom's distrust of the Reynoldses, she still seemed to have faith in James.

Sam called my old burner phone at noon. I was on the treadmill and called him back on my new phone so he'd have the number.

"I tried to buy us some time with Cain," Sam said. "Told him I thought you needed a few days off. He was completely sympathetic. Was so concerned about your fitness for work he suggested you see Dr. Penn. He even offered to set up an appointment."

"Shit!" A dull headache pinched the back of my skull.

"Yup, and unless you can think of another way to prove that we're still capable, happy ICO employees, we're going to have to take a case."

Another case meant another plate to spin. "I suppose he has one picked out? Something to showcase another of my *skills*?"

"Surprisingly, no. He's either content to let me choose or he doesn't want to tip me off to the fact that something's changed."

"All right," I said, unable to see a way out of it. "Guess we're taking on a new case. Do you have one in mind?"

"Maybe. A few days ago, a low-level diplomat working out of the Chinese embassy on Granville Street lodged a complaint against a Chinese-Canadian investor to whom he'd entrusted a large sum of money. No one in the department wants it. There's a sea of paperwork to wade through, but he's a foreign diplomat. Cain can't say no. It fits all his criteria."

"Sounds perfectly boring. I hope you aren't counting on my extensive investment knowledge to help with the analysis."

"No, you're safe. We'll ride it out on someone else's coattails for a change. I've got a forensic accountant in mind. A civilian."

We agreed to meet for lunch with the accountant the next day, and Sam would fill us both in on the case.

Chapter Eighteen

At six thirty in the morning, I watched the sky brighten from the balcony with a coffee in my hand. Light danced on the ocean, where distant seagulls spread their wings. In one of the tall pots at the balcony's edge, mauve and purple tulips bobbed gently in the breeze, putting me in mind of Easter eggs. Mornings like this made it possible to imagine a kinder world. I lingered in that fantasy until the cool April air chased me back inside.

When Mom emerged, I made her an omelette. We tested the conversational waters with benign talk of weather and local news. The friction between us, though not gone, had subsided. I wanted to ask her if she'd canned her PI but couldn't bring myself to shatter our truce. Not yet.

We left the condo at the same time. Mom headed to the Apple store downtown for a lesson on her new iPad. I headed to The Teahouse in Stanley Park to meet Sam's accountant friend.

I'd never been to The Teahouse but knew it by reputation. The path to the front door divided a lush, green lawn. Manicured gardens surrounded what was originally an officers' mess. Renovations had turned it into a sprawling upscale restaurant—a definite upgrade from Denny's.

Sam was alone and seated when I arrived. He stood to greet me.

"A suit?" I said, impressed. The restaurant's windows behind him framed a spectacular view of the ocean.

"I was at the embassy this morning," Sam said, as if that explained it. "Took Zhang's statement. He may be a Chinese national, but his English is better than mine."

The table was set with a crisp white cloth, heavy cutlery wrapped in matching linen and an orchid.

Sam flipped through his notepad and sketched out Zhang's complaint, quoting dates and names and large sums of money. I tried, unsuccessfully, to keep up.

"I filed our new case with Cain," Sam said. "Should get him off your back about Penn." A waitress arrived and I ordered iced tea.

When she left, Sam reached for my wrist. "Is your tracker in there?" he asked, absently examining the locket on my new bracelet."

"Yeah," I said.

Sam nodded. "I pushed Cain on the names of the men who were operating the drones that spied on us." I raised my eyebrows in query. He released my wrist. "He's not disclosing their identities. Says it's taken care of."

"Which means he knows who they are," I said. "And who sent them."

"Yup."

Movement at the corner of my eye caught my attention. Sam followed my gaze to the woman approaching with a confident stride, her eyes locked on Sam. She wore a perfectly tailored houndstooth suit. Sam smiled and stood, banging his knee against the table and rattling the china. The woman had a briefcase in one hand and a small purse on a chain over her shoulder. He shook her hand.

"Thanks for coming," he said. "Naomi Russel, this is my colleague, Emelynn Taylor."

She extended her hand. Sam pulled out a chair for her. I couldn't help but notice her arrival had caused a stir with the neighbouring diners. It might have been the figure she cut, but to me, her most striking feature was the white hair she wore to her shoulders. It didn't match her age: she didn't look older than thirty-five.

The waitress delivered my iced tea and took Naomi's order—an espresso.

When we'd resettled, Sam handed her a file and dove into the details of the case. Naomi opened her briefcase on an empty chair and took notes with a pen that looked like a piece of art. She told me it was a Bentley, a gift from her father, and I made a mental note to look it up.

She interrupted Sam to ask a question. He leaned over and flipped through the file to find what she needed. Something about the way he remained pitched forward even after he'd finished his summary drew

my attention. She offered a theory. He nodded thoughtfully. She out-
lined a plan. Sam accepted the details as if they were gifts. He returned
every one of Naomi's smiles, and she was generous with them.

I bit back my own smile. Wow. Sam and Naomi, sitting in a tree.
Now I understood the suit and the luxurious surroundings. Naomi had
likely never seen the inside of a Denny's.

After Naomi left, Sam remained standing until she was out of sight.

"How do you know her?" I asked.

He retook his seat. "She had a break-in."

"That's a little below your pay grade, isn't it?"

"Not when the subject is heading up the forensic audit of one of
the city's biggest money launderers."

"She's very beautiful."

"And smart."

"You going to ask her out?"

"What's the latest on ICO from your people?"

"Don't think I didn't notice that stealthy change of subject, Detective. No word from Mason or Stuart. Or James, come to think of it. But
I did see Dr. Coulter." Sam seemed relieved to hear Avery's perspective
on my stolen eggs, and changed gears.

"Naomi has bought us a week or so. I'll interview Zhang's portfolio
manager this afternoon. You take a few days off. Enjoy some time with
your mother."

I heard from Mason that evening. His email lit up my new phone's
screen. He'd been calling the burner phone and got concerned when he
couldn't reach me. I texted him my new number with an apology and
told him I'd call in five minutes. I excused myself from my mother and
Anderson Cooper and walked to the bedroom.

"How are you?" he said, when he answered.

"Antsy, but don't worry. It's normal post-trauma shit. What's up?"

"Good news. We know who the Redeemer sold out to. He found a
CIA director willing to deal. Told him he'd witnessed something
extraordinary at Cairabrae. The director followed up and was smart
enough to smell a cover-up. He's also one of the very few who know
about ICO. Sadly for the Redeemer, the director was more interested in
getting the top spot at ICO than he was in keeping his word and anni-
hilating the Tribunal. Looks like it's not going to work out for either of
them, but you know what they say—treachery is what treachery gets."

　　　　　　　　　　　　　　　　　　　　　　　JP McLEAN

The CIA? ICO? Who wasn't trying to screw with us? "I didn't know they said that."

"They will now."

Mason sounded smug, which bothered me. People would lose their lives over this. "How many others know about us?"

"I don't expect many. The CIA guy followed the need-to-know rule to protect his territory."

Small mercies. "What's next?"

"That's actually why I called. Sebastian has convened the Tribunal to get consensus on dealing with ICO, and thanks to your mother's private investigator, I can't use my computer for the video conference."

"Why not?"

"Because as soon as I learned the idiot was trying to hack my computer, I seeded a drive with enough misleading information to keep him busy until your mother called him off. She hasn't yet."

"I'm sorry. I asked her to do that two days ago."

"Well, until she does, I can't use the computer. Not for this anyway, and I don't have the time to organize a new one. I need to use yours. I know James set it up. It'll have the level of encryption I need."

"Okay. I'll bring it to you. Where are you?"

"No. I need privacy for this. I'll come to you."

"My mother is here."

"Well then, I can ask her myself to call off her PI."

"Don't you dare! When is the meeting?"

"Eight o'clock."

"I'll arrange for Mom to go out. Will half an hour be long enough?"

"Yeah. Should be."

It was 7:15 p.m. I hung up, changed into my nightshirt and robe and headed back to the living room.

Mom glanced over but didn't comment. Twenty minutes later, I asked, "Want to watch a movie?"

"Are you tired of CNN?"

"They've been on the same loop for a while. Have you seen the new one with George Clooney?" I knew that would tempt her. I found the movie on the streaming box and clicked on the icon.

My mom held out her hands, weighing her options. "Anderson Cooper or George Clooney," she said, juggling her palms. "Tough choice, but I'll go with Clooney."

She drew a chuckle out of me. I quickly looked away so she wouldn't see the hurt behind my smile. I loved her laughter, her wit, and not because she was my mother and beautiful and smart. It was because I liked her. I wanted more of these quiet nights with her. But this night, like our entire adult relationship, was built on a lie. Sadly, I wasn't done lying.

"If only we had one of those fancy sundaes to go with it," I said.

"From Frankie's? That place over by the university?"

"That's the one. We went there the day you arrived."

"I remember. They were good."

"The best," I said. I sighed for show then straightened. "Ready?" I said, with my finger hovering over the play button.

"No. Let's go get a sundae." She checked her watch. "Do you think they're still open?"

"Now? I'm in my pyjamas. I don't feel like changing."

Mom grabbed her tablet from the coffee table. "Look. They're open until nine o'clock. How about I go get us each one?"

"You would? I'd love it!"

Mom took my order, stood and headed for the hall. She dipped into her room and five minutes later called out to me. "I'll be back in a jiffy," she said, and the apartment door opened and closed. Fingers crossed her jiffy lasted thirty minutes.

I checked my watch. It was 7:56, but Mason was already here. I'd sensed him when I suggested the sundaes. He took form in front of the TV.

"She's a beautiful woman, your mother. Too bad she's a thorn in my side."

"Keep your eyes off my mother," I said. I walked him to the dining room table and turned on the laptop. He folded his jacket over the back of a chair and sat down. When I had the browser open, I swung it around to face him. "Do you need anything else?"

"No. And this is a video call, so be quiet and don't get behind me into camera range. They don't need to know you're here."

I left him and returned to the living room to silence the TV and my phone. But curiosity made me return. I stood in the entrance and leaned against the frame.

I recognized Sebastian's voice starting their meeting by checking that all nine Tribunal members were present. "I'd like to open the meeting with an update on the Redeemer situation. Mason?"

"No further news on that front," Mason said.

"You've got a Redeemer who was at Cairabrae in your possession and Redmond Moss at your disposal and you haven't put a lid on it yet?" The sneer in Sebastian's voice made it clear he considered Mason incompetent.

"As you know, these matters are delicate. So as I said, no news."

Sebastian huffed and then continued. "Before we address this business with ICO, I propose we clear up some old business. I call a vote to remove the Tribunal Novem's offer of a seat on this body to Emelynn Taylor."

I'm sure my jaw dropped. Mason pounced. "That issue is hardly critical. We have limited time and urgent business to attend to."

"I disagree," Sebastian said. "Emelynn Taylor is directly responsible for the mess with ICO. She's not fit to take a seat next to us. She should never have been offered it."

I was stunned speechless, but Sebastian's vitriol rolled off Mason without leaving a mark.

"So you've said," Mason countered, his voice calm. That he was able to keep his cool reminded me that he'd dealt with Tribunal politics all his life. "And you also know there are opposing opinions which will take precious time to hear. You can make your case at the next meeting. The urgent issue at hand is ICO."

Another voice concurred. "I agree. Table it, Sebastian."

"Aye," another voice piped in.

"Yes," said another.

"Let's get on to this ICO matter," added someone else.

That was five voices to move on, not that I was counting. Sebastian dutifully caved.

I'd known he didn't support the vote to offer me a seat—he'd told me as much—but he knew damn well the "ICO mess," as he called it, was a shit storm he'd had a hand in creating. The bastard was twisting the truth to make an end run around a seat I wasn't interested in. Why?

I had no time to digest Sebastian's motives before he dove into a summary of the events that led up to James and me ending up in the back of a semi. Our stolen reproductive material wasn't mentioned. Giving no credit to Mason, Sebastian provided the details about the rogue CIA director and the Redeemers' failed attempt to have ICO do their dirty work.

"Cain may not be directly involved," Sebastian said, "but he's aware someone in the CIA infiltrated his ranks. He chose not to share this information with us, but his investigation has proven quite helpful. Regardless, Cain knowingly left us exposed. ICO has unequivocally broken their contract with us. Does anyone here not favour ending this farce of a deal?"

Silence ensued. Sebastian continued. "Good. I anticipated as much. I've already identified two people in Cain's intelligence orbit who need to go. Another one on the civilian intelligence side."

A male voice asked, "What about the players here in the States?"

"I've assigned Stuart Reynolds and James Moss to find the traitors inside ICO."

Assigned? Bullshit! James initiated that, not Sebastian. I nearly convulsed, but Mason didn't react.

Sebastian didn't miss a beat. "Moss's handler, Beale, is most certainly involved. They're working their way back from Beale to identify who else we need to address on that end. Dillon Marshall has agreed to monitor everyone they ID. Dillon, give us a progress report."

I remembered Dillon Marshall from Cairabrae. He was new to the Tribunal, having taken over for his cousin, Carrie, who'd been killed by one of Manse's Redeemers. Dillon wasn't a friend of the Reynoldses.

Dillon cleared his throat and spoke in a clear tenor. "Beale and his boss are being monitored, same with the CIA director. But that's all we have. Moss hasn't been forthcoming with further information. Perhaps I could incentivize him?"

I pushed off the wall. Mason didn't move his eyes from the screen. "I'll speak with my father," Mason said. "Make sure the lines of communication are cleared up."

"Have you assigned anyone to work on the data angle?" another voice asked.

"I ghosted one of our IT people into Cain's war room. He hacked into a computer, found their server and opened a portal. He's now running algorithms remotely. All contaminated data is being tagged. We'll do the same in the States as soon as we find the right computer to gain access. When I give the go-ahead, the tagged data and anything created from it will be wiped without a trace."

"Beale will know whose computer to use," someone said. "Get Moss on him."

Again, I surged forward, incensed that they seemed to feel James was theirs to manipulate.

"Is that wise?" Mason said. "We'll have to eliminate Beale if we use Moss. That may tip our hand and drive the others underground."

"True," Sebastian said. "This operation is far too important to risk raising any flags."

"How long until we're ready to roll?" said a voice I didn't recognize.

"We can't rush this. It's big. It'll take another few weeks to ensure we have all the data trails nailed down and at least that long to set up the final scenarios, get the people we need in place to pull them off."

"It's going to take more than the nine of us," a female voice added.

"You're right," Sebastian said. "I want two Ghosts on each person we identify. This has to come off with precision. There's no room for error. Call in your best contacts. Send me their information. I'll coordinate it."

"What's the end game?" came another voice I couldn't identify.

"Simultaneous elimination of every target," Sebastian said. "Same with the digital sanitation. It'll be difficult to keep it contained, so it's critical that James Moss and Emelynn Taylor remain in their roles with ICO. No one's to tell them in advance of me pulling the trigger. I don't want any leaks."

"What about paper copies of the data?" someone asked.

"The metadata on the digital files will tell us if a copy has been printed," someone answered.

Sebastian's plan, if it was even his, was indeed thorough. After the trigger was pulled, it would be as if time had rolled back to a point before the massacre, when ICO wasn't in our lexicon. Too bad we couldn't bring back the lives lost there.

The meeting wrapped up quickly after that. Mason signed off the conference call. I checked the time. Mom would be home any minute.

"Why didn't you call Sebastian on his bullshit?" I said.

Mason chuffed. "Which particular offence are you referring to?"

"He didn't *assign* your father and James to anything. James was already working the Beale angle and your father volunteered to help."

"Yes, and Sebastian knows it, but he's a politician. He doesn't gain any political currency presenting it that way."

"It's dishonest. So was taking credit from you for uncovering the CIA director."

"He didn't get that without a price," Mason said, and he closed the laptop. I cocked an eyebrow. "He's agreed to a date for the caucus. I'm announcing it as soon as I talk to Dad and clear my schedule."

"Seems Sebastian isn't the only politician. Congratulations. You've been waiting a long time."

Mason stood and reached for his jacket.

"I'm worried about James," I said. "If he doesn't get payback from Fuente and the people who held him captive, he's going to implode. And Dillon still thinks of James as a Tribunal employee. If Dillon tries to pull rank, I'm afraid of what James might do."

"Dillon won't pull rank. Not with my dad involved." Mason shrugged into his jacket.

"Sebastian doesn't know my eggs were stolen."

"He knows. Despite what you think of him, he's not a total cad. He and his men are actively searching for them."

I was taken aback and Mason knew it. "He'll respect your privacy to the point it impacts the Tribunal."

Ah, that was more like the Sebastian I knew. "And what point is that?"

"If he can't find them. We're not there yet." Mason stuffed his hands into his pockets. "I have other news but you have to keep quiet about it until the caucus." He waited until I nodded. "Redmond came through. He helped us identify the last Redeemers. By this time tomorrow, the Redeemer nightmare will finally be over."

It took a moment for his words to sink in. No more Redeemers. No more looking over my shoulder, checking the shadows. I'd be free.

"Did you hear me?" Mason said.

"Yes, but are you sure?"

"Their leadership has been wiped out. Every Redeemer who was at Cairabrae has been eradicated like the vermin they are. And tomorrow, the two remaining recruits will breathe their last. One of them I'm taking care of personally. So yes, I'm sure. It's over."

It's over. With those words, my life jumped tracks. I imagined people who'd won the lottery felt the same shift of tectonic plates. Carson Manse's legacy was finally dead. Neither he nor any of his rabid followers would be coming for me, for my mom, for my covey. Yet the relief I wanted to feel eluded me. It would take time, I supposed, for the reality to take root. I'd been living in fear, hiding from them, for so long, I'd forgotten what life before constant vigilance felt like.

"If the threat we've all been living with is really over, I don't understand why you aren't announcing it right away. This is welcome news."

"It is, and Sebastian would like nothing more than to claim credit for wiping out the Redeemers under his leadership. But that's my victory. I'll share the news at the caucus, after I'm sworn in. It'll set the right tone, be a good start to my leadership of the Tribunal."

"Political currency."

"You're learning."

Sadly, I was, and it was further confirmation that the Tribunal was a snake pit. Jump in there and you'd get a nasty bite.

"Thank you, Mason. From the bottom of my heart, thank you. We can't ever let something like that happen again. You have to make sure of it."

"I will. In time. But the more pressing issue is—"

We both turned to the sound of a key in a lock. Mason looked at me. "Not a word about the Redeemers until the caucus," he said, and then he disappeared.

My mother called out, "Sundae delivery!" I heard her keys drop into the dish on the hall table and moments later she arrived in the kitchen. "You should have seen the lineup."

"Looks yummy." I helped myself to the one with peanut butter chunks. She took the caramel. It wasn't until we were seated on the sofa that I sensed Mason leave.

"Do you feel all right, sweetheart? You look a little flushed."

"Do I? I feel fine," I said, and pushed the play button.

Chapter Nineteen

Though I watched the movie, I didn't see it. Mom stood and stretched when the credits rolled up, and I reached for the controls. I remember pecking Mom on the cheek and walking to my bedroom, closing the door. I tasted toothpaste, so I must have brushed my teeth. I stared at the ceiling above the bed for a long time.

Typhoid Mary had left the building. The threat of death by Redeemer no longer dogged me or cursed those close to me. I had my life back, and ICO's grip on my freedom was fading fast. I could reach out to the covey again, and Molly. Maybe Eden would come for a visit. With each new revelation, my smile grew. I could breathe again. When I visited Avery, neither of us would worry what might follow.

The only precautions I'd have to take were the same ones any other Flier or Ghost would take.

The spinning plates were slowing down.

When morning broke, fresh excitement bubbled up in me. I leapt out of bed, rushed to the bathroom and practically skipped to the kitchen to make coffee. Neither the grey day nor the drizzle outside dampened my spirits. In fact, if I didn't get out for a run and bleed off some of this energy, I'd be keyed up all day. I dressed, ate a granola bar and headed downstairs.

This time I consciously chose my route and ran one of the loops around UBC. I slowed at the children's park. It was deserted. Water pooled beneath the sling swings and dotted the painted bench the mothers usually occupied. How was Sebastian's search for my eggs going? I wondered.

I sat on a lower rung of the monkey bars and dialled Sam. I told him what I'd learned about the CIA director, but I kept Mason's confidence about the last Redeemer.

"This CIA guy tapped Beale but not me? I gotta say, I'm feeling a little left out." Sam laughed, and it sounded a lot like relief. "Did Sebastian say what Cain's role was in this?"

"Only that Cain knew ICO personnel had been involved and that he's actively investigating. Sebastian seems to have access to the investigation."

"Did anyone mention whether Cain knew I'd been holding back?"

"No. Your name didn't come up. And believe me, that's a good thing."

"Yeah. But I'd sure like to know if Cain's aware I've been holding back, or what I've been holding back."

Mom was dressed and in the living room with a coffee when I emerged from the shower.

"You were up early this morning," she said, looking up from her iPad.

I poured another coffee, refilled hers and she read me the morning headlines from the CBC Brief in her inbox.

Sharing the news over a coffee—this was how mornings should be. We were back to normal. It gave me the courage to ask her if she'd called off her PI.

Mom kept her eyes on the iPad. "He hasn't returned my call."

"Call him again. Please."

"Sure," Mom said, and before I could press the issue, my phone rang.

"Turn on CNN," Sam said. "Right now."

At the urgency in his voice, I lurched to the edge of my seat and grabbed the controller.

"What is it?" my mother asked.

The screen lit up with footage from a helicopter. The crawl at the bottom identified a massive explosion and possible terrorist attack in California. Charred bits of debris were strewn over a large area.

Breaking News flashed on the screen, and the feed cut to an announcer—but I didn't hear her. I stared in disbelief at the pristine roadside sign for Vector Labs to her right and the columns of smoke still rising from its ruins behind her.

I raised the phone to my ear. "I'll call you back." I hung up on Sam's protests and immediately dialled James. He didn't pick up.

I dialled Stuart. It went to voice mail. I dropped my hand to my lap. One thought took up all the space in my head: Were they hurt?

I dialled Mason. No answer.

"Isn't Vector Labs the company you mentioned a few days ago?" Mom asked. "The one you'd gotten some calls from?"

My phone rang. I willed it to be James. It was Sam. "Get out. Take your laptop and your phone and get out of there."

"What's happening?" I asked.

"I don't know yet, but if someone at the CIA or inside ICO is cleaning up, you'll be on their list. Leave your tracker behind. I've dispatched a car to your service entrance. Go. Now!"

Panic quickened my pulse. I hung up and turned to Mom.

"What's wrong?" she said.

"Sam has sent a car for us. We have to go."

"Go where?"

I stood and inhaled a deep, calming breath. It didn't work. "I don't know."

"What are you talking about?"

"Take your phone, your iPad, some clothes. Hurry. Meet me at the door in two minutes."

I raced down the hall to my room knowing I would never forget the look of terror on my mother's face.

I grabbed my bag, threw in some clothes and my laptop and tossed the bracelet toward my pillow. When I arrived at the door, Mom wasn't there. I ran to her room. She'd pulled out her suitcase and was scrambling to fold the clothes that lay scattered on the bed.

"There's no time." I jammed the garments in and closed the lid. She winced as I yanked the zippers closed. "Come on. We gotta go." I grabbed her suitcase and ran back to the door. Mom sprinted behind me, struggling into her jacket with her purse in her hand.

I locked the door and turned to find Mom punching the elevator button. "Stairs," I said, and passed her, hurrying to the stairwell door. We ran down five flights then cut back into the building and called the elevator.

Sweat beaded Mom's forehead. "It'll be all right," I said, taking a stab at reassuring her.

From the underground parkade, we took a little-used service hall.

I cracked open the door. A grey unmarked waited for us. Roberta Montgomery sat behind the wheel. I opened the back door and Mom crawled in. I tossed in our bags and followed her.

"How about you ladies duck down," Roberta said, as she shoulder checked and calmly pulled out around the garbage dumpsters. Roberta had helped hunt down Carson Manse. I hadn't seen her in six months, but she hadn't changed—still wore a suit and no-nonsense short hair. Mom and I folded over our bags.

"Where are we going?" I asked.

"I'm still awaiting word. Until then, we're on a scenic tour, and I'll make sure no one's tagging along."

"Thank you for coming."

"Just like old times."

"I didn't think Sam worked with your team anymore."

"Not since he got kicked upstairs, but he has friends. We've got each other's backs."

"Thank god for that. Mom, this is Roberta Montgomery. Roberta, Laura Aberfoyle."

"Pleased to meet you, Laura."

"You too," Mom squeaked, and she reached for my hand. I held on tight, trying desperately not to think about why James hadn't picked up.

Roberta's running commentary kept us abreast of our route around UBC. She circled between East Mall and West Mall and finally made her way onto Northwest Marine Drive. She left the university's grounds and passed Spanish Banks. When she reached Locarno Beach, she pulled into the parking area and turned off the engine. "You can sit up. No one followed."

My mother tidied her hair as she darted furtive glances out the windows. "Will someone please tell me what's going on?"

Roberta glanced at me in the rear-view mirror. I answered. "I can't, Mom. Not until I talk with Sam."

Mom pursed her lips. I knew she wasn't happy with my answer, but I also knew she wouldn't cause a scene in front of Roberta.

Roberta's attention was drawn to a beep from her onboard computer. She reached for the ignition. "We have an address," she said, and pulled out.

We drove east to Cambie Street and then south to Twelfth Avenue. She crossed Kingsway and zigzagged through an old neighbourhood in Kensington. We slowed to a crawl in front of a row of three Vancouver

Special homes then turned into the back lane. The garage door of the middle two-storey stuccoed home was open. We pulled in and the door trundled down behind us.

Roberta released the door locks and got out then opened the door for my mother. The stretch of Roberta's arm pulled her jacket aside, exposing her gun and the shield she wore on her hip. Mom was staring at her hardware when I scrambled out the other side. The interior door to the house opened, and I froze until Dino Martinez stepped out.

"Let me help you with that," Dino said, lumbering over to grab my mom's suitcase. Dino was as big as ever; his belly was always first into a room.

"Mom, Dino Martinez. Dino, this is my mom, Laura Aberfoyle." He nodded his greeting and Mom mumbled something I didn't catch. Roberta led the way inside and Dino locked the interior door behind us.

I'd never been inside one of these 1960s-era Vancouver Specials. We walked the length of the house and up the stairs. Dino dropped Mom's suitcase in the kitchen.

"What is this place?" Mom asked.

"It's a safe house," Roberta said. "No one but us and Jordan know you're here."

Dino reached for his phone. "It's Jordan. He's at the door. Take them into the living room," he said, as he pulled his gun from its holster. Alarmed, my mother grabbed my arm and Roberta ushered us around the corner. Dino headed down the stairs to the landing and moments later, I heard Sam's voice.

Sam and Dino thundered up the stairs, Dino with a paper grocery bag in his arms. Sam looked to me and then my mom. He halted. "Laura, nice to see you again. Emelynn? A word." He turned and headed toward the back of the house. I rushed to follow.

He stepped into a bedroom at the end of the hall and closed the door behind me. "Any word from Moss?"

"No answer," I said. "Same with Stuart. Same with Mason."

"All of them?"

"I'm scared, Sam. After what we've just been through, there's no way James wouldn't return my call."

"Goddamnit!"

"Anything from ICO?"

"Nothing." He rubbed his face with his hands. "How much does your mom know?"

"I told her ages ago about the calls I received from Vector. She connected the dots right away when she saw the news coverage."

"Does she know about ICO?"

"No. She thinks you're still working on Manse's missing accomplice."

With his hands on his hips, Sam stared at his shoes. "We can work with that, but the less she knows, the easier it will be for us."

I told myself it wouldn't be a new lie, just a perpetuation of an old one. "All right. I'll follow your lead."

Back in the living room, Mom and Roberta were having a quiet conversation. Dino sat at a monitor in the kitchen watching feeds from security cameras around the house. Mom and Roberta looked up as Sam approached. He sat opposite Mom and leaned forward with his elbows on his knees.

"I'm sorry for all this. It's just a precaution. You know about the explosion at Vector Labs?"

Mom nodded.

"It may well turn out to be an accident, but I thought it best to be proactive, just in case."

"In case of what, Detective?"

"Call me Sam, please. Emelynn told us about the calls she received from Vector Labs. Given that we still haven't apprehended Carson Manse's associate, in the unlikely event the two are connected, we thought it best to get you both out of harm's way."

Mom frowned. "You think Manse's associate found my daughter?"

"Until we know what caused that explosion, we'll take every precaution."

"How long until you know?"

"A day or two." Sam stood. "Detectives Montgomery and Martinez are two of our best. You'll be safe here."

Mom thanked him and he addressed me. "I'll check in later. Keep your phone on."

"Where are you going?" I asked.

"Walk me out," Sam said. Neither Roberta nor Dino moved.

When we were out of earshot, Sam stopped. "I've got someone watching your building. If anyone tries to target you there, I'll know."

"What about you? If I'm a target, so are you."

"That's why I'm going back to the office. I doubt ICO or whoever this is will blow up the station, and the only other way they can get to me there is to arrest me, which would draw too much attention."

"Shit."

"Yeah, that about sums it up. Let me know the minute James calls."

If he calls, I thought, fighting back the fear. "I will. Thanks, Sam. Be careful."

I made us a dinner of sandwiches from the groceries Sam had brought. Afterwards, Roberta went to lie down so she could relieve Dino at midnight. Mom and I took up a game of rummy. Twice I phoned James from the bathroom. By nine o'clock, Mom and I gave up trying to play cards and each picked a bedroom.

With my phone in my hand, I curled onto my side and willed James to call. I dozed, and my dreams circled a drain to hell. I woke with a lurch at every unfamiliar creak of the house.

When my phone vibrated, I lurched awake once again. "Hello?"

"It's James."

Swamped with relief, I inhaled a ragged breath. "What happened? Where are you? Is Stuart with you? Why didn't you call?"

"Hey, slow down. I'm okay, so is Stuart."

"I can hardly hear you."

"I'm in a hotel bathroom running the shower. Beale suspects. I couldn't call. I think he's using a listening device."

"Did you do it?"

"Damn right. But I couldn't have done it alone. Thanks to you, I didn't have to."

"Well thanks to you, Mom and I are at a safe house. My mom, James! You could have texted. Done something to warn me."

"I'm sorry. We were on the fly. Still are, and Beale's dogging me."

"Are you in danger?"

"Not if I stay ahead of Beale."

"Does he know it was you?"

"I can't be sure. The day I left Cairabrae, he shoved a missing-person case down my throat. He's been monitoring me ever since. Makes me wonder if he's on to the fact that I know he betrayed me. But he can't connect me to Vector. Every move I've made is in connection with the missing-person case. I gotta go. I'll call when I can."

"Stay safe," I said, and hung up. I kept a cap on my anger, going over James's explanation, convincing myself that he wouldn't have put me and my mother through this trial without a good goddamn reason.

Sam didn't put as much emphasis on James's reasoning as he did his methods. "If Moss knows Beale suspects him, Moss will keep moving, at least until the cause of the explosion is determined. Looks like we're going to find out how good Moss is," Sam said, and warned me to stay put.

I couldn't get back to sleep. Roberta was at the monitor when I left the bedroom. It was four o'clock in the morning. "Can I make you a coffee?" I asked.

Sam called again an hour later. "A body's been found in the rubble," he said. "It's Fuente. They IDd him a few hours ago."

My stomach sank. James hadn't told me. Worse, he'd unknowingly jeopardized the Tribunal's methodic plan of attack on ICO.

"Any talk of murder? Foul play?"

"None. The main blast occurred in the lab closest to Fuente's office. He was the only casualty," Sam said. "The employees who made it out said an alarm had gone off."

"Has the cause of the explosion been identified yet?"

"Not definitively. The gas company repaired a leak a few weeks ago. Investigators are speculating a faulty repair."

"When will we know for sure?"

"By the end of the day, I expect. Hang tight."

"You too." I hung up and pulled on my Pollyanna pants.

Dino relieved Roberta at six in the morning, and the waiting continued.

By the time Mom wandered out of her room, word of the casualty had hit the mainstream news outlets. The recent gas-line repair, however, had yet to come out, and the cause of the explosion was still fodder for endless speculation.

Stuart checked in at 8:00 a.m. Neither Dino nor my mom said a word as I retreated to my room and closed the door. "Are you in one piece?" I asked.

"I'm fine. Sorry to have worried you, my dear, but it couldn't be helped."

He filled in the details that James, in his rush to get off the phone, hadn't mentioned. Maybe I was over-sensitive, but I couldn't quite shake my disappointment that James hadn't tried harder to get a message to me.

"Have you heard from Mason?" I asked.

"No, but I didn't expect to. He was tied up yesterday with a disposal issue I'm sure you're aware of."

"Yes, I know. The last Redeemer. Politics hardly seems like a good enough reason to hold back that information from the coveys. The Redeemers have terrorized all of us."

"Mason knows what he's doing. Staying vigilant a little longer than strictly necessary will be seen as a wise precaution."

I hadn't thought of that, but then again, I wasn't a politician. "Did you hear about the Tribunal's meeting?"

"No. What happened?"

"I don't think they're going to like what you and James have been up to." I told him about their plan for simultaneous elimination of the threat.

"Ah yes, best-laid plans and all that," Stuart said, sounding rather more casual about it than I'd expected. "That explains Sebastian's message."

Stuart assured me he could handle Sebastian's wrath. We hung up after I promised to keep him apprised of my whereabouts.

With my hand on the door handle, I paused, thinking about my mother. She was on the sofa out there, pale and frightened, pretending to read something on her iPad. A lifetime of lies lay between us. The lies had been simple in the first few years after Jolene gifted me. *I like sitting in the dark. I tripped. I fell.* After I moved back to BC, the lies had spun so far out of control that our relationship was now more lie than truth. I ached to strip away the lies, to go back in time and tell her about the day on the beach when Jolene changed my life forever. But that was impossible. The damage was done. All I could do was pray I could keep her safe—from me, my lies and from my world.

Shortly after five that evening, my prayers were answered: the explosion was deemed an accident and Fuente's death, a tragic loss.

Chapter Twenty

Roberta drove us home.

Back in the condo, Mom and I sat like zombies on the sofa staring out the window before us.

"I hadn't realized this is what your life has been like these past few months," Mom said.

Another apology tumbled out of my mouth, and I reassured her that the last two days' events were not the norm.

"Was it Vector Labs that you and Sam went to see in California?"

There was little point in denying it. "Yeah. It was."

"Maybe you should rethink the work you're doing to help Sam. It's putting you in danger."

I had no response for her. My work—what I was—put me in danger on more levels than I cared to think about. Denying any of it would be yet another lie.

Mom stood. "I need to stretch my legs, get some air," she said. "I'll pick up something for dinner."

She hadn't invited me to join her. I didn't blame her. She probably needed a break from me and my drama. Hell, I needed a break from me and my drama.

After she left, I did what I always did when I couldn't turn off my mind: I cleaned. Something about the mindless tasks calmed me. I sparkled the bathroom, made my bed, found the tracker bracelet and slipped it on. I cleaned the kitchen sink, sorted the laundry and after I put away the vacuum, I boiled the kettle. While tidying, I'd found the invitation to Molly's baby shower. It was a Jack and Jill, so the husbands and boyfriends would be there. Just one more slice of normal I'd never taste. I tossed the invitation into the garbage and made a cup of camomile tea.

My first sip was still in the cup when I sensed Mason's arrival. "Mom's gone out," I said, and he materialized. I was tempted to scold him about not using doors, but one glance at his scowl and I knew something was wrong. So much for the calm I'd managed. It had lasted all of two minutes. "What is it?"

He tossed a laptop on the sofa beside me. I shot my hand out and grabbed it before it bounced to the floor. Clearly, the computer was not his. "Take a look," he said, and peeled off his gloves.

I set my tea down. The screen lit up when I opened it. On it was a spreadsheet. I scrolled through a long list of names I didn't recognize, next to addresses from all over the world and amounts of money in the fifty-thousand-dollar range.

"What am I looking at?" I said.

"Confidential details about the recipients of the Reynolds Family Trust."

That was a surprise. I looked up. "You have a trust?"

His scowl remained firmly entrenched. I didn't know why. "It supports the most vulnerable of our kind."

"Impressive." I referred back to the spreadsheet. There were over a hundred names representing a half million dollars, all distributed last year. Why would that piss Mason off? What they were doing through the fund was admirable, generous. Looking for clues as to Mason's ire, I took a closer look at the names, the addresses, emails. Nothing popped out.

And then something did.

"Whose computer is this?"

"It belongs to Michael Draper. Your mother's private investigator."

Oh no. "How did he get this information?"

"How he got it has been taken care of. The pertinent question is why is he still digging?"

"I don't know. I thought Mom had called him off. Wait . . . how did you get his computer? What did you do to him?"

"He's alive. Unconscious but breathing. When he wakes, he'll find his computer missing and his phone and cloud account wiped clean."

"Jesus, Mason. Now he'll know for sure he's on to something."

Mason leaned in. "Which wouldn't have happened if your mother had fired the man when I first brought him to your attention." He'd bit out the words through pursed lips.

I leapt up and met his aggression head-on. "Back the hell off. It's not like I can make her do it, and after the business with Jolene and spending last night at a safe house, trust between us isn't exactly at an all-time high."

"Damn it, Emelynn! You're so busy digging a hole you can't see how bloody deep it is. Now it's caving in and you're standing in the pit of it. Stop fucking digging! Tell her about us!"

"I won't. I can't. God, there are so many lies. She'd never speak to me again."

"Fine! Then kindly tell your mother the next time I find Michael Draper in my business, he won't survive. And that's not a lie." Mason grabbed the computer and disappeared.

My heart thumped as I stared into the empty space Mason had vacated.

When I turned around, my mother stood in the doorway, her face ashen.

Plates and their spindles came crashing down around me.

My feet grew into the floor, paralyzing me. My mind caught little anomalies: mom's lopsided coat collar, grease stains on the paper bag in her arms, the shoes she would normally have kicked off.

"Where's Mason?" she asked, her voice barely a whisper.

I said the only word that came to mind. "Gone."

"He was here. I heard you two arguing."

How much had she heard? I grasped at the slender hope she hadn't seen what I feared. Maybe I could salvage this. "Let me take that," I said, and stepped toward her.

She jerked away from me and walked into the empty space Mason had left. She stood there, swivelling her head from side to side. She then walked into the kitchen and set the bag down. She stared at the arm of her coat where the grease had soaked through.

"Mom?"

She didn't look up. "Am I losing my mind?"

"What are you talking about?"

She looked up slowly and something raw in her eyes stared back, something I'd never seen before. "He's not in here, not out there. Not on the balcony. Where is he?"

"You . . . you must have missed him."

Mom spoke slowly, reinforcing her words with steel. "Don't fucking lie to me."

I had no words.

"I just watched a man vanish. Men don't do that. Nothing does that." Tears rimmed her eyes and then spilled over. I stepped forward but she stopped me with her hand and fierce determination on her face.

"He said, 'Tell her about us.' You tell me. Right now."

I desperately wanted to soothe her. Tell her it would be all right. But it wouldn't be all right. It would never again be all right.

My worst fear was unfolding and I couldn't stop it. I wrapped my arms around myself. "You'd better sit down for this." I turned and walked blindly to the bank of windows in the living room. I stood before them, numb, as I stared into the darkening night.

In the window's reflection, I saw Mom inch into the living room and gingerly lower herself into one of the chairs. She stared at my back.

"I met Jolene when I was twelve."

It was the start of a very long conversation, though conversation implies two people talking, which wasn't the case. I talked, she listened. She didn't move, she didn't ask a single question. It took an hour to get through the lies that had defined my high school and university years, and to explain my decision to return to the cottage. She sat stone-faced through it all.

During the second hour, I told her about how Avery found me; how Jackson, Eden and Alex taught me how to fly; how Avery trained me. I told her about my covey; how Avery and Jackson had both discovered Jolene Reynolds's identity; how I'd learned that I could ghost, just like Mason had. I felt as though I was sacrificing everyone I knew and loved to justify my lies. It left me sick.

I never got to the ugly side: the Tribunal, Redeemers, ICO. She stood, walked to her bedroom without looking back and closed the door. I didn't know which detail had broken her, or if it was the accumulated weight of it all that had proven too much.

I went to my room, turned off my phone and curled into a ball on my bed. There were no tears. *Shame, regret, remorse* were mere words with no needling emotion. This was what empty felt like.

Sometime in the night, I woke. I padded down the hall. Her door was open, her room empty except for her phone, which she'd left on the dresser. I crawled into her bed and fell asleep in her scent.

There are times in life when the mind can be fooled for a brief moment upon waking, a blissful reprieve before reality comes crashing down. This wasn't one of those times. The morning brought with it no illusion. I wasn't fooled, not even for a split second. I felt as empty upon waking as I had when I'd closed my eyes.

I checked every room, but Mom hadn't returned. My lies had driven the final wedge between us. I didn't blame her. What I'd done was unforgivable. I couldn't protect her from me or my lies. She should put as much distance as possible between us.

It seemed pointless to change into clean clothes. Curled in the corner of the sofa with a blanket over my legs, I watched the sky lighten. Childhood memories flooded in: collecting shells on the beach; Saturday-morning laughter in the cottage; my father with a stack of papers in the study; Nanny Fran.

Every time the words *if* and *only* connected in my head, I pushed them out and dug deep for another memory: Mom and Dad dancing in the living room; Mom kneeling in the flower bed wearing gardening gloves; Nanny Fran making gooey grilled-cheese sandwiches. I closed my eyes, thankful for so many good memories. Hopefully, when the pain of my deception passed, Mom would also remember the good times and not so much the bad.

A knock on the door broke me out of my reverie. What now? I debated not answering it but eventually stood and wrapped the blanket around my shoulders. I hadn't made it to the door before I heard a key in the lock and halted. The door opened and Sam burst into the hall ahead of Colin.

He stopped and dragged a gaze from my head to my feet then turned to Colin. "Thank you. I'll take it from here."

"You need to get your phone fixed, Ms. Taylor," Colin said. "We can't reach you otherwise."

"I will. Sorry for your trouble."

The door closed and Sam put his hands on his hips. A lecture hung in the air. So much for *take a few days off, enjoy time with your mother.* I turned and headed back to the living room dragging a corner of the blanket behind me.

Sam followed, stomping. "What the fuck is going on? Where's your phone?"

"I needed a break. I turned it off." I reclaimed my seat in the corner of the sofa.

Sam ranted behind me. "Well, that's just fucking terrific! What the hell is wrong with you?"

He left me and I heard him clomping through the condo, opening every door, muttering threats and obscenities. When he returned he stood before me. "Where's your mother?"

"She left."

"Where'd she go? When?"

"Some time last night. I don't know where."

Sam ran his hand through his hair. "What happened?"

"Mason came by last night. We argued. She heard some things she shouldn't have. And then she saw something she shouldn't have."

"Damn." Sam folded into the closest chair. "You told her?"

"I didn't have much choice. She thought she was losing her mind."

"How did you leave things with her?"

"Not very well. I unpacked all the lies from the time I met Jolene. Mom didn't ask a single question. Didn't say a word. I told her everything—well, almost everything. She walked out before I could finish. Went to her room. She was gone when I checked this morning."

"Do you want me to find her?"

"No. She doesn't want to be found. She left her phone behind."

Sam leaned forward, puffed out his cheeks on an exhale. "She'll come around. She needs some time is all."

"Thanks, Sam, but she's not coming back. I don't blame her. I don't blame Mason. This is on me. At least she knows the truth now."

"It wasn't so long ago I was in your mother's position. That night at Cairabrae, when we got into that helicopter and you ghosted me out of it before it crashed. Saved my life. I didn't appreciate the whole saved-my-life aspect for days. All I could think about was this world of yours I hadn't known about that existed all around me. I'm a goddamn detective, and I hadn't picked up on a single clue. It's a lot to process, Emelynn. Give her time."

I didn't realize I was crying until Sam picked up a box of tissues and shoved it in my general direction. "Got any coffee in this joint?" he said, and headed to the kitchen. I didn't follow. If he wanted coffee bad enough, he'd figure it out.

He returned sometime later with two mugs and handed me one whitened to the exact shade of caramel I liked. Guess he'd paid attention all those times at Denny's.

He sat beside me. "Stuart phoned me," he said. "You hadn't checked in. He couldn't reach you. I just texted him, but you should call him."

"I will."

He held his phone in his left hand, the coffee in his right, and swiped across the screen with his thumb. When he'd found what he was looking for, he held it up to me. "Have you seen this guy before?"

The photo had been taken in a morgue. Even though his hair was slicked back and his eyes were closed, I knew who it was. It was the man from the other side of the glass wall; the man with wiry, unkempt eyebrows and shiny black shoes.

"I don't know his name, but yeah. He was in the semi with me, outside the glass wall. What happened to him?"

"James, I suspect. What about this woman?" He held up a different morgue mug shot.

"No. I don't recognize her. How'd they die?"

"Drowned. Kayaking accident. Believable, except the woman's husband is telling authorities she was afraid of the water."

"James is being reckless. He's going to tip them off."

"Or he already has. This business with ICO isn't over. Cain's on his way."

"Here?"

"Yup. Wants a face-to-face. On the tarmac at the south airport."

"What's wrong with your usual protocol? Your secure channel?"

"Cain believes it's been hacked."

"By us?"

"He wasn't specific, but it's the face time that concerns me. He's flying in on a Challenger jet, but I also know a CP-140 Aurora flew into Vancouver last night. It's a long-haul military aircraft. Makes me wonder if Cain is aiming to apprehend me and take me somewhere I doubt I'll want to go."

"You can't meet with him."

"I don't have a choice. Which is why I need you back in the game. Put aside what happened with your mother and focus."

"When are you meeting?"

Sam looked at his watch. "In two hours. I want you there. I need you to cover me."

"As a Ghost."

"It's what you do best. If Cain's intent is to take me into custody, can you get me out of there?"

"I don't know. Is his jet airtight?"

"No. It's the first thing I checked."

"Then I can do it."

"That's what I was hoping you'd say. We've got to get a move on. I want to get to the airport before he lands, see if he's flying with an escort and see who's coming or going from his jet before our scheduled meet and greet."

I pushed the blanket off my shoulders and stood. "Then I'd better have a shower and get changed."

While Sam finished his coffee, I showered, retrieved my phone and turned it on. I'd lost an entire morning. It was already past noon. Stuart had called four times, Colin twice, Sam three times. Nothing from Mom. I dialled Stuart and put him on speakerphone while I got dressed, and told him what had happened with my mother. Like Sam, he tried to reassure me that she'd come around. But neither Sam nor Stuart had been deceived for years by their own child, their only flesh and blood.

"Sam told me two kayakers have been found," I said. "One of them looks familiar. Do you know anything about it?"

"Heard it was an accidental drowning."

I raised an eyebrow. "You sure about the accidental part?"

"Quite."

"I don't suppose the male victim knew where my eggs ended up?"

"Sadly, he wasn't able to enlighten us."

"By *wasn't able*, do you mean wouldn't or couldn't?" I asked.

"Sometimes it's best not to ask those questions."

"Please don't tell me James isn't even asking. This is important to me."

"I know, but try to understand, there's very little room for flexibility in situations such as these."

Which meant the answer to my question was *couldn't*. I tried not to dwell on the critical piece of information that might have drowned along with Shiny Shoes.

"How did Sebastian take the news that you and James were colouring outside the lines?"

"As expected, but we came to an understanding. James will have his retribution."

"You're not done yet?"

"Not quite. I told Mason I'd return to Cairabrae by week's end. He's anxious to plot our course."

"Mason's been anxious for five years. I have other news. Cain's on his way here. He wants Sam to meet him at the airport, on board his aircraft." I glanced down at the bracelet on my wrist and removed it. "I'm going with him in case he needs me to get him out of there."

"Call Sebastian. He's probably on top of it, but make sure he knows."

"Even if I had Sebastian's number, which I don't, I wouldn't call him."

"I'll text it to you. And don't even think about not making the call. We all have to step up, even you."

Calling Sebastian made me want to vomit, but Stuart ensured I couldn't shirk it by copying Sebastian on the text. So much for the promise I made to never call him again, I thought, and dialled his damn number.

Sebastian hadn't known. Cain's flight and his meeting with Sam weren't on Cain's official schedule. As far as Sebastian knew, Cain was addressing new recruits in Hangar 11 at the Ottawa airport.

"How fortuitous for us that you're tagging along. I'll have a package delivered to you within the hour. It's a bug. Plant it on Cain. Let me know when it's done."

I stared at the phone. He'd hung up. No *would you mind*, or *please*, or *thank you*. Sebastian at his finest.

CHAPTER TWENTY-ONE

S am wasn't pleased we had to wait for Sebastian's package. He paced behind the sofa with his hands on his hips. "Cain is skirting official channels. He knows someone's tracking him, which means he's already sweeping regularly for bugs."

"If he checks after your meeting, he'll find Sebastian's bug," I said. "He'll know where it came from."

"Yup. It's what I'd do."

"Sebastian's slipping."

"From what I've heard about the man, he'd consider it a calculated risk."

"Yeah, and you and I are expendable."

"If Cain's plan isn't to arrest me, he'll do a pre-departure sweep after I deplane. If the aircraft's clean, I'll be off the hook. After the sweep, that's when you can plant Sebastian's bug."

As promised, the package was delivered within the hour. Two bugs, not one. I tucked the tiny bugs into my pocket, and Sam and I headed to Cowley Crescent, near the airport, where a viewing platform had been constructed to get aviation enthusiasts off the shoulder of the road.

Sam parked, locked his side arm in a case in the trunk and handed me a pair of binoculars. He pulled the strap of his long-lens camera over his shoulder. An elderly gentleman in a wool sweater and cap nodded hello as we mounted the platform's stairs. The young boy with him had a scope to his eye.

"Have you spotted the Aurora?" Sam asked.

The boy turned to Sam, his face lit up. "An Aurora's here? Where?"

"North and west, past the hangars," Sam said, pointing.

The boy raced to the northwest edge of the outlook. "Wow, Gramps! Look at that," he said. "That's a CP-140 Aurora. Don't see that one very often."

"Good spotting," Sam said, and he raised his camera. "And it hasn't moved," he added, under his breath. We had a perfect view of the incoming air traffic.

Sam swung his lens in a wide arc. He'd already briefed me on the size and shape of Cain's Bombardier Challenger. "It'll come from there," Sam said, nodding to where several specks above the horizon approached. Each speck turned into an aircraft as it got closer and lined up for landing.

Sam never lowered his camera. After another ten minutes, he said, "He's here." As the dull grey jet turned, I caught sight of the Canadian Air Force insignia emblazoned on its flank and the Canadian flag on its tail. I watched as the jet landed. Sam lowered the binoculars and turned to me. "No escort."

We said our goodbyes to the boy and his grandfather and trotted to the car. After we'd buckled up, Sam floored it. When we got near CCTV range of the parking lot, he slowed and I disappeared. After Sam parked, I drifted alongside him into the terminal. He'd brought his camera. We were twenty minutes early for his meeting.

He wandered to a bank of windows overlooking the runway. The Challenger was on the tarmac in the distance. She wasn't at a gate and her door remained closed. Sam took a quick glance around. "Go charge your batteries. I'm going to stay here and watch. The special services counter behind me will arrange my transport out there. I'll text you when I'm leaving."

"I'll be in the ladies'," I said, and breezed to the washroom. I blew through the restroom door and re-formed inside the stall at the far end. I'd have to thank Sam later. Working was infinitely better than dwelling on events I had plenty of guilt about but no control over.

When Sam's text came in, I ghosted and pushed out of there. He'd already passed through the special services area and exited through a back door. I caught up to him as he hoisted himself into a golf cart. His camera was gone.

"Gotcha," I whispered into his ear. His escort was an armed man in uniform. As we headed out to the tarmac, the Challenger's door lay open, her steps extended.

I kept pace with the golf cart. When it stopped, I was first on board.

The interior was luxurious despite the insignia which suggested austerity and the absence of flight attendants waiting to take coats and hand out flutes of champagne. I pushed into the cockpit. The pilot and co-pilot were seated with their headsets on.

Back inside the body of the aircraft, plush leather seating divided the interior into two sections. In the first, a sofa lined one wall, and opposite were facing seats, two abreast. The second section had seating for eight, four on each side, facing each other, with tables between them. In this section, a rail of a man with a ring of white hair sat alone. He wore a crisp uniform. Cain. Had to be.

I drifted past him and into the rear of the plane. Beyond the plush seating was a washroom with a toilet, sink and shower. Opposite the biffy was a fully-equipped kitchen. And beyond the kitchen, a closed door. I drifted through it to find two men plugged into computers. They had a visual of Cain, and their headsets suggested there was an audio feed as well. Both wore side arms and stun guns, and those were just the weapons I could see.

When I drifted back out, Sam was inside, walking toward the general. Sam's face gave nothing away. His gait was sure, his shoulders tense. The general stood. He shook Sam's hand and invited him to sit.

"I'm sorry to say it, but you and your operative have been exposed."

Sam straightened and sat forward. "When?"

"We can't pinpoint an exact date. At least three months ago."

"And you're just telling me now?"

"We needed to be sure you weren't involved."

"And how did you determine that?"

"You told me about the drone operators. They're CIA special ops. You won't find them. You're welcome to try."

"You have their deets?"

Cain opened the file before him, removed two sheets of paper and slid them across to Sam. Sam glanced at the sheets, folded them and tucked them into an inside pocket.

"You know who hired them?"

"Someone outside ICO. He's CIA, but he's aware of our organization. Something or someone prompted him to investigate a disturbance at Cairabrae. He knew more than he should have. We don't know how. Opened his own private investigation."

"Who's the CIA insider?"

"I can't tell you that, but we're on to him. We'll shut him down when we know who's in his network."

"Does that network include insiders at ICO?"

"I'm afraid so."

"Who?"

"That's classified."

Sam sat back, keeping his eyes on Cain. "The night I told you about the drone operators, you already knew that the baby boy who'd been kidnapped had been located. Who told you?"

Cain hollowed his cheeks. He didn't look away. "You think I'd put two unknowns into the field without having some checks and balances in place? I've been in this business a long time, Detective. The only sure thing about it is someone's going to try to outmanoeuvre you."

That explained the tracker he'd had Penn put in my arm.

"Who's your check and balance?" Sam asked.

"That's classified. As is this conversation."

Sam took a moment, rubbed his chin. "Who hacked our secure video line?"

"Classified."

Sam drummed his fingers. "This leak is a terminal breach of ICO's contract with my operative."

"Your operative and the people she reports to don't know there's been a leak, and that's how it has to stay. We can't lose their cooperation. They're too valuable an asset."

As much as I admired Cain's patriotism, his integrity had just suffered a fatal blow.

"My operative and her counterpart under Beale were both unwilling guests of these people. They know there's been a leak."

"No. They know someone else knows their secret. They have no idea who. It's critical we keep it that way."

"They may not know who yet, but you can bet their people are looking."

"Yes, and we're a step ahead of them. When we're ready to move, the leak will be plugged, the people involved will be charged with treason, and any information they collected from their drones and their ill-advised incarceration of our operatives will be safe with us. Their Tribunal will never connect ICO to the leak."

If ICO got hold of that information, they'd have their hooks into us so deep we'd never be free.

"As long as this rogue CIA player is out there, Emelynn Taylor and James Moss are both in danger."

Cain sat back and pressed together the tips of his fingers. "Taylor can kill a man at twenty paces without a weapon and I've seen Moss's file—he's a good as they get."

"Didn't stop them from being taken and drugged."

"What more can I do? You tell me Taylor won't relocate. Refuses a security detail. She's working a low-profile case, one you hand-picked, from the safety of her home. What do you suggest?"

"Take them out of service. At least until the danger has passed."

"You want to wave that red flag? Keeping them working, in our orbit—that's where they're safest."

Sam settled back in his seat. "How soon until you move on this CIA player?"

"Weeks, not months. That's the best intel I have right now."

Sam exhaled and turned to gaze out the window.

"She trusts you," Cain said. "That's why you're handling her. We're counting on you."

Sam turned his head back to Cain. "I'll manage her. Are we done?"

"Almost," Cain said. "What can you tell me about Sebastian Kirk?"

Sam pulled off an award-winning puzzled expression. "Name sounds familiar. Can't place him."

"He attended a charity fundraiser last year at Cecil Green House. Emelynn Taylor was there as well. The Cooper brothers' case?"

Sam nodded as if a light had come on. "Yes. Kirk bought a godaw-ful mask as I recall."

"He did," Cain said. "But at least one of Emelynn's table compan-ions seemed to think Emelynn knew the man."

"She's not mentioned him. Is he involved in the breach?"

Cain smiled. "What breach?"

"Of course," Sam said, right on cue.

Cain stood, signalling the end of the meeting. Sam rose and fastened a single button on his jacket. They shook hands. Sam thanked him for his time and left the same way he'd arrived: confident, tense.

I remained behind. Cain watched Sam leap into the waiting golf cart, and didn't move until Sam was inside the terminal building. At that point, the door to the room at the back of the plane opened and one of the two men emerged. The jets fired up to a high-pitched whine.

"Did you pick up on anything?"

"His heart rate went up when you mentioned Sebastian Kirk."

Apparently great acting wasn't good enough when you played with the big boys.

"Did it?" Cain said, nodding sagely. "Well then, I'd say we have a new target."

And I'd say Cain didn't trust Sam nearly as much as he'd let on.

The man from the back activated a device the size of a cellphone but thicker. "Let's see if he left anything to remember him by," he said, and just as Sam predicted, he started scanning Sam's seat. I beetled to the back of the bus, unsure if the bugs I carried would set off the device.

Cain rose and walked to the kitchen. While he helped himself to a cup of tea, I drifted through the open door into the back room. The man remaining was tracking Sam through the terminal building. I watched over his shoulder as Sam bypassed the exit and joined a long line in the coffee shop. It was a stall tactic. Sam had the patience of a nun when it came to surveillance, but he wouldn't wait in a lineup for the Holy Grail.

The voice of the man doing the sweep drifted into the room. "It's clean. He didn't drop anything." I peeked out as he turned off his scanning unit and exhaled. Cain glanced at his cellphone. I was close enough to read the incoming text: *Taylor's stable. Switching to Kirk.*

Though I wasn't entirely sure what it meant, it didn't sound good for Sebastian.

Cain, still in the galley, picked up an intercom. "Let's go," he said. Moments later, the whine of the jets accelerated. Shit! I'd been so preoccupied I hadn't considered where to plant Sebastian's bugs. The plane began rolling on its approach to the runway. Cain teetered down the aisle and took his seat.

He crooked his left wrist, pushed his sleeve back and checked the time. I had two bugs and nowhere to put them. If I dropped one in Cain's pocket he'd find it. It was a little too big to go unnoticed stuck to his watch. He hadn't pulled out a computer, and his phone was inside his jacket. I ducked and gazed out the window. We were speeding along a bumpy road. It occurred to me a military jet with a general on board wouldn't likely have to join a queue. He'd be pushed to the front of the line for takeoff.

Cain hooked his thumbs under his belt buckle, leaned back and closed his eyes. The jet slowed and turned its nose into the runway. I re-formed my hand and pressed one of the bugs into the raised insignia on Cain's belt. The whine of the jet engines accelerated to a deafening pitch. I pressed the second bug into the stitching on his left shoe.

The brakes released and the jet started to bullet down the runway. I raced for the back of the aircraft and threw myself at the emergency exit, praying Sam was right about the jet not being airtight.

Wisps of my ghost were torn apart in the jet's wash, and they scattered like ash. I'd never experienced such a violent vortex. Gathering myself together took more concentration, more effort than I'd ever needed before.

I flowed in the direction of the terminal building. Dizzy and nauseous, I tumbled into the last stall of the ladies' room and re-formed. Immediately I threw up, and because that was so much fun, I threw up again. The one-ply bathroom tissue disintegrated in the sweat from my forehead.

When I finally felt well enough, I ghosted once again and ventured out to the parking lot. Sam wasn't in his car. I pushed inside to the back seat. I shouldn't have; the heat triggered my nausea and a dull headache.

Sam finally approached with his camera over his shoulder, a caffeine buzz in his eyes and a brand-new paperback. Stalling 101 apparently included shopping. He unlocked the car, tossed the book on the passenger seat and settled in behind the wheel.

"Thank god," I said. "Let's go."

"In a hurry?" Sam muttered, starting the engine.

"Not if you don't mind me tossing my cookies in your car."

"Oh, shit no." Sam slammed the car into gear. The tires screeched as the car picked up speed and bounced out of the parking lot. The engine raced. "Hang on. One more minute."

I re-formed lying down. Sam caught a glimpse of me in his rear-view mirror.

The car lurched around a corner and came to an abrupt stop. I pulled the handle, tumbled out and retched. Sam was at my side in a flash. When the nausea passed, he helped me into the front seat and got back behind the wheel.

"What the hell happened?"

"You were right about the sweep," I said, and then I told him what had transpired inside the jet after he'd left. When I'd finished, I asked, "What do you think the text *Taylor's stable. Switching to Kirk* means?"

"I'd say he's moving his resources—shifting them from you to Sebastian Kirk. At least, as long as you remain stable."

Sam dropped me close to home and I snuck back inside, where I slapped on my bracelet and gave it a kiss. Remaining stable had become my new objective.

I wandered the condo rubbing my arms against the cold. Did I really need all this space? Seemed a waste to heat it, and a lot for one person to clean. And it was far too quiet. I turned on some music and poured a glass of wine.

The phone call to Sebastian wasn't as painful as it could have been. I'd thought he'd be pleased I'd waited until after Cain's sweep to plant his bugs, but he didn't think to mention it. So I chose not to mention what I hoped was Cain's change of focus. I did, however, tell him about the drone operators, as Sam had asked. Sam had told me he had an idea of how to find them, but he wanted to check it out first.

Dinner was a pizza delivery. I poured another glass of wine, took it to the balcony and sat in the lounger my mother favoured. Where was she tonight? I looked up to the stars. Perhaps she'd gone to Paris. She'd attended a conference there years ago and always wanted to go back and explore the city properly. That's where I imagined her, eating croissants, touring the Louvre and snapping photos of the Eiffel Tower. I wiped a tear away.

CHAPTER TWENTY-TWO

The phone woke me. I tried to ignore its persistent vibration, but like a mosquito in a tent, it wouldn't let up. I reached for it and squinted to focus. James.

"Hello?" I said, putting the phone to my ear. A dull ache bloomed behind my eyes. I closed them against the light that made it worse.

"Did I wake you?"

I cracked my peepers, held the phone at a distance and checked the time. 10:47 a.m.

"No," I said. His laughter and apology told me I needed to work on my delivery.

"It's good to hear your voice," I said.

"You too. I have news."

"Good or bad?"

"That depends on your perspective." Somehow, I doubted that. "Beale suffered a stroke this morning."

I shot up in bed. The contents of my stomach lurched in protest. "What have you done?"

"Whoa! That bastard set me up. He had to go."

"Fuente, Vector, the kayakers and now Beale. The Tribunal is going to flip."

"You think I give a fuck about the Tribunal? Stuart's backing me— why the hell aren't you?"

I pinched my forehead. A mother of a headache thumped at my temples. "I'm sorry. That didn't come out right. Of course I support you. But you gotta know you're undermining the Tribunal's plan."

"If this is all it takes to undermine the fearsome Tribunal then I have nothing to worry about."

When James was being flippant, there was no talking to him. I veered away from what would only end in an argument.

"I hope you're right," I said, and then changed the subject and told him what had happened between my mother and me. It was sufficiently jarring to tear him away from his Tribunal rant. I topped that off with what had happened on the tarmac yesterday.

"Dad told me Mason capped the last of the Redeemers."

"He'll announce it at the caucus," I said. "He's setting it up now."

"ICO is on its deathbed. You and I are about to be unemployed."

"So it seems."

"As soon as it's over, how about you and I take a break from this shit? Go somewhere far away, quiet."

"Sounds like heaven," I said.

After we ended the call, I lay in bed another ten minutes fighting my headache. I didn't win. I crawled out of bed and downed a handful of Tums and two extra-strength aspirin before making my way to the kitchen. The empty wine bottle made me want to gag. I made tea and dry toast and carried my breakfast to the living room. The toast settled my stomach. I stretched out on the sofa and fell asleep again.

When I woke next, it was past noon and my hangover had faded.

After I showered and changed, I almost felt human again. I dialled Stuart. He needed to hear what had happened last night.

"Hello, dear," he answered. "Would you hold just a moment?"

Stuart apologized to someone, and his footsteps carried him to another location. "My apologies," Stuart said.

"I can call back if you have company."

"No need. I have a few minutes."

Stuart was glad for the update. "Phoning Sebastian was the right call. As distasteful as the man can be, we're stronger when we work together."

"Speaking of which," I said, "how are you and James making out?"

"Very well. We've finished with the initial cull. But there's more to come, as you know."

"You're getting along?"

"Like old chums. We make a fine team, your James and I. Is there anything else?"

"No, you're up to date. Get back to your company."

My stomach rumbled. I hung up and walked directly to the fridge. Omelette, I decided, just as Sam texted: *I'm in the neighbourhood. Have something to show you.*

I texted back: *Come on over, I'm making omelettes.*

The eggs were in the pan and a fresh pot of coffee was brewing when Sam knocked on the door.

"You're looking better," he said, and closed the door behind him.

"Amazing what a bottle of wine will do," I said, and chuckled as I headed back to the stove. "You hungry?"

Sam and I ate in the kitchen with his tablet between us.

"The way I figure it," Sam said, "at least one of our drone operators is likely an enthusiast. You know, someone who goes to the drone competitions to show off. He wouldn't use his real name, but we don't need his name—we have his face. And look," he said, swiping through an endless roll of YouTube videos, "all over the world, everyone with a smartphone films these events. That's how we'll find them."

"Good thinking, Sam. Can I help?"

"No. I need something to do. You know how sitting around waiting drives me stir-crazy."

"Have you thought about what comes next for you?" I asked.

"I imagine whoever is left at ICO will want to have a chat with me. Try to figure out what the hell happened. I'm not worried. James is making sure I'm not connected to any of it. Then I suspect they'll have me sign an iron-clad nondisclosure agreement and cut me loose."

"Will you go back to your unit at the police department?"

He stared into the bottom of his empty mug. "I think I'll take some time off. How about you? What are you going to do?"

"Travel somewhere. James wants to get away for a while."

"Heard anything from your mom?"

"No." And I wasn't expecting to and thinking about it hurt. I refocused and stood to clear our dishes. "What's the latest on the complaint from Zhang at the Chinese embassy?"

"I'm meeting Naomi later today for an update."

"Over dinner?"

"It's work, not a date."

I razzed him a bit then promised to stay close to the condo and not vary my routine.

"Check out Iceland," he said, as I saw him out. "It's the newest hotspot for hipster vacationers."

In the following days, I did just that. I also looked into France and Italy. England looked interesting. Ireland and Scotland with their moors and castles pulled at my imagination. Maybe a beach vacation somewhere warm.

Updates trickled in from Sam, but otherwise, my phone remained quiet.

One day I ran, another, I kayaked. I worked out in the gym, caught up on a lot of movies and started a new book, a thick one that would take a long time to read. Each day I took a long, lazy bubble bath.

And I flew. Each time, I'd leave the bracelet behind, ghost off the roof and re-form over the Pacific. I wallowed in the freedom, the bliss, and sent grateful thoughts Jolene's way.

The moment Mason made public the news about the Redeemers, I'd arrange to see Eden. If she couldn't come to me, I'd go to her, stay with her and Alex. I couldn't wait. And I couldn't wait to see the covey again. Maybe Avery could be talked into setting up a game of laser tag. I couldn't remember the last time we'd trained together.

I was on the balcony in the late afternoon with a blanket and my new book when Colin called. "There's a Stuart Reynolds here to see you."

Why hadn't he called ahead? "Thanks, Colin. Let him up." At least we were finally using a door. I set my book and the blanket aside and took a quick peek in the fridge. I could offer him cheese, I thought, and took out the ripe brie and a package of crackers.

When the knock came, I raced down the hall and opened the door.

But it wasn't Stuart I saw. It was my mother. She stood on the threshold, her hands clasped in front of her. Stuart stood a pace behind with my mother's suitcase in one hand.

Though I tried, words refused to form.

"You going to invite me in?" Mom said.

I stumbled backwards and held the door. Mom directed Stuart to leave her bag in the hall. He obliged and then followed her to the living room.

She stopped in front of the door to the balcony but didn't turn around.

Stuart passed behind her and turned to me. "Spacious," he said, nodding his approval. "Panoramic view. Not so bad, if you have to live in a city."

My mother squared her shoulders and continued staring out the window. Seeing them together in the same room felt disquieting. I looked at Stuart. "Not to sound rude, Stuart, but what are you doing here?"

He made a show of glancing around the room. "Thought it was about time I came to see this condo I've heard so much about."

"Mom," I said, turning to her. "What's going on?"

She cleared her throat. "After our last discussion, I had questions, as you can imagine. I decided to go to the source for the answers."

"You went to Cairabrae?"

Mom nodded. "Stuart has been very accommodating, considering. Thank you, again," she said to Stuart. "I know how difficult I've been. I had no idea."

"Don't concern yourself. I've got the hide of an armadillo. Now I must go."

"Where? You just got here."

"We'll visit another time. I have work to do. Laura, it's been a pleasure."

Mom nodded. I had to rush to keep up with Stuart as he headed down the hall to the door.

"Are you sure you won't stay?"

"Quite." He gave me a hug and kissed the top of my head. "I must say, your father had very good taste in women," he said. "Now go mend some fences."

The door closed with a quiet click. My gaze slid from the back of the door to my mother's suitcase on the floor. Had she returned to stay or to say goodbye?

Dread accompanied each step back to the living room. Mom had wandered out to the balcony. I stopped shy of the open door, took a deep breath and joined her.

She looked up. "You're reading a new book?"

"Yeah. Can I make you a cup of tea?"

"No."

"I'm sorry, Mom. A thousand times over, I'm sorry."

"So am I," she said. Her eyes brimmed with tears. "Stuart told me about Carson Manse. I wish I'd known."

"Knowing wouldn't have changed anything." I'd still have the scars. The cottage would still be gone.

She wiped at a tear that threatened to fall. "It's cool out here," she said. "Let's go inside."

We sat on opposite ends of the sofa and talked for hours, some-times through tears. This time, it was a real conversation with two people participating.

She told me about the morning she arrived at Cairabrae, riding a wave of fury, and how understanding Stuart had been, how he'd patiently untangled the mess I'd made and let her see the possibilities of the gift. He made her understand that I'd been protecting her as best I could, and then he showed her Dad's research. He played on her scientific training and walked her through the anatomical diagrams Dad had drawn of a Flier's eye and the second lens. And when Mom understood the scope of the threat Dad's research posed, Stuart told her how Paul Rossi had recovered the research from Edgar Stein, the doctor she'd unwittingly passed it on to. Mom was crushed to learn that it was Dr. Stein who'd arranged for someone to search her apartment. She couldn't believe he was capable of such deceit.

We made a late supper of the brie and I finally brewed that pot of tea.

Stuart had been selective in his education of my mother. She knew we could shed gravity and fly. She knew we could ghost by transforming into molecules too small for the human eye to see. She knew we had perfect night vision. What she didn't know was that we could deliver deadly jolts and painful sparks. And she didn't know that we were ruled by the Tribunal Novem, which meant she knew nothing about the Redeemers or ICO. I was grateful for that. For now, it was enough that she knew about Carson Manse. She didn't need to know he'd organized a band of lawless thugs to overthrow the Tribunal, or that there were others like him who would go to extremes to steal the gift. Those details could wait.

I remembered my own initiation into this world, how confusing it had been, how distrustful I'd been. It had taken me a long time to appreciate the wonder of the gift, the freedom, the power. My mother was walking that same path. It was difficult enough to move from acceptance to wonder—I wanted that wonder firmly rooted before she learned about the dark side of this gift. The inescapable side we were now both a part of.

Mom agreed to stay. I took her suitcase to her room and we embraced, said our good nights.

Somewhere between sleep and me, a nagging thought burrowed in: my mother was an intelligent woman, and probably sooner than I'd like, she would ask how our kind had managed to keep our existence from the rest of the world. Therein lay the ugly truth I had yet to reveal—that, and the fact that I'd killed a man.

In the middle of the night, I checked her room. She was still there.

When the sun rose, I made coffee, and when she woke, I made us oatmeal with cinnamon and vanilla. She thought my rendition tasted better than hers.

We wrapped ourselves in blankets and sat outside. She told me how hurt she'd been. How the shock hadn't worn off yet. I apologized countless times, told her how much I wished I'd told her years ago. How good it felt now that she knew. We talked about forgiveness and moving forward. We vowed to find a new normal together in a world where normal didn't apply. And finally, she asked me to stop apologizing.

EPILOGUE

Well, it's official," Mom said, looking up from her iPad. "I'm unemployed. Just got a letter from the dean accepting my resignation."

"Congratulations!"

"I'm sure not looking forward to going back to the lab, but it can't be helped. I'm the only one who can do the handover of my research. I don't know what I'll do if I run into Dr. Stein."

"Be polite. Flirt a little. It'll drive him crazy."

Mom laughed. "You sure you don't mind me moving in here until I find my own place?"

"You can stay as long as you like. The condo's too big for me anyway." I screwed the cap back on the nail polish. "What do you think?" I asked, showing off my lavender pedicure.

"I like it. We'd better get dressed or we'll be late."

Not wanting to smudge the polish, I hobbled to my bedroom in the toe dividers. I slipped into a dress Mom had picked out for me on one of our many shopping trips of late. It was sleeveless, high necked and had a full skirt. Yellow embroidery almost covered the grey background. I slipped into my sandals and went searching for Mom.

She emerged from her bedroom in a pale-blue form-fitting dress that took her out of the *she's-my-mom* ranks and dropped her into the *definitely-datable* category.

"Wow. You look beautiful, Mom. Would you zip me?" I said, and turned around.

Her fingers found the zipper and she hesitated. My scars had been wounds hidden beneath gauze and tape last time she'd seen them. The white lines that now criss-crossed my back were a permanent reminder of Carson Manse. She finished zipping me and patted the zipper flat. "That dress looks good on you. Do you need a sweater?"

"I have a wrap right here," I said, and draped it around my shoulders. "You know where you're going?"

"Yes. I've got the GPS with the route right here. You sure this is safe?"

"Absolutely. I wouldn't go if it weren't. Ready?"

Mom took a deep breath and nodded. I squeezed my crystal and vanished. "I will never get used to that," she said.

"Sure you will. See you soon."

Mom took the MGB. I kept her in my sights until I was certain she wasn't being followed, and then I breezed into the passenger seat with a warning. "I'm back." She jerked, regardless, but stayed safely in her own lane. I re-formed when traffic was at a safe distance.

Mom drove out to Summerset and parked. I didn't know who was more nervous as we walked up to the door. Helium-filled balloons tied to a garden gnome bobbed in a light breeze. I knocked, and when the door opened, laughter spilled out from inside.

"Laura!" Mrs. Connolly said, holding the door. "It's been years— welcome. Emelynn, good to see you again. Come on in."

Molly's mom led my mother inside and added our gift to a table piled high with cotton-candy-coloured gifts. Mom and Mrs. Connolly slid into reminiscing and catching up. I waved to Molly's father, who joined them, and I carried on to the kitchen. Molly and Cheney's storybook home was everything I'd imagined, with its diamond-paned windows, arched doorways and built-in cabinetry in every room.

Cheney's friends from Fast Eddies monopolized the beer cooler by the back door. It had been months since I'd been to the bar they called theirs, and I was unsure of their names. They didn't hold that against me as I reintroduced myself.

"Is Dean here?" I asked. His was the one name I'd not forget.

"Yeah, I think he's outside."

I glanced out the back door and knew him from a distance. He had a butt I'd long admired, and we'd dated briefly. He'd been best man at Molly and Cheney's wedding. I excused myself and sauntered into the backyard.

Dean stood with his back to me laughing at something the woman beside him had said. No one could accuse him of being a slave to fashion in his plain white T-shirt and heaven-sent Wranglers. He hadn't changed a bit.

He turned when he saw me, and surprise flitted across his face. "Emelynn!" he said, and he reached an arm around my shoulder and gave me a squeeze. He swung his head to clear a lock of hair that had fallen forward, and I caught a glimpse of the scar that ran from his temple to his jaw. It took nothing away from him. "You look terrific," he said.

"Thanks. So do you."

He introduced me to Heather, a cheerleader type with a ready smile. She hooked a territorial arm in his and told me how he'd introduced her to motorcycling.

Cheney's voice came from behind, and I turned. "I heard you were here," he said, and pulled me into a hug. His soft linen shirt smelled of Old Spice. "How are you? We missed you in Vegas."

"I know. I'm so sorry." Backing out of being the best woman at the wedding had been one of the hardest sacrifices I'd had to make thanks to Carson Manse.

He pulled me aside and concern clouded his sky-blue eyes. "Is it over now? They caught the guy?"

"It's over. He won't be bothering me anymore."

"Thank god for that—"

A voice interrupted our hushed conversation. "Emelynn?"

Cheney's attention immediately fell to Molly. "Let me get you a chair."

"Thanks, sweetie, but I've been sitting for an hour. Need to stretch the gams." In keeping with her favourite 1950's style, she wore a hair band to match her blouse.

James had nicknamed Molly *Short, Dark and Bubbly*. It was a pretty good summation. Her dark curls had grown longer, but her ready smile beamed.

"Wow," I said, taking in the girth of her. "Big as a house is a real thing."

She swatted me on the arm, and we held on to each other for an embarrassingly long time. "I've missed you," she said. "Are you really safe now?"

"I'm still taking precautions, but yeah, I'm safe."

Mom and I left the party arm in arm and took our time strolling to the car. The night had cooled, and we both wore our wraps.

"I'm glad you have Molly and Cheney in your life," Mom said. "It's good for you to keep normal friends—ones who aren't involved in that other world."

How long would it be, I wondered, before Mom understood that for me, "that other world" was my new normal?

"I didn't realize Molly's parents were both retired now," she said.

"Did you meet the Rumble sisters, Ruth and Anne? I worked for them before the fire."

"I remember. And I did. Told them I'd be sure to visit their bookshop."

"You know, we're pretty close to Cliffside. Want to drive out and see the property?" I asked. Mom hadn't seen it since the fire. Whether it would be painful for her or not, I couldn't guess.

"I wouldn't see much right now."

"The moon's bright, stars are out. It'll be perfect."

Mom gave me an indulgent smile. "All right. If you'd like."

She found our old street without a misstep, pulled into the driveway, right to the top, and parked. She turned off the headlights and we let the dark and quiet settle in around us.

"The place looks strange without the cottage, doesn't it?"

I nodded my agreement. "I miss it."

"You always did love it here."

"There was a time when you used to love it too," I said.

We got out of the car and walked to the edge of the cliff. Moonlight sparkled on the water like a spray of diamonds.

Mom closed her eyes and inhaled a deep breath. "I've never forgotten the sea air. It feels cleansing, doesn't it?"

"If you want—if you'd like to try—I can take you up there," I said, looking up to the treetops toward the neighbouring park.

Mom followed my gaze. "It's incredible, this gift Jolene gave you. Hard for me to fathom, really." It wasn't awe I heard in her voice; it was a hint of bitterness.

"It's difficult to put the wonder of it into words. I think it's something you have to experience to believe."

"Wonder, certainly, but danger as well. Jolene had no right." Mom turned back to the sea. "You're not afraid of heights?"

"Not anymore. You get used to it."

"I suppose you'd have to."

Mom's words had an undertow. I felt it whenever she talked about the gift. She remained circumspect, suspicious.

We listened to the wash of waves on a high tide below.

"Maybe another time," she said. "I'm not quite ready for that."

We headed back to the car. Mom stopped halfway and turned to stare at the empty space where the cottage once stood.

"I have some other news," I said. She looked over at me. "James asked me to marry him."

Mom hesitated. "Have you given him an answer?"

"Not yet, but I will. I'm going to say yes. I've decided not to let fear stop me."

A slow smile spread across Mom's face. "Don't keep him waiting."

She turned back to the ocean once more. "Maybe we should rebuild," Mom said. She turned to me. "I think your father would like that, don't you?"

Thank You

Thank you for reading *Deadly Deception*. If you enjoyed it, please tell a friend or consider posting a short review where you purchased it. Reviews help other readers discover the books and are much appreciated.

—JP McLean

Excerpt from Book 6

WINGS OF PREY

Emelynn suffered a devastating betrayal at the hands of the clandestine government organization that was supposed to protect the secrecy of the gift. And now Emelynn's mother is a party to that secret. But Emelynn's mother has some secrets of her own—secrets that will set Emelynn on a collision course she may not survive. Will Emelynn be able to protect her family in a world where operatives and Tribunal titans are above the law?

Read on for an excerpt . . .

Three weeks had passed since my mother learned that another world existed within her own. A world where the laws of gravity weren't so much laws as suggestions. A world where a select few who shared the right gene could dissipate into molecules too tiny for the human eye to see and then re-form, unaffected. A world of Fliers and Ghosts.

Years of hiding the truth from her were behind us, and yet I felt her doubt, her skepticism. It seemed as if she was waiting for me to say *just kidding* and then life would return to normal. Normal: the most overrated place in the world.

"Where's your mom?" James said, leaning against the kitchen door jamb. He raked his hand through still damp hair that touched his shoulders. Last night it had been my hands running through his hair. He was dressed in dark colours. They made him look leaner, lankier. Sexier. He stared at the belt of my robe.

I pulled my mind out of the bedroom and picked up the note she'd left. "At the university again. 'Back tonight,' it says. You know what she's doing, right?"

He pushed off from the jamb and sauntered over. "Looking for proof?"

"It's the scientist in her. She can't help herself."

James pulled two mugs from the cupboard and reached for the coffee pot. "There's always the hope the university will pull her library privileges."

"With her credentials? Fat chance." We took our coffees to the living room and settled on the sofa. Outside, the Pacific shimmered under a weak May sun.

"I did the same, you know," I said. "Before I knew. Back in Toronto."

"Did you find anything?"

"Not unless you include witchcraft and mystical rapture. Then there's always demonic possession and shamans. And let's not forget cults and alien space invaders."

James gave me the laugh I was looking for. "Abnormal behaviours are your mom's forte, are they not? Maybe she'll be the one to figure out the science behind the *gift*."

"More likely a drug to cure it." My mom, Laura Aberfoyle, was a respected behavioural research Ph.D. She'd resigned from her post at the University of Toronto a few weeks ago.

"Cure it?"

"It wouldn't be the first time she pioneered an anti-psychotic med. Mom's furious that Jolene did this, gifted me, put me in this position. She thinks the gift is dangerous." I traced a dribble of coffee up the side of my mug and licked my finger. "She doesn't know the half of it."

"When are you going to tell her?"

"I don't know. I'd hoped the gift would win her over. She should be curious, but she's resisted every offer to experience it for herself—from Stuart, from me. Without that cushion, it's going to be a blow when she learns about the Tribunal Novem and our enemies."

"I wish I could stay and help, but it's going to take from now until the caucus to set up the security."

Next week's caucus was a big deal. The entire Tribunal Novem, their families and allies would be in attendance. Security measures would be unprecedented.

"I have to tell you, I'm surprised Mason asked for your help."

"I sense Stuart had a hand in that."

"He tells me you two work well together."

"The guy's got balls. Pretty nimble for an old cowboy. I owe him."

That old cowboy was becoming more like the grandfather I never had with each passing day. He'd pressed James's right for revenge with Sebastian and then helped James track down and assassinate the two amoral vultures responsible for stealing our genetic material. He'd then helped dispatch James's handler, Tim Beale, the man at International Covert Operations who'd set James up.

I smiled. "Stuart's probably taking advantage of your new unemployed status."

"Unemployed. I like the sound of that. But I'm not idle. Took a private contract before I showed up on your doorstep."

James toyed with one of the lockets on my bracelet. Inside the locket was the RF transmitter International Covert Operations had implanted in my arm. James had one just like it—not the bracelet, the transmitter. ICO wasn't aware we'd found them, and we were counting on them not knowing we'd had them surgically removed. Now we were in control of how much they knew of our whereabouts.

James twisted the bracelet and checked the second locket—his locket. I'd agreed to keep his tracker with me while he was working with Mason on security for the caucus. We couldn't risk ICO knowing where the meeting was taking place.

"I'm glad you came."

"Me too." He took my hand in his. "I was worried your mom would toss me out when I showed up."

"Are you kidding? She thinks you can do no wrong. I was the one who kept her in the dark and insisted everyone else do the same. You, she loves."

A playful smirk crossed his lips. "I am damn near perfect." I rolled my eyes. He raised the back of my hand to his lips. "Thank you for saying yes."

My smile faded. "We're taking it slow, remember?"

"Like I'd forget that conversation."

An awkward silence fell. He rubbed his thumb over my knuckles. "We aren't the first couple to have to work out a few snags, Em."

"Snags?"

"Tiny," he said, squinting at the small gap between his thumb and forefinger. "My father's law firm will work out the legal issues with me being American and you Canadian. And as far as the Reynoldses go, I've already made my peace with Stuart, and Mason will come around when we tell him."

"And that little snag to do with children?"

He cocked his head to one side and frowned. "You want kids, right?"

"Eventually."

"Then it's just a matter of timing, that's all."

That's all. He said it as if it were an easy fix, a little tweak. I wasn't so sure. The thought of having kids sent me into cold-sweat territory.

"Speaking of kids, isn't Short, Dark and Bubbly about to pop?"

"Next month if she can hold on, but I don't think it's contagious," I said.

James laughed, knowing I'd caught his not-so-subtle play. Short, Dark and Bubbly was James's nickname for Molly Connolly, though she was Molly Meyers now. She and I had been best buddies when we were kids. She was still my closest and dearest friend in the non-Gifted world.

"I've got to get moving," James said.

"You'll keep in touch?"

His gaze dropped to my hand. "As much as I can. Yes."

James was a man of few words, but his habit of cutting off communication when he worked a case had moved beyond annoying. I had the same job, so I understood the risks, but not knowing if he was alive or dead, not being able to reach him or warn him, had cost us both— dearly. Now someone at ICO had a piece of us they shouldn't have, and the Tribunal had issued a death warrant for the operatives within ICO who knew of our existence.

After breakfast, James put his Dopp kit in a black leather satchel that sat on the floor inside my bedroom door. I tried not to take offence that he kept it perpetually packed, ready to grab and go at a moment's notice.

"If the Tribunal doesn't deal with ICO before you head to the caucus, leave the trackers here."

I nodded patiently at his reminder, the third one he'd given me since stringing his tracker on my bracelet. He kissed me one last time and then left for the airport to board a plane headed to San Francisco, where he'd meet with Mason. The exact location of the caucus wouldn't be disclosed until twenty-four hours beforehand. After the massacre at Cairabrae, no one on the Tribunal was taking any chances.

The home gym I'd set up in the third bedroom of the condo would feel too confined today. I needed space to burn off energy. I dressed in workout gear and ran a ten-kilometre circuit around the university.

At six o'clock that evening my mother still hadn't returned. I ate a dinner of ham and scalloped potatoes alone and then dished her a plate. This felt like our old life in Toronto, when I was going to university and she worked at the lab. Once again we occupied the same home but rarely saw each other. I texted her but it went unanswered. If she was in the library, she probably had her phone turned off.

When Mom finally came home, it was eight thirty. I set my book aside and listened to her slow footsteps approaching from down the hall. She plodded into the living room and dumped her shoulder bag as if it weighed fifty pounds.

"Tough day at the office?" I asked.

She shrugged out of her trench coat. "Has James left?"

"This morning."

Mom headed to the kitchen. I heard the creak of the oven door and the wrinkle of tinfoil. Moments later, she carried the plate I'd kept warm to the dining room table and took a seat. "This is good," she said, swallowing a mouthful. "Thanks."

"How was the library?"

"Good. I hired a grad student today. He starts tomorrow."

"Why?"

She raised a sardonic eyebrow. "Have you seen UBC's library?"

"Which one?"

"Exactly. I'm spending more time running around buildings and stacks than I am researching."

Alarm pricked the back of my neck. "You haven't told him any-thing . . . about the gift . . . have you?"

"No! You think he'd agree to work with a woman of questionable sanity?"

"Tell me what you're looking for, Mom. Let me help."

"Thanks, sweetheart, but the young man I hired is a master of library sciences student. He'll be far more efficient than either of us, and I'm only here until the end of the week."

Her avoidance of my question reinforced my belief that she was looking for evidence of the gift. I wanted to tell her she wouldn't find it, but she'd learn that for herself soon enough. "You're coming back, right?" I'd invited Mom to move in with me, at least until she found her feet on the coast.

Mom screwed up her face as if I'd asked a ridiculous question. "Of course. I'm going to hand off my research and pack up the condo. Shouldn't be more than ten days."

"You planning on working late again tomorrow?"

"For a few more days, yes."

"How about I meet you tomorrow? Say eight o'clock? We'll go for dinner."

"Tired of cooking?"

"Tired of not seeing you. It feels a little too much like our time in Toronto."

"Well then, let's try to fix that. Dinner tomorrow it is."

The next night, I took the usual precautions to ensure I wasn't followed. ICO knew where I lived, but I'd gone to extreme measures to hide who my mother was. I didn't trust them not to use her to get to me. Koerner Library was a twenty-minute walk away. I pulled my collar close, stayed alert and made it there without incident.

"Impressive," I said, when I found Mom. She'd managed to commandeer a carousel in a study room on the first floor, two floors below the main entrance.

Mom jerked her head up from behind a stack of books and journals. "Is it eight o'clock already?"

I tilted my head to read the books' spines. Mom twisted the pile away from my quizzical gaze. "You're researching ocean tides?"

"You should have called. I'd have met you upstairs." She scraped her chair back and grabbed her coat and bag. "Let's go," she said, nudging me ahead of her.

How did ocean tides tie into the gift? Perhaps I'd been wrong about her research subject. I dismissed the matter and we started out for the Point Grill, a ten-minute walk away. James and I had eaten at the Point a few times. We liked the casual atmosphere, and most nights the restaurant was busy enough to render us anonymous and mask our conversations.

After we were seated, Mom pulled out her tablet and showed me the real estate listing for the Toronto condo. "It went up this afternoon," she said. "The agent's showing it this weekend. She figures we'll have offers by Sunday."

Through dinner, we talked about her upcoming trip and impending move. The gift was the impetus behind all of it and yet that very subject never crossed our conversational threshold. It wasn't because of the public venue; the gift had somehow become a taboo topic. *Verboten.* As if talking about it made it more real.

We left the Point and stepped into a cool, starlit night. Mom tucked her hand in the crook of my arm as we strolled along the street, our footsteps the only sounds.

"I'll head off at the next corner," I said. She nodded, having gotten used to my routine. "Meet you back at—"

High-pitched yips startled us. A woman screamed. I dropped my mother's arm and raced toward the ferocious snarling around the corner.

At the forested edge of a small greenspace, a coyote had cornered a small fluffball of a dog. The dog held its ground, but it had been hurt and the coyote smelled blood. The only things keeping the coyote at bay were the screams and cartwheeling arms of the young woman standing too close. She stood to my right gripping an empty leash. The coyote was on my left and the injured dog straight ahead.

Without a second thought, I drew on the gift and, with a toss of my head, drilled a potent *spark* into the coyote. It yelped and turned on me, baring its teeth.

"Go on! Git!" I said, and stomped my feet. But the coyote had a meal within reach and wasn't keen to let it go. It lowered its head and snarled. I hurled another spark. It yelped again, and this time it charged me.

My next spark wasn't a warning. Its hind end collapsed, stopping it in its tracks. I took a step forward and the animal quickly righted itself and limped off into the bushes, abandoning its dinner. I bent over with relief.

The young woman raced for her dog and scooped it up. "Thank you," she said. Tears streamed down her face. Blood stained the white fur of the dog that quivered in her arms.

"He's probably in shock. Keep him warm," I said.

Mom appeared at my side. "I called campus security," she said, and to me she whispered, "We gotta go." She tugged my coat and I stumbled to follow. I stole a glance behind me. The woman ran to the street, where a vehicle with flashing lights approached. I turned and hurried after my mother into the shadows.

She marched west, opposite the direction of the condo. Neither of us said a word until we were across Northwest Marine Drive.

"What the hell was that?" she said, still marching forward.

Even with a brisk stride, I could barely keep up with her. "Have you not seen the warning signs around campus? About coyotes?"

"That's not what I'm talking about and you know it!" Anger fuelled her pace.

"Mom, stop," I said, and halted in my tracks. The *no good deed* axiom ran through my mind. My actions had forced a conversation I'd been dreading, but there would be no stopping it now.

The moment Mom realized I wasn't following, she turned. "I thought you were done keeping secrets."

I closed the distance between us and blew out a breath. "It's another facet of the gift. It's called a spark."

She frowned. "Another facet? How many more *facets* haven't you told me about?"

"I can't change any of this, Mom. Only Fliers born with the gift can give it away. I don't have that option. There's no getting rid of it. It's part of me."

"None of that has any bearing on you lying to me. Again. Or should I say *still?*"

"It has everything to do with it. I know you hate Jolene and what she did to me, but it's not curable. I can't be fixed. This is me now, warts and all, and it would be a lot easier for me to tell you about the warts if you'd accept some of the good things about this damned gift."

Mom stepped close. "There are no good things about that gift. Everything it allows you to do will get you killed."

"That sweet dog would be dead if I hadn't been able to scare off that coyote. That's something good."

She flung her arms into the air. "And what if you hadn't been able to scare it off? It could have been rabid. What if it had attacked you or that young girl?"

I lowered my voice. "Then I would have killed it."

My mother's face went slack. I'd gone too far.

"How?"

I straightened, confused. "What? You want a demonstration?" She jutted her chin. Not once had she asked for a demonstration of the gift, and she was choosing this?

She jutted her chin. "Show me. I want to see."

I knew that look. It meant there would be no escaping her stubborn determination. Exasperated, I blew out a breath. "All right. There," I said, nodding toward a sign with a white *H* on a blue background; a directional sign for the hospital. I called on the crystal that powered my gift and gathered the strength I needed for a powerful *jolt*. Mom's gaze turned slowly toward the intersection where the signpost stood. When the jolt was molten hot, I hurled it at the sign with a flick of my head. The post snapped and the sign blew loose and landed with a crash in the bushes.

Mom gasped and stared at the jagged stump of the post for a long minute. "I suppose that explains why your father was so fascinated with that second lens in Fliers' eyes."

"He never intended to share that information." It was Mom who'd unwittingly passed on his research to one of her colleagues.

"I know that now." She turned to face me. "We need to talk. I'll meet you at home." She stuffed her hands in her pockets and walked away.

I watched her until she crossed the street. Indeed, we needed to talk. Tonight she'd learn the rest of the terrible truth. For her, there would never be the awe and wonder of the gift to offset the Tribunal and what it did to protect us from those who would do us harm.

Unseen, I stepped off the path and into the forest, squeezed the crystal that lived alongside my soul, and ghosted.

Acknowledgements

Although it's the writer who imagines and writes the story, by the time a book is in a reader's hands, the story has been shaped and influenced by many collaborators.

This time around, my gratitude goes to Elinor Florence, who was instrumental and supportive throughout the rebranding of The Gift Legacy series.

Nina Munteanu's brilliant editing of *Deadly Deception* brought out the best in the story (https://ninamunteanu.me). Nina is also a writing coach and author. Copy editing was provided by Rachel Small of Rachel Small Editing. Rachel's editing is second to none and makes the story shine (www.rachelsmallediting.com).

Thanks to the design team at JD&J Designs for *Deadly Deception's* enticing book cover design.

The beta readers' influence on the story cannot be understated. Thank you once again to Jean, Eleanor, Kathy, John, Gee and Sue.

Thank you to the owners and staff at Abraxas Books on Denman Island. Their support of local and independent authors is unstinting.

My gratitude goes to the Denman Writers' Group, whose members graciously provided early vetting of critical scenes. Thanks also to Sussan for resolving a vexing plot problem that had me stumped.

And finally, thanks to my husband and family for your unwavering support. I couldn't do this without you.

All errors in the research and writing of this novel are entirely my own.

Glossary of Terms

Covey: A group of Fliers who are geographically connected. Older coveys were and still are connected by family rather than location. All Fliers belong to a home covey and are expected to check in with coveys in areas they are visiting. Coveys are a source of information and are trained to protect their Fliers.

Crystal: All Ghosts need a crystal to achieve ghosted form. The two exceptions to this are Emelynn Taylor and the woman who gifted her, Jolene Reynolds.

Flash: Fliers can use the second lens in their eye to produce a flicker of light within the eye that other Fliers recognize.

Flier: A human either born or gifted with a mutated gene that allows him or her to shed gravity and take flight. The gene can also manifest with additional facets, such as memory reading and telekinesis. The mutation produces a second lens in the eye.

Founding families: The nine founding coveys are comprised of the oldest and strongest families within the Flier community. Centuries ago, these family coveys founded the Tribunal Novem to police the Flier ranks.

Ghost: A Flier with the ability to dissipate into molecules too small for the human eye to see. Ghosts are rare. The process of turning into this form is called ghosting. All members of the Tribunal Novem are Ghosts.

The Gift: The mutated gene that allows a Flier to shed gravity. The mutation produces a second lens in the eye. The gene can also manifest with additional facets, such as memory reading and telekinesis.

Gifting: The process of transferring the gift, in whole or in part, from one Flier to someone else. The receiver can be any human. The process strips the donor of the element gifted. When the entire gift is given, the process weakens the gift-giver and is fatal half the time. Giftings are strictly controlled by the Tribunal Novem. A Flier who has been gifted is considered a second-class Flier.

Jolt: Fliers can use the second lens in their eye to produce a wave of energy along a spectrum from sparks, which are like static shocks, to jolts, which are painful and can even be fatal. The degree of energy produced depends upon the Flier's particular gift and varies from weak to strong. A fatal jolt causes a brain bleed (hemorrhage or aneurysm), which is medically classified as a stroke.

The Redeemers: A group of Fliers who feel they have been wronged, or are not represented, by the Tribunal Novem. Their goal is to replace the Tribunal Novem. They are led by Carson Manse.

Rush: Fliers can use the second lens in their eye to produce a stimulative energy that falls within the low-end of the spectrum of energy they are able to produce. It's sexual in nature and used to heighten sexual arousal. Referred to as the/his/her rush.

Spark: Fliers can use the second lens in their eye to produce a wave of energy along a spectrum from sparks, which are like static shocks, to jolts, which are painful and can even be fatal. The degree of energy produced depends upon the Flier's particular gift and varies from weak to strong.

The Tribunal Novem: Judge, jury and executioner in the Flier world. They are comprised of one representative from each of the nine founding coveys. They are always Ghosts. Their identities are not known within the Flier community. The Tribunal's leadership rotates every five years. At any given time, five Tribunal members provide day-to-day investigation and enforcement.

DISCUSSION QUESTIONS

Spoiler alert: These questions contain spoilers that will ruin the story for those who haven't yet read the book.

1. The opening scene in Deadly Deception has Emelynn learning how to pull off a successful B&E under Sebastian Kirk's tutelage. They gauge the value of a target based on the security signs in windows or on lawn stakes. Do you think these security signs are a good deterrent to would-be thieves or not?

2. Who would you cast in the James Moss role for the movie version of Deadly Deception?

3. Closed-circuit television cameras (CCTV) are installed and in use in many public places recording people whether they know it or not. In Deadly Deception, Emelynn and the detective use film gathered from CCTV to help track a kidnapper. Do you think CCTV should be used in public spaces? Is it an effective tool? Is it an effective deterrent?

4. Drones are used by the police and by criminals for surveillance in Deadly Deception. How do you feel about the use of drones? What, if any, restrictions should be placed on their use? What are the pros and cons of drone use in modern society?

5. Many employees at one point or another have had to bite their tongue when working for an arrogant boss. Sebastian Kirk is Emelynn's arrogant boss. Is she handling him effectively? How would you advise her to deal with him?

6. Legitimate businesses whether knowingly or not, sell products and services to the criminal set. If you were the owner of such a business and had proof of their criminal activity, would you report the criminal? Some businesses are legally bound to report criminal activity. Do you think they should be?

7. Emelynn's parents never told her about her father's son who had died. Do you think they should have? If Emelynn had known about her half-brother sooner, would it have made a difference in her life?

8. The scene inside the Tex-Mex bar where Emelynn is harassed came close to being cut from the book. Do you think this scene should have stayed or been cut?

9. When Emelynn delivers a ghosted James to Redmond's room at the hotel, he jolts her. Was his reaction justified? Do you think it was out of character for Redmond?

10. When Emelynn's mother learns about the gift and Emelynn's cover-up, she packs her bags and leaves. Do you think Emelynn's mother overreacted? If you were her mother, how would you have handled Emelynn's revelation?

11. If you could ask the author one question, what would it be? Would your organization or group like to arrange an author appearance in person or online? If so, please contact the author at jpmclean @jpmcleanauthor.com.

A printable version of these discussion
questions is available at jpmcleanauthor.com/extras.

About the Author

JP (Jo-Anne) McLean writes addictive supernatural fiction. She is an Eric Hoffer award winner, a two-time silver medalist in the Wishing Shelf Book Awards, a finalist in the Chanticleer International Book Awards and the Independent Author Network Awards. She is a B.R.A.G. medallion honoree and four-time Literary Titan Gold Award winner. Reviewers call her books *addictive*, *smart*, and *fun*.

JP holds a Bachelor of Commerce degree from the University of British Columbia's Sauder School of Business, is a certified scuba diver, an exploratory chef, and an avid gardener.

Raised in Toronto, Ontario, JP now lives with her husband on Denman Island, which is nestled between the coast of British Columbia and Vancouver Island. When she's not writing, you'll find her cooking dishes that look nothing like the recipe photos or arguing with weeds in the garden. She enjoys hearing from readers. Contact her via her website, jpmcleanauthor.com, or through social media.

 Sign up for her newsletter ~ jpmcleanauthor.com

 Find her on Goodreads ~ goodreads.com/jpmclean

 Like her on Facebook ~ facebook.com/JPMcLeanBooks

Follow her on Twitter ~ @jpmcleanauthor

www.ingramcontent.com/pod-product-compliance
Lightning Source LLC
Chambersburg PA
CBHW021314190726
48288CB00003B/839